Karen

THE BAD REPUTATIONS

— Karen V. Robichaud —

THE BAD REPUTATIONS
Copyright © 2023 by Karen V. Robichaud

All rights reserved. Neither this publication nor any part of this publication may be reproduced or transmitted in any form or by any means, electronic or mechanical, including photocopying, recording or any information storage and retrieval system, without permission in writing from the author.

This is a work of fiction. Names, characters, places and incidents either are the product of the author's imagination or are used fictitiously, and any resemblance to actual persons, living or dead, businesses, companies, events, or locales is entirely coincidental.

Printed in Canada

ISBN: 978-1-4866-2500-0
eBook ISBN: 978-1-4866-2501-7

Word Alive Press
119 De Baets Street Winnipeg, MB R2J 3R9
www.wordalivepress.ca

Cataloguing in Publication information can be obtained from Library and Archives Canada.

For Linda and Kevin,
my sister and brother-in-law, with all my love.

PROLOGUE

August 17, 1930

Rays of morning light shine through the barred window and fall across my face. I'm already awake and dressed, sitting on my bunk. I'm waiting for the guard to open my door so I can fall in line with the other prisoners to walk to the dining room for breakfast.

A twenty-two-year-old Christian is the least likely person you'd think would be serving a four-year-sentence in a maximum security penitentiary. But here I sit in an eight-by-six-foot cell in the northwest cellblock at the women's wing of the Kingston Penitentiary in Kingston, Ontario.

It's a bare, dank room. It has only a narrow bunk, lidless toilet, and sink that are all bolted to the grey cinderblock wall. A stainless steel desk and chair are bolted to the floor and a stainless steel shelf is bolted to the wall over the desk where I keep my Bible, a few books, and some photos.

There are thirty-two single occupancy cells on two floors and two double-occupancy cells in the hospital ward. I'm introverted, so having my own cell is one thing about being in prison that isn't horrible. Just the one thing.

The entire cellblock is cold and damp. Yesterday I watched a fat, grey rat scurry across the floor and vanish under my bed. I got down on my knees and saw a hole in the putty between two cinderblocks just big enough for the ugly rodent to pass through. I've heard stories of rats crawling on prisoner's faces while they sleep and chewing their noses off. I don't know if that's true, but I sleep facedown, the blanket pulled up over my head.

The food is appalling and the only activity to pass the time is needlework. I hate needlework, and at first I refused to do it. But after three months of reading the same three books over and over, I took it up. So far I've produced a yellow wool baby's sweater and now I'm working on a matching yellow hat.

The worst thing about this prison is solitary confinement, where one is locked in a six-by-six-foot cell in the even damper basement of the building and fed only bread and water. I haven't been in solitary. It could happen, though. Many of the women in here are inclined to violent outbursts. A few are cold-blooded killers who show no remorse.

It doesn't take much to trigger a rage in them. Just yesterday, an inmate in the supper line went berserk because the older inmate behind her accidentally bumped into her. The younger woman told the older offending inmate to apologize. The older woman laughed. The confrontation escalated rapidly, and in a rage the younger inmate lifted her food tray up in the air and started bashing the older one repeatedly on the head. Blood spurted everywhere. It took four male guards to wrestle her to the floor, handcuff her, and carry her away to solitary.

In two more years, I'll be moved into the new women's penitentiary, which is being built across the road behind the warden's residence. I pray that it'll be warmer and drier, that the food will be better, and that I'll have other activities besides needlework.

Going to prison shocked some who knew me, but many more weren't surprised at all. It broke the hearts of those who loved me and thrilled the hearts of those who loathed me. When I was led down Whaleback Cove's wharf in handcuffs, some townspeople gathered to watch with triumphant sneers. A few watched with sorrow. A friend released a horrible high keening wail that echoed up and down the streets of town and, some said later, made it sound like even the buildings were crying.

But what happened, you wonder? What led to my ruin?

My story begins in the early spring of '29.

CHAPTER ONE

April 2, 1929, 4:57 a.m.
Whaleback Cove, Nova Scotia

"Love, you'd better go now," Blade says, eyes fixed on Waterfront Street, the town's main road.

I set the heavy wooden lobster trap on top of the stack and look toward the vehicles just as they turn right and start down the wharf road toward us.

I frown. "This is stupid. I won't jinx them just because I'm a woman."

Blade smiles, his warm brown eyes crinkling under the glow of the spotlight above the wheelhouse door. It lights up the boat from the wheelhouse to the stern where we'd stacked the traps.

"I know, my love," he says. "It's a foolish belief, but we're fighting centuries of tradition."

I put my hands on my hips and glare at the approaching vehicles. "I'm not afraid of them. I'm not running home just because they're here."

Blade puts a hand on each shoulder and turns me gently to face him. "I know you're not, but there's no sense stirring things up worse than they already are. We've made them angry enough already. You've helped me a lot. I can manage things alone now."

"But there's still traps that need mending."

"I'll finish them. Go home now and get some rest."

"You said you need to work on the engine. I'll mend the traps while you do that."

"I can do both."

"What does it matter to them, Blade? Most aren't even fishing, they're rum-running. Why do they care if I help you make an honest living fishing lobster?"

"What they do is no concern of ours." He gives me a tender smile. "Please, love. I haven't made enough this month to pay the bills. I want to get everything done so I can head out to the fishing grounds, not waste more time arguing with these guys."

Our eyes meet and hold. My heart tumbles in my chest. I reach up on my tiptoes and kiss him on the cheek, his skin cold and bristled. "Fine."

"Thank you. Take the truck."

"Okay, but I'll be back after work to pick you up."

"No need. I'll walk home later," he says, then adds. "I might be late, though. I want to bring in a good catch today. Don't worry if I'm not home in time for supper. Go ahead and eat without me."

I open my mouth and start to protest but see his eyes shift to the rapidly approaching vehicles. I close it again.

Lines etch his face. Lobster season so far has been poor and the bank is at his throat, threatening to take the boat.

"All right. I'm going." I nod my chin toward the trucks barrelling down the wharf road. "But this is ridiculous."

"I know it is." He leans forward, pulls me into him, and kisses me softly on the lips. His lips feel rough, chapped from fishing at sea in cold weather. "What time do you work today?"

"Noon till five."

"Good. Let's meet at Pruett's at eleven and have an early lunch together before I head out and you start work."

I glance over at Pruett's Eatery. The lights just came on; the cook is starting up the coffee and frying thick slices of bacon and fat sausages for the early morning rush of fishermen. It's the diner the locals all patronize. Tourists prefer The Bluenose, with its crystal glassware and white-bone china. You won't find a bottle of ketchup on a table in there.

"That's a late start for you," I say. "Half the day will be gone before you get to the grounds."

"It's fine. The engine work will take awhile anyway. I want to be sure it's running good before I go out."

"I already packed you a lunch. It's in the wheelhouse."

He grins. "I'll eat that in addition to lunch at Pruett's. If I stay out late, I'll be able to eat a horse. It won't go to waste."

"But Blade, we can't really afford it. Let's not bother with that. You eat your packed lunch and I'll eat at home."

"No, you've helped me so much this week. I want to treat you." He runs his finger along my cheek. "I'll get a good catch today. It'll be fine, I promise."

I understand this is his way of apologizing for sending me home.

"All right." I hug him tightly. "But let's meet at ten-thirty, so you can head out sooner. We've both been up since three, so we'll be hungry by then."

"Deal." He embraces me back and I can feel his heart beating against mine. It stirs me. I breathe in his scent. He smells good, tangy like the sea, fresh and invigorating.

I have a sudden disquieting feeling that I need to hold him against me and never let him go.

He kisses the top of my head and then releases me. "Go, quickly now, my love."

I walk across the deck to the side of the boat, ready to jump over it to the wharf road when the roar of engines grows louder and headlights shine on us. The vehicles, two pickup trucks, brake hard in front of our boat. I'm too late.

"Shoot," Blade murmurs behind me.

Frank Defoe and his son Johnny jump out of the first truck. Clint Taylor, captain of the *Bianca Lynn*, and his cousin, Burke Taylor, jump out of the second. They stand under the circle of light from a lamp pole on the wharf.

Frank steps over to the wharf railing and glares down into Blade's face. "You allowing your woman on the wharf and on your boat is going to jinx us, Doucette."

Blade frowns. "Now, Frank."

"Look, it not only can jinx us, it endangers your own safety," Frank retorts. "It endangers all of your fellow fishermen's safety, too."

Clint and Burke come up alongside Frank.

Blade shields his eyes with a hand and squints up at the men. I do the same, but the headlights still blind me.

"That's just a superstition from the old days, Frank," Blake says. "There's nothing to it. Besides, there's not that many of us from town actually fishing these days, is there?"

"Doesn't matter what we're doing out at sea," Frank spits. "We're all trying to make a living, and your woman will jinx us. You forgetting what happened two years ago to Clem Hollister when he let his woman go out with him? His boat capsized and both died."

Blade shakes his head. "That was a tragic accident, nothing more. A rogue wave flipped them over. It happens, and usually for no reason we can understand."

Burke Taylor jabs a finger at Blade. "Why do you think the rogue wave hit them? Because he took his wife out with him, ya moron! We're only trying to help you. Fine, go ahead and have something bad happen to you. You'll learn the hard way. But if something happens to me or any other fisherman from town, you'd better watch your back."

A hot flash of anger rises in me. I step forward, but Blade's hands hold my shoulders and gently stop me. I go still.

He turns me around to face him. *Go home now, please, Duska,* his eyes plead.

I nod and he releases me. I cross the deck and jump over the side onto the wharf road. I'm passing the four fishermen when Frank and Johnny step sideways and block me.

Mustard yellow light from the streetlamp falls across Frank. He's a small compact man, leather-faced from years out at sea in the wind and sun. He has coal-black hair and round dark eyes that look like two black cherries. His son Johnny could be his twin.

"Girl, haven't we warned you before about coming on the wharf?" Frank snarls.

Blade takes a fast step across the deck. "Frank, let her by now."

Frank and Johnny sneer at me but move. I cross the wharf road to our pickup truck and climb in. As I drive away, I look back over my shoulder through the cab window and wave goodbye. Blade waves and then turns and goes into the wheelhouse.

I drive up the wharf road, the red orb of the sun just starting to rise in the east. I pass two more pickups heading to the boats. The first pickup's bed is filled with lobster traps and is driven by an older fisherman, Charlie Adams, who, like Blade, is one of the few true lobster fishermen in town. The second pickup has nothing in its bed; my headlights illuminate the driver and two passengers, their white pinched faces glowering at me. It's unusually mild, with a sultry breeze, and the truck's windows are down.

As the second truck nears me, it slows and a male voice yells out, "Stay off the wharf, woman. We catch you again, and we'll throw you into the harbour!"

I keep my eyes pointed straight ahead and roll up my window to muffle his shouts.

At the end of the wharf road, I turn left and drive south out of the centre of town. Predawn mist hangs like an oilcloth over the road, dulling the glow of my headlights.

After a mile, I turn right, off the highway onto Rowboat Road, where our house sits at the end of the lane. Our only neighbours, the Sutters, live in a tiny house on the lefthand side at the entrance of the narrow, dirt road. Our house sits near the end of the dead-end lane on the right.

I turn into our driveway, the tires crunching on the scallop shells that Blade and I lined the driveway with when we moved in. I park in front of our two-story house with periwinkle blue cedar shingles, white windowsills, and wooden shutters. The cozy home has a wide porch and lush yard in front, with a large back porch that looks out over the water. I like to sit out on the deck, take in the vast ocean, and drink coffee in the mornings.

A narrow path leads down the long, grassy back yard to our private white sand beach with turquoise water so clean you can see crabs scuttling over the bottom. Wild rose bushes line the north side of the property and lilac bushes line the south, their wonderful mixed scents saturating the air, and, when the windows are open, making their way into every room in the house.

Many of the poorer families in town, like the Sutters, live in shacks. For Blade and me, we feel so blessed to live in our little paradise.

I yawn as I pull up in front of the house and shut off the engine. I've been getting up at 3:00 a.m. for the past three nights to help him get the *Duska Mae* ready before he heads out in the morning. Blade's deckhand broke his leg after falling off a ladder four days ago. After that, Blade decided to work alone, since the season has been poor. I offered to help, and at first Blade flatly rejected my offer, but he reluctantly agreed when he remembered that we couldn't lose any more fishing days. To avoid the fishermen, we'd slipped down in the dead of night and worked while they slept.

Years ago, Blade worked for two years in St. Andrews, New Brunswick, on a fishing boat captained by a woman. Blade found her to be an intelligent, fair captain, and nothing bad happened in those two years, not to the boat or anyone on it. In fact, they'd had the biggest catches of all the lobster boats in town. That experience had only cemented Blade's opinion that women had as much right as men to fish.

In the past three days, I'd cleaned the small wheelhouse, the tiny head, and mended and stacked traps. Today I'd stacked the mended traps and cut up mackerel for bait. While I worked, Blade oiled and greased all the parts that needed it and helped me repair the damaged traps.

Though it's been a bleak season until now, Blade's in a good mood. He's sure the engine only needs minor maintenance and then will run well. And the forecast for the next two weeks is favourable. It's looking to be a good end to the season.

I walk into the house, totter up the stairs, and collapse facedown on the bed fully dressed, falling asleep in seconds.

CHAPTER TWO

A swath of warm sunlight cuts through the curtains and falls across my face, waking me three hours later. I hear the long, slow roar of the sea, the screeching of gulls, and the wind rattling my bedroom window. I look at the clock on my nightstand. 9:00 a.m.

I jump out of bed and go to the open window, which looks out on the water. Salty, fresh sea air fills my room and invigorates me. After a quick sponge bath, I head downstairs to the kitchen and make a cup of coffee. I retrieve the newspaper from the front step and then carry it, the coffee, and a banana muffin out to the back deck. I want to save my appetite for lunch.

I sit on the wooden deck chair and set my coffee and plate on the circular wooden table next to it. I hear the waves rushing up on our beach. My heart thumps as I survey our property, like a child taking in the gifts piled under the tree on Christmas morning. There's a garden shed and small boat shed at the left side of the property. Both sides of the property are bordered by a tall line of pine trees to block the wind. The grass on the back lawn is just turning green and slopes down to the beach. There's a row of lilac and wild rose bushes at the lawn's far edge with a wide gap in the centre that opens to the beach and gives me a magnificent view of the water. The sea sparkles a pristine sapphire blue under the bright sunlight.

I turn to the front page of the town's newspaper, *The Whaleback Cove Bugle*, and my stomach plunges. The headline screams that Quinten Dover, a young fisherman from town, was arrested five miles off the coast of Maine on the rum-running boat, *Triple Threat*, two nights ago, by the United States Coast Guard. He's now in a jail cell in Portland.

Quinten, his wife Beryl, and their two young sons are members of our church. I'm not entirely shocked. So many fishermen from town are so desperate due to the low prices on lobster that they're involved in rum-running.

Blade, though, refuses to do so, even though he isn't making enough money lobster fishing to pay our bills. He believes and trusts that God will provide, but I struggle with it. Sometimes I'd give my right arm just for a sliver of his faith.

I fold the paper and set it down on the table. I sip my coffee and gaze out at the water. The breeze coming off the water is warming up and so salt-laden that I can taste it on my lips. It promises to be a gorgeous early April day.

I think of my Blade with his sandy-brown hair, soft brown eyes, and slow, crooked smile. It was his gentle manner that drew me to him. Many of the fishermen in town are good men, but some are rough and bark at their deckhands constantly. Blade's a good boat captain who treats his deckhands fairly and with respect. We've been married for three years and every time I see him my heart tumbles, my breath catches.

Blade is a lifelong resident of Whaleback Cove, but I grew up in a small seaside town on the southeast tip of New Brunswick. My grandfather, father, and my two brothers are fishermen in town. I helped my dad on his boat from a young age. There are female deckhands, and even a few women who captain their own boats.

But Whaleback Cove is different. It's a smaller town south of Halifax and slightly west of Yarmouth. Around two thousand people live here, and everyone is either related or knows everyone else. In the summer, the population doubles with the influx of tourists. The fishermen stick hard by their centuries-old-traditions, one of which is that they don't believe women should be anywhere near the wharf, and most especially they should never fish on any of the boats. There are no female deckhands or captains in this town.

Blade is two years older than me. We met when he came down to visit a friend of his. I was working at a book store on Shoal Street, A Novel Idea. He came in to buy a book for his mother's birthday. After three months of him showing up in town every few weeks to visit his friend, and coming in and buying a lot of books he likely never read, he finally gathered his courage and asked me out. A year later we married, bought the cottage on Rowboat Road, and I moved to Whaleback Cove.

Together we pooled our savings and bought our first boat, a new thirty-five-foot cherry red and white Razorback. Blade named it the *Duska Mae*. Instead of the sail and small outboard engine he'd had on his old dory, this boat has a single inboard diesel engine and a small enclosed wheelhouse that protects him in bad weather. The outer walls of the wheelhouse have handrails around the top and bottom that Blade can grasp during stormy seas to keep his balance and not fall overboard. Fastened to the port side of the wheelhouse is a small wooden dinghy in case of an emergency. The boat also has a hydraulic winch and snatch block to make setting and hauling up the traps easier.

Most fishermen in town name their boats after their wives, daughters, or mothers for good luck. Something I find mind-bendingly ironic. Whaleback Cove is a desperately superstitious little town.

I go back inside and do my chores. Then I dress in a navy blue skirt and white, long-sleeved cotton blouse. My boss at Saltwater Books, Sophie Carter, requires that we dress in dark blue skirts that fall four inches below our knees and white blouses.

I clean my teeth, brush my hair, and leave the house. The sun is high and blazing down from a cloudless crystal blue sky. I decide to walk the mile to town, enjoying the sunshine.

They say when two people are connected powerfully by love, one can sense if something bad happens to the other. As I'm walking along the shoulder of the road, I feel a wave of foreboding that stops me dead in my tracks. I look around, puzzled, then keep going.

Near town, I feel a sharp pain in my temple, like someone's hit me with an axe. I gasp, stop, bend over, and press my hand to my brow.

What in the world?

I straighten up and continue on, but faster, feeling uneasy.

Entering town, I hear shouts coming from the wharf and then the shriek of sirens. Numbness slides through me and I run down Waterfront Street as fast as I can. I reach the entrance to the wharf and race toward our slip where I see a cluster of people gathered around it. An ambulance is parked right in front of the *Duska Mae*.

Sophie, standing at the back of the crowd, turns around and sees me coming. She hurries toward me, arms out, to stop me. Her face is a ghastly white and her hands are trembling.

"Stop, Duska, please."

I try to see around her, but too many people block my view. "What's happened, Sophie? Where's Blade?"

Her voice breaks. "Duska, there's been an accident. A terrible accident."

My breathing stops. "What accident?"

She puts a hand on my shoulder to hold me. "Stay here with me."

I shake off her hand. My pulse throbs in my temple. "Where's Blade? Is he okay?"

"No, no, he's not okay," she says in a strangely helpless tone. "Something happened with the engine. They're saying it blew up. Don't go over there."

Sheer terror makes my skin go cold. I can't see through the crowd in front of me.

"Blade!" I shout. "Blade!"

Then the crowd turns at once to look at me, and suddenly, through an opening between two men, I see two ambulance attendants carrying a stretcher across the deck of the *Duska Mae* with a person on it. He's covered with a red blanket. Only a pair of men's black rubber fishing boots are visible at the foot of the stretcher. Balancing the stretcher between them, the attendants step carefully off the boat onto the wharf road.

"Blade!" I start toward the stretcher.

Sophie lunges out with her arms to grab me. "No, Duska, stop!"

I dodge her and run for the gap. I burst out of the crowd and reach the stretcher. One attendant is at the front and the other at the back, guiding the stretcher to the waiting ambulance. I dart aside before either attendant can react, my arms outstretched.

The wind picks up then and lifts the blanket off the man's upper body. I freeze, my hands only inches from his face, and feel my heart stop. On the stretcher, face up, is my Blade. His gentle brown eyes are open, vacant, staring lifelessly at me. A small chunk of bloody, mashed flesh is all that's left of his nose. In his left temple is a two-inch hole. Around the edges of the hole is torn crimson flesh and jagged white bone. Inside the gaping hole, I see the blood-streaked fragments of grey matter.

The world tilts. A shock of horror goes through me, so violently that I cry out and collapse to the ground like I've been shot. I hit the wooden-planked road hard. I sit there, stunned, unable to take my eyes off Blade's mangled face. A sudden and grave silence sets in as blood streams in rivulets down his left cheek. In the quiet, I hear the terrible *plonk-plonk* of the blood dripping onto the stretcher.

The attendant at the back lifts a hand from the stretcher to try to pull the blanket back up over Blade's face. When he does, the stretcher tilts to the side and Blade rolls a little toward me. One arm slips off the stretcher and sways in the air, the fingers of his hand splayed, as if reaching out for me.

My heart stutters in my chest, and then for a second it stops beating. Black spots swim in my eyes. Though I'm sitting and my hands are planted on the ground, I begin to fall backwards... but then a pair of hands grab my shoulders and catch me from behind.

"Get him in the ambulance!" says a man's voice behind me. I turn my head to see a Mountie, who gently lifts me to my feet. "I've got you, ma'am."

Weak, in shock, I lean back against him.

"Let's get you to my car..."

I twist sideways, trying to pull free of his grip. His hold is gentle but firm.

I shake my head, trembling and weeping uncontrollably. "No! I need to go to the hospital with my husband."

He turns me around, his blue eyes filled with sorrow. "I'm so sorry, ma'am. Your husband's dead. They're taking him to the morgue. You don't need to go there. You've had enough shock already."

Sophie comes over and hugs me and I slump against her. She leans into my ear and says soothingly, "Let's go home, Duska. I'll go with you."

The Mountie looks at Sophie. "Do you know her family? Are they here in town?"

Sophie steps back and frowns at the crowd. "Her husband's family lives here, so most know already. Her family's in New Brunswick. I can call them or help her to call them."

"Thank you." He nods. "Can you stay there with her until someone in her family arrives?"

"Yes, of course. I just need to lock up my store first and then I'll be right there." Sophie looks at me. "Duska, I'll meet you at home shortly. Will you be okay until then?"

I'm too dazed to answer. Then I look over to my right and watch the attendants drop the wheels of the stretcher and roll it to the back of the ambulance. I see Blade's body under the blanket and think I will die right there on the spot, the pain in my heart is that excruciating.

Sophie heads for the bookstore and the Mountie guides me forward. We reach the ambulance just as they slide the stretcher into the back. I look into the ambulance window and see my own reflection, noticing that my eyes are wide and glazed over with shock.

The Mountie moves me quickly past the ambulance. Blade's brother, Callum, stands a few feet in front of us. His head is lowered, arms hanging loosely at the side. He lifts his eyes to me. His face is a bloodless white, grief-stricken. Then it hardens. A vein bulges in his neck and his eyes burn accusingly. The quiet cold of his anger shocks me.

Callum steps forward, but the Mountie raises a hand, palm out, in a warning. Callum halts, tightens his jaw, and turns his back to me. My heart feels shredded, like he's slashed it over and over with a razor blade.

The Mountie leads me down the wharf road to his waiting cruiser. We pass a group of fishermen collected at one side of the wharf. Burke Taylor and his cousin Clint stand in the centre of the group.

Burke's eyes are like glass. Silently, spitefully, he mouths the words, *We warned you, but you wouldn't listen.*

I glance at the other men, seeing anger, hatred, and blame in their clenched jaws, raised neck cords, and narrowed eyes.

The Mountie opens the passenger side door and helps me inside. Then he walks around the car and gets behind the wheel. He removes his hat and sets it on the seat between us.

I notice that the nametag over his shirt pocket reads *Constable A. Hayes.*

As we drive off the wharf, I look out of the passenger seat window at the gathered townspeople. Everyone watches me, a few with pity but most with accusing expressions.

Constable Hayes turns his head. "Pay no attention. You didn't cause this."

But it strikes me like a thunderclap. *Dear God, they're right. I caused this. It's my fault that my beloved Blade is dead.* I clench my hands together in my lap to keep from grabbing the steering wheel and wrenching it right off the wharf into the harbour.

---•---

Later, while sitting at the kitchen table with Hayes, we wait for Sophie to arrive. I've stopped weeping. I'm silent and shattered.

"Would you like a glass of water, Mrs. Doucette?" he asks gently.

I shake my head.

"Why don't I make you a cup of tea then?" He doesn't wait for a reply but gets up and goes to the stove.

A minute later, he sets a cup of hot tea in front of me. He sits back down and looks at me, his eyes filled with compassion.

There's a quick knock and the sound of footsteps before Sophie enters the kitchen. She hurries over and wraps her arms around me. And that sets me off weeping again.

Hayes picks up his hat from the table, puts it on, and heads out of the kitchen. He stops at the open doorway, then turns and gives me a sad nod before leaving.

CHAPTER THREE

April 3, 1929, 12:30 a.m.
Whitecap Lane, Whaleback Cove, Nova Scotia

The sound of bootsteps on the front porch wakes Larkin Wade first. When she hears the doorknob rattle, she closes her eyes again, thinking it's just her dad. Something must have woken him and he's gone outside to check.

But then the footsteps continue and the boards of the porch creak under the weight. Over it she hears muted voices.

There's more than one person.

Larkin jumps out of bed and goes over to the window to peer outside. A veil of whisper-thin fog hangs over the property. Under the glow of the porchlight, she sees two men dressed in dark pants, black overcoats, and dark fedoras. Their faces are hidden by the brims of their hats. One man wears white and tan shoes, and the other black and white wingtips.

She frowns. This is a town of fishermen. Like her dad, they only wear suits to church or funerals, and go out in fishing clothes the rest of the week. In fact, she's never seen any man other than the town's doctor and bank manager dressed like this. And neither of them would be skulking around the Wades' house in the dead of night.

The intruders stand directly under the light, only their eyes showing over the dark handkerchiefs covering their faces. Both are holding handguns.

The taller one moves to the living room window, then cups a hand against the glass to peer inside. The shorter man removes the handkerchief from his face and wraps it around his hand. When he looks up at the light, Larkin sees his face. His head is shaped weirdly. His jaw juts out and his eyes are slits. It's like lifting a rock and seeing a snake looking back at you.

Her breathing stops. The skin on her arm prickles like an icy wind has blown through the room, holding her in place.

The man reaches up with his wrapped hand and Larkin hears the muffled sound of glass breaking. The porchlight goes out.

She forces herself to move. She slides her feet into slippers, throws on her housecoat, and runs into her father's bedroom. She shakes him awake. "Dad, Dad, wake up!"

He sits up and blinks at her. "What is it?"

"There's two men on the front porch."

"Oh, just somebody lost or having car trouble. Probably need to use the phone." He tosses back the blankets and swings his legs over to the floor. "You go back to bed."

"Their faces are covered with handkerchiefs, and they have guns. One of them broke the porchlight."

"No!" Her father vaults out of bed. "Wake Bash and bring him in here and lock the door!"

"Who are they, Dad? What do they want?" she asks, her voice trembling.

"I don't know," he says, but a tightness has crept into his voice that makes her think he does know exactly who they are. "Get your brother and stay in my bedroom. But if you hear gunshots, get out of the house. Go out my bedroom window onto the porch and climb down to the back yard. Hide in the woods across the road until I come for you." He squeezes her shoulders to make sure she's paying attention. "If I don't come within a half-hour, go to the Steeles' place, understand?"

A chill sweeps up her back. "What? Dad, no!"

"Just do as I say please, sweetheart."

He turns and runs out of the bedroom, heading down the stairs to the living room, barefoot, in only his pyjama bottoms and a sleeveless white undershirt.

Larkin quietly follows her dad downstairs. She stands behind him as he parts the curtains and peers out the window. The boards of the porch groan as the men move around. Then the doorknob jiggles and her heart jumps into her throat.

One of the men moves quickly to the window. Her dad lets the curtain go, leaping back, but not in time.

"There you are, Ethan," the man shouts. "Come on outside now. We have some business to discuss with you."

"Get off my property or I'll call the police!"

The man laughs. "Kind of hard to do that when the phone line's cut."

Her dad goes silent, his hands clenched in fists at his sides, his breathing loud and ragged.

"Come on out or we're coming in, last warning," the man yells. "We know you've got kids inside, so come out and we'll go for a drive and talk about this."

"We can talk tomorrow," her dad yells back at him. "I'll meet you at the diner in town. Pruett's on Waterfront Street at eight o'clock."

"Not happening. We're here now. Come on out, Wade. We don't want to hurt your kids," says the man gruffly.

"My children aren't here. They're visiting their grandparents in Halifax."

Then one of the men boots the door so hard that the wood splinters a little and Larkin cries out.

Her father whirls around. "Larkin, what are you doing here?" he says in a low voice that only she can hear. He puts a finger over her lips. "I told you to wake your brother and take him into my bedroom. Never mind, go get my shotgun and a box of shells and bring them to me, quick now!"

The angry tick at the corner of her dad's mouth, the sour odour that rises from his armpits petrifies her. Heart pounding, she runs out of the room and down the hall to the locked gun cabinet that stands against the wall in the mudroom across from the kitchen. Moonlight slants in through the sheer white curtains and she clearly sees the gun cabinet. She reaches up on top of the cabinet and grabs the key, then unlocks the door. Inside, a sixteen-gauge hangs from a hook.

"Larkin, hurry!" her dad says, keeping his voice to a whisper.

She grabs the gun, cradles it under her left arm, and reaches up on the top shelf for the box of shells. She hears the angry male voices yelling at her father again, followed by another boot to the door. That, and the panic rising in her dad's voice frightens her so badly that she drops the box. The top bursts open and shells roll across the wooden floorboards. She bends down, swiftly picks them up, and shoves them back in the box.

Carrying the box of shells in one hand and the shotgun in the other, she hurries back into the living room. She hands the gun and box of shells to her dad, who quickly loads it. He parts the curtain a half-inch with the end of the shotgun, aiming at the men on the porch. His fingers shake so hard that his wedding band clacks against the barrel of the rifle.

"Time's up, Ethan," the man shouts and starts booting the front door.

"Leave now or I'll shoot!"

The sound of a gunshot shatters the quiet night air, spooking the nightbirds. With a rush of flapping wings, they burst from the trees and fly off.

Larkin screams, stumbles back, and falls to the floor.

"Larkin! Why are you still here?" Her dad turns and lifts her to her feet. He pushes her firmly toward the stairway. "Go upstairs and take Bash into my bedroom. Make both your beds so it looks like they weren't slept in. Then climb out through my bedroom window and hide in the woods. Go, now!" His tone of voice will brook no further disobedience.

"Ethan, come on out or the next shot won't be in the air," one of the men hollers.

Her dad swallows loudly. He turns to her. When he speaks, his voice is so broken that it terrifies her. "Larkin, if something happens, promise me you'll look after your brother for me."

Her eyes well up. "Dad, no!" she sobs.

"Sweetheart, I need you to be brave and strong. Take care of Bash always. Promise me."

His words petrify her more than the men outside. "I... pro... promise," she stammers, her entire body quivering.

He pulls her into him and embraces her tightly, kissing the top of her head. "I love you and your brother with all my heart, remember that."

He gives her a gentle but firm push toward the stairway.

"I love you too, Dad."

Larkin dashes out of the room and up the stairs but stops halfway up to look back. She squats down in the shadows and watches her dad come out of the living room and lock the door behind him. He hurries over to the guest bedroom across the hallway and shuts and locks that door too. Then he hurries across the hall to the dining room, again shutting and locking the door.

He sprints down the hallway to the kitchen at the back of the house, shuts the door behind him. Larkin hears the click of the lock.

She runs up the stairway into her bedroom and swiftly draws the blankets up over her pillow. She then runs into her brother's bedroom. He's sitting up in bed, knees drawn up to his chest.

"Larkin, what's wrong? Who's shooting?"

She places a hand lightly over his mouth and shakes her head. "Bash, shhh," she whispers.

His eyes are so wide that the whites shine in the moonlight streaming into the room. But he nods, so she removes her hand.

"Where's Dad?" he asks in a low voice.

"Downstairs. Listen, we have to get out of the house and hide in the woods. Dad will come and get us after."

Larkin pulls her little brother out of bed and helps him put on his housecoat and slippers. She makes his bed, then leads him into their dad's bedroom and over to the window. She slides it up, sticks her head out, and surveys the back yard. It's all quiet. The men are still at the front door.

She knows she has to move fast, in case the men decide to come around the side of the house to break down the back door.

She pulls her head back in and looks Bash in the eye. In the moonlight, she sees a paleness in his cheeks, a frightened look in his eyes.

"It's okay, little guy. Come on. Let's go."

A man's voice suddenly roars outside. Then there's a terrible, bone-jarring explosion of noise as his booted foot kicks repeatedly against the front door. The door splinters and gives a little. The men will soon be inside.

Bash cries out, but Larkin quickly places a hand over his mouth and shakes her head. "Quiet."

He nods and she drops her hand. She swings a leg up and climbs over the sill to the small roof over the porch. She holds her hand out for him. He takes it and she helps him climb out onto the roof. She shuts the window, and then, holding hands, they creep carefully across the shingles to the roof's edge.

Larkin points at the porch post. "I'm going to shimmy down the post to the ground. You get on my back and wrap your hands and legs around me."

He nods, and she crouches down so he can climb on her back.

She drops her legs over the edge and wraps her arms and legs around the wooden post. With Bash clinging to her back, she shimmies down to the ground.

Bash slips off her and they stand there for a moment. She hears more heavy thuds against the front door and it finally gives with a loud crack. Footsteps thunder on the floors inside the foyer. The men are inside.

Then comes the crack of an inner door being kicked open. The living room door. Then a second door cracks and easily gives. The guest bedroom door.

She hears a third door splinter open, followed by men's voices, harsh and angry. The dining room door. She stops breathing. The only door left is the kitchen, where her father waits alone.

Only seconds later, the men start booting on the kitchen door. She squats down on her hunches, pulling Bash down with her.

"You men stop right there, or I'll shoot!" her dad yells.

Larkin looks over at the kitchen window and sees that it's open a few inches. Her dad must have forgotten to close it before he went up to bed. Luckily, the men hadn't started out by slipping around the back of the house before anyone inside heard them.

"Put the gun down, Ethan," bellows one of the men, his voice ringing in Larkin's ears. "We only want to talk to you."

"Stop right there! I mean it!" her dad shouts back. "Don't come into this room!"

"I warned you, Ethan. No more chances. We're coming in."

Her dad shouts again, but Larkin's pounding heart drowns out his voice. She holds her breath, trying to slow it down as she squeezes Bash's hand so hard that he lets out a cry. She softens her grip and listens.

Right then, she hears the sound of the kitchen door splintering. There's a boom, the sound of her dad's shotgun exploding in the house. It carries right out the kitchen window.

Only seconds later, this is followed by another gunshot and her dad moans in pain. A shudder of fear tears through Larkin.

She hears the thudding of heavy footsteps in the kitchen.

"No, no!" her dad screams.

Then there's another shot, softer, like a pop. Then a beat of silence, more footsteps. Seconds later, another pop. And then there's only silence. A terrible hollow silence.

Razor-cold fear slices up Larkin's spine, freezing her to the spot. Every part of her wants to go back inside the house and help her dad, but she promised him that she'd take Bash and run.

Bash lets out a choked gasp. "Was that Dad? Is he hurt?"

Larkin gulps back a moan. "No, no. It was just a nightbird."

She hears the creak of floorboards as the men move through the kitchen. She takes Bash's hand, yanks him to his feet, and starts walking.

"That wasn't a bird," he sobs, dragging his feet. "That was Dad."

"Shhh." Crouching down, they creep under the kitchen window. The stench of gunpowder wafting out is so strong that it nauseates her. There's another odour mixed in with it, something metallic that she, with a rising horror, recognizes as the same smell as when Bash has one of his frequent unexplained nosebleeds.

She forces the realization from her mind. It's too horrific to accept.

Larkin holds Bash's hand tightly and pulls him around the side of the house. His hand is so small and as cold as ice. She leads him across the front lawn to the road. It's deserted and dark, so they race across it and dash down the ditch. The gravel gives and she loses her footing and falls, hauling Bash down to the bottom of the ditch with her.

Bash rubs his arm. "Ow."

She lays still and gestures to Bash with a finger over her lips to stay quiet. Heart thrashing, she listens for any sign that the men have heard them. But the only sound is the chirring of crickets and the buzz of insects in the bushes.

She helps Bash to his feet. They climb the ditch and duck into the woods, where they drop down to their stomachs behind a wide oak tree. Larkin peers around the tree to the house. She sees the shattered front door and dark windows. Nothing moves.

Suddenly, the living room window lights up. A man's profile, tall and slim, crosses in front. He disappears, and then a few seconds later the guest bedroom light goes on and he crosses in front of that window. Upstairs, the lights go on in the front two windows. Her and Bash's bedrooms. The silhouette of a shorter man crosses in front of those. Both are wearing hats. Neither of the men are her dad.

The understanding that her dad could be badly wounded and dying while she hides in the woods turns the blood in her veins to ice.

The men are searching the house room by room. Larkin knows the men will see the empty, made-up beds in her and Bash's bedrooms. She prays they'll believe that she and Bash really are away. If not, they'll come outside soon to look for them.

But her feet feel like they're enclosed in cement. She can't move them to flee.

What if Dad isn't badly wounded? What if he comes outside to get us after the men leave?

The night air is chilly and she shivers uncontrollably. Her housecoat, which she'd grabbed from the end of her bed before waking her father, is thin, her feet bare in her slippers.

She hears a strange noise that sounds like marbles hitting each other in a bag. She looks at Bash and sees that it's his teeth clacking together.

"I'm freezing," he wheezes, shivering from a combination of his asthma, the cold, and fear.

Larkin removes her lavender housecoat and drapes it over him. Then she skooches over next to him so that their sides touch. It'll help to both warm and calm the two of them. She puts her arm around him and peers around the left side of the tree to watch the house again.

Astoundingly, a few minutes later, Bash is asleep. Desperate, Larkin closes her eyes and prays in a whisper, "Oh Lord, please help my dad. Please protect him from these men."

When she's finished, she stays awake, her eyes not leaving the house. The lights stay on, yet inside it looks silent. At times she briefly sees a man's profile cross in front of a lit window.

Finally the two men come out of the broken front door and stand on the porch. Larkin clamps her hand over her mouth to stop a frightened gasp. They light cigarettes and she hears the low murmur of their voices as they talk and smoke.

They finish their cigarettes, dropping them onto the porch and grinding them out with their shoes. They then move from one side of the porch to the other, looking into the trees that line either side of the house. Next, they come down the porch steps and separate. One goes left and the other goes right. They disappear around the back of the house. Minutes later, they come around to the front again and walk down the short driveway to the road.

"There's no one else here," she hears the shorter one say. "Let's go."

The taller one points right in her direction. "He has two kids. They might be hiding somewhere. We should look around some more."

"Nah, he said they were away. Their beds were made; the rooms were tidy."

"What if he was lying?" the taller one grumbles. "They're witnesses."

They both stare across the road right at where she and Bash are hiding. She hears a harsh catch in her throat and feels her heart convulse. Though she knows she's concealed, it seems like they're looking right at her. She goes stone-still and holds her breath.

"No," the shorter one says. "They're just kids. They wouldn't have had the foresight to make their beds. They would've been terrified and hidden under the beds or in a closet. We searched every room. The house is empty."

"I don't know."

"I have four kids. I do know." The shorter one laughs, then turns his head and hacks and spits on the ground. "Besides, even if they were here, the idea of shooting youngsters leaves a bad taste in my mouth. And Giuseppe didn't say to kill the whole family. And how old are they? From the pictures, the boy looks five maybe, the girl sixteen."

"That's plenty old enough to identify us."

"Still, we don't have time to look for them. Someone's bound to have heard the shots and called the cops. Let's go. Giuseppe will understand. He won't want us to risk getting pinched for this."

"All right," the taller man grumbles. "But if we're wrong, you tell him it was your decision for us to leave."

Larkin hears their voices fade as they walk off into the darkness. She rises again and peers around the tree. The men are heading toward the highway. She watches until they're lost in the shadows.

A few minutes later, she hears a car engine start up and then fade as it pulls onto the main highway and drives away. The men must have parked on the road in the darkness. She prays their neighbours, the Steeles, heard the shots and called the police.

But then she remembers that they're both elderly and hard of hearing. Her heart sinks.

Larkin stays behind the tree, waiting and fervently praying for God's help, for her dad to come and get them.

He doesn't.

And as the hours go by, the police don't show. She waits until the sky lightens in the east and birdsong fills the air. The branches stir and the wooden sign on the front lawn with their family name written in black paint swings in the breeze. It makes an eerie creaking sound.

Bars of sunlight break through the canopy of trees, falling across Bash's face. She hears the rustle of a squirrel scurrying over dry leaves on the forest floor.

Bash moves, opens his eyes, and blinks twice.

Larkin forces a smile. "Hey, little guy."

He smiles, but then remembers where they are. His smile evaporates. "Are the bad men gone yet?"

"Yes, they're gone."

He sits up. "Can we go in now? I want to see Dad."

"No. Not yet."

He gets on his knees and peers around the tree toward the house. "Where's Dad?" His voice is raspy.

Larkin bites her lower lip to keep it from trembling. She fights back tears, having the same horrible thought.

Bash reaches out and clutches her forearm. His hand feels like glacier ice. His pupils are dilated.

Larkin puts her free hand over his. "It's okay, Bash," she says in her most reassuring voice. But in her heart, she knows it isn't okay. Nothing will ever be okay again.

"Let's go in the house, please," he says. "I'm cold and I need to use the bathroom."

"Put my housecoat on over yours and go to the bathroom here in the woods."

"I'm not wearing a girl's housecoat!"

Two crows scream in the trees overhead and Larkin flinches.

She draws in a breath to calm herself. "Bash, please, stop."

"But what if he's hurt and needs our help?" His breaths are weaker and raspier.

Larkin squeezes her eyes shut, trying to decide. Bash is struggling to breathe. He needs his asthma medicine. If he stops breathing, it will be life or death. She has to go back inside the house to get his medicine.

"Fine. But first I'm going to look in the kitchen window. And only I am looking. I want to make sure it's safe before I go in. If it's safe, I'm going in, not you. Agreed?"

"Okay." Bash nods and hands Larkin her housecoat. "I'm not wearing this."

Larkin sighs and puts it back on and ties the sash around her waist. Then she takes his hand and leads him out of the woods to the house and around the back to the kitchen window.

She eases Bash down to his knees on the grassy lawn.

"Stay down."

She takes a breath, bolstering the strength for what she fears she'll find. She gets to her feet as her heart throbs in her chest. She stands on her tiptoes and peers in through the kitchen window—

—and sees her dad. He's sprawled on his back. His eyes are open and gazing lifelessly up to the ceiling. There's a hole in his right shoulder, and two holes in his temple. Red blood pools in two lines from his shoulder and head, flowing in a thick line over to the side wall.

She stares in acute horror and shock, then she stumbles back and sinks to her knees beside Bash. Her heart is beating so violently that it feels like it's going to come right out of her chest. There's a ringing in her ears. She feels dizzy, sick, and fears she's going to vomit.

"Larkin, what is it? Did you see Dad?"

Fighting back the nausea, she closes her eyes and places her hands on the grass to steady herself.

Bash puts his hands on her arms and shakes her. "Larkin, can we go in now?"

"Bash! Stop it!"

He drops his hands, presses his lips together, and looks near tears.

"I'm sorry, Bash," she says in gentler voice. "No, you can't go in, remember. I'm only going in long enough to get your asthma medicine. After that, we're going to the Steeles' house for help."

"What about Dad? Is he coming with us?" He looks up at the window, his face pale and stricken. "Dad! Dad!"

But there's only silence. Horrible, ghastly silence.

Bash turns to her, tears pouring down his cheeks. "Dad's dead, isn't he?"

"Yes," Larkin says, her voice breaking with grief. "I'm so sorry, little guy. Dad's dead."

Bash drops down onto his knees and weeps, his thin back heaving with gulping sobs. Larkin puts her arm around him and draws him into her in a tight embrace. She looks up at the glorious sunrise painting the sky in stunning bands of plum, fiery orange and magenta. It's so perversely incongruous with the horror inside their home.

She drops her head as tears pour down her face. Her own strangled sobs mix with her brother's and fill the early morning air.

CHAPTER FOUR

Blade's funeral is held three days later on a beautiful Saturday morning at our Baptist church. The sun shines golden in a crystal-clear sky, which seems to me obscenely cruel on my beloved Blade's burial day. Where are the black storm clouds? How can the sun even shine today?

The church is packed with my dad, stepmom, and two brothers. Blade's parents, his brother and sister, some cousins, and his friends and fellow fishermen sit in the front pews on the other side of the church. Blade's mom, when she first came in, stood keening over his coffin, her wails echoing through the church. Pity rose in me. But she will neither look at nor speak to me or my family.

Other mourners, unable to find an empty pew, stand outside. But whether inside or outside, I know that many have only come so they'll have something to gossip about later.

A second funeral, for a fisherman who was murdered the same night, is being held across the road at the Lutheran church. I'm aware of it, but only barely; everything around me passes in a grey blur.

The anger and resentment toward me in the church is palpable. I'd have to be unconscious not to notice it. I hear murmurs and whispering and know what they're saying… that I'm responsible for Blade's death. I feel their glares burning into my neck like hot pokers. It doesn't matter that Blade was killed due to a freak accident. The throttle stuck on the big diesel engine, and the engine accelerated uncontrollably until it finally exploded, causing a blast of such magnitude that two pieces of jagged metal flew like bullets. One struck Blade in the face, destroying his nose. The other, the largest, penetrated deep in his skull, piercing his brain and killing him instantly. A horrendous, unbearable tragedy.

Yet to these people, it's entirely my fault.

When the time comes to walk behind Blade's casket down the aisle and out of the church, I notice their terrible stares. Some hold sympathy, but many of their eyes are glazed with loathing. Already shattered by grief, their hatred feels like razors to the heart, leaving me barely able to stand, barely able to walk. My mom died years ago, and if it hadn't been for my brothers and my father tightly gripping my arms I would have sunk in a sobbing heap onto the church's floor.

———— • ————

Three days later, as the weak early evening sunlight shines into the kitchen with little warmth, I sit at our table, studying our finances. My father and brothers gave me a little money before they left to go back to New Brunswick, but they're just getting by themselves. They can't help me much. It's only enough for food.

There's bills and more bills. The biggest are the boat loan and the mortgage on the house. Thankfully, Blade bought the truck four years ago for cash after a very good fishing season. Unlike most vehicles in town, it had an electric start, which I loved.

Blake had no life insurance. We'd talked about it but decided to wait since the premiums were so steep, fishing being a high-risk occupation. We needed a new boat more. And like most young people, we thought we'd die in our old age.

I feel a pounding in my head, prop my elbows on the table, and drop my face into my hands. I'm on my own. The boat payment, already behind, is due in a couple of days. The mortgage is due on May 1. I need money and a lot of it, but I can't sell the boat because the bank owns it. It will likely be repossessed soon. Besides, no local fisherman would be interested in buying it with only seven weeks left in the season. Especially not now that the engine is destroyed.

And they blame me for Blade's death.

Even if someone is interested, they would likely think the boat is jinxed. I'm sure most of the fishermen hope I lose everything and have to move out of town, teaching me a lesson. Like losing Blade isn't enough!

I close my eyes, trying to summon the strength to endure this excruciating pain, to keep from coming completely undone.

Despite the sunlight, the day is cool and windy. The sea is covered with whitecaps. Gusts rise off the water and slam into the house, howling through the rooms like a ghoul.

I throw my coat over my shoulders and go out onto the back deck. I smell the ocean and, over that, my neighbour's woodsmoke. I stand in the chill purple dusk and stare out at the churning waves, mulling everything over.

I let out a sorrowful breath. I have no other option but to let the bank take the boat. I can sell the truck and make one more mortgage payment to buy time. But I don't make enough working part-time at the bookstore, and it's all Sophie can offer me. I won't be able to cover the utilities, buy wood for the stove, and purchase groceries.

If I don't make more money, and a lot of it, I'll have to move.

My dad has told me I'm welcome to come back home to live with him, but I'm not crazy about that. He lives with his new wife and her grown adult son.

I could stay with my oldest brother until I find an apartment, but he has five kids and doesn't need another person around.

My youngest brother is single. He works as a welder in a shop in Moncton and boards in a rooming house, so that's no good.

There just aren't any other jobs here in Whaleback Cove. The town is too small.

If I do lose the house, I suppose I could move to Halifax where there are more opportunities. Maybe I should go anyway. How can I stay in a town where I'm so despised?

The first thing I'll do, I decide, is go down to the wharf tomorrow and gather some of Blade's personal effects from the boat before the bank takes it. Callum cleaned up the blood and destroyed engine parts, so I can go aboard without being further traumatized.

The thought of going onto the boat to collect Blade's things shatters me and a sudden pressure builds in my chest. I fight for air, feeling like I've sunk down to the bottom of a lake and can't resurface.

My fault… my fault… my fault.

Tears scalding my eyes, I push my chair back from the table and stand. My legs shake as I go upstairs into our bedroom and climb into bed. I pull Blade's pillow into my face, breathe in his scent, and weep in the horrible, empty silence.

CHAPTER FIVE

That night, I jolt awake at 4:00 a.m. and reach out for Blade. He's not there. At first, I think he's just gone fishing, left without waking me, and I close my eyes to go back to sleep.

But then my mind clears and reality hits. Blade is dead.

The shock of that knowledge nearly stops my broken heart. My throat closes with the horror and images of that day. My grief is unutterable. Once again, I can't get my breath.

A foghorn blares out in the bay, the awful sound low and mournful, compounding my agony. I can't face another day without Blade. I bury myself in the blankets and close my eyes. God forgive me, but I wish I would fall asleep and never wake up.

An hour later, I give up, throw the covers off, and sit up. I sleep with a window cracked open to let in the fresh sea air. The room is chilly. I swing my bare feet onto the cold floor and stand, sliding my feet into my slippers and pull on my housecoat.

I pad across the room to the window, then cup my face, press it against the glass, and peer out to the back yard. In the milky predawn light, the boughs on the trees sway back and forth in the wind. Beyond the yard, the sea is rough, roiling and topped with whitecaps.

I dress fast, the air in the room making me shiver. I go into the bathroom and splash cold water onto my face and pat it dry with a towel. The sharp scent of Blade's aftershave fills the room. I open the medicine chest and see his razor, his shaving cream and bottle of aftershave. I loved burying my face into his neck, inhaling the spicy scent after he shaved. Tears flood my eyes.

I slam the door shut and hurry down to the kitchen, feeling like I might slide into madness if I stay in the house one second longer. I can't wait for the fishermen to leave the wharf before I go down to gather Blade's personal things. I have to get out of here.

I stir the red-hot coals in the cast-iron cookstove and add some kindling. Once the kindling catches, I add a few chunks of hardwood, fill the kettle from the water pump in the kitchen sink, and put it on to boil for coffee. I have no appetite and don't want breakfast.

When the coffee's ready, I drink a quick cup and pour the rest in a thermos. I set the thermos in an empty cardboard box and carry it to the front door, where I pull on my shoes and lined jacket.

Carrying the box, I step outside into a cold, dark morning. I walk to the truck and my stomach churns from the coffee I drank.

Though it's officially spring, there's still a bite of winter in the air. Smoke from the stove saturates the property as fog rolls in off the water, covering the ground like a white, gauzy veil. My hair's damp in the time it takes to stride down the walkway to the truck.

I get behind the wheel, turn the key, and the engine roars to life. When it slows to a rough idle, I push the clutch in and put the gear in first.

The fog's so heavy as I drive that the headlights only illuminate a foot or two in front of me. I leave the window open, tasting the briny air on my lips.

Soon I'm on Waterfront Street, and through the fog I make out the glow of the streetlamps on the wharf. Normally at this time of day the streets and sidewalks are empty, the houses dark. But not today. Many homes are lit up. A lot of vehicles are parked in Pruett's lot and on the wharf next to some of the fishing boats. There are even two trucks ahead of me, one with lobster traps stacked in its bed. They're making their way to the harbour.

Shoot. I didn't get here early enough.

I look at the streets and sidewalks of town and wonder how the fishermen, the townspeople, who knew Blade can just go on with their lives. How can they drink coffee and talk together in Pruett's and then head out to sea as if my Blade isn't dead? It's irrational, I know, but I want the town... I want the world to stop, like mine has.

I don't want to drive down the wharf road and park at our slip. The fishermen will see me and might harass me. It'll be easier to park near the wharf and try to make my way to the boat unnoticed. I pull into an empty space at the far edge of the parking lot of Pruett's, which sits on the land side of Waterfront Street, facing the wharf.

I roll up my window, cut the headlights, and kill the engine. I grab the cardboard box and step out into the cold dawn. The wind stirs the tree branches and carries the smell of coffee and bacon. Then the wind rises and carries the fog away.

I look over at the diner. It's lit up and I see through the big-plate glass window that it's packed with fishermen buying coffee and sandwiches to take on their boats. I see a few women inside too… the fishermen's wives. Many drive their husbands down to the wharf in the morning. That's mainly because not all fishermen are going after lobster, returning later today. Some are heading to the French Islands of St. Pierre and Miquelon to pick up liquor to sell off the east coast of the United States, called Rum Runners Row. They'll be gone for days, maybe even a week or more, and their wives drive them in so they can take the vehicles back home.

I start out of the parking lot feeling only half-alive, like half my heart is gone.

I hear the door to Pruett's open and bang shut, then look back to see two women with scarves tied around their hair and wearing wool skirts and flannel coats. As they exit the eatery, I cross the road. But they see me and pause under a streetlight, as close to the wharf as they dare. They stand with their arms crossed over their chest, glaring.

"What do you think you're doing, Duska?" Doreen Jolly shouts in her high, shrill voice. She's stout and cross-looking. By no stretch of the imagination could she be regarded as jolly.

I just keep my eyes locked on the *Duska Mae*, swaying on the water in our slip about two hundred feet away.

"Maybe you didn't value the life of your man, but we do," Mary-Agnes Harding hollers.

I thought I was used to their vicious condemnation, but her words stop me like a slap. Hurt and angry, I glance back over my shoulder and stifle a retort.

"Duska Doucette!" Doreen screeches. "Don't you dare go on that wharf!"

It's like hearing a fox caught in a snare. Wincing, I face them, shivering. "Leave me alone."

My mind reels with astonishment and sadness. In one way, I understand their fear, but in another I'll never fathom how the hypocrisy and silliness of the tradition doesn't bother them. In fact, they even help enforce it. I draw in a deep breath, garner my courage, and walk to the wharf entrance.

Upon reaching the wharf, I see a group of four fishermen. One of them is Blade's brother, Callum. They've all turned to scowl at me.

Callum holds up a hand, palm out. "Whoa now, Duska. Where do you think you're going?"

"I'm going to get Blade's things off the boat before the bank takes it," I reply without slowing.

He shakes his head as if this is the most ridiculous thing he's ever heard. "I'll take care of that. Just tell me what you want."

My heartbeat thuds as I look past this group of men to the other fishermen on the wharf. They've been busy getting ready to head out, and all stop to stare at me from the wharf. Some have emerged from Pruett's and are walking past us, muttering under their breaths, casting me ugly glares.

Callum gives his chin a brisk rub. "Give me the box and tell me what you want. Go wait by your truck. I'll bring it over to you."

My eyes burn hot. "I don't even know what I want yet, and anyway, they're not your things to root through, Callum. They're my husband's and I'm the only one who will touch them."

We fall silent. The wharf is charged with tension. Over us, three seagulls soar past, screeching to one another.

Aiden Poole, standing beside Callum, is a mountain of a man with a lugubrious face. He's shy and quiet and was a good friend of Blade's. He attends the same church and is a long-serving deacon.

He removes his wool hat and scratches his bald head and gives me a sympathetic look. "I understand, dear. I don't have a problem with it myself, but it's the other fishermen. You're spooking them. They think you're going to jinx their fishing."

"Jinx their fishing? That's a good one. Half of them are rum-running."

Aiden allows a small smile at that. "Still, they're sure you'll jinx them. Wait until all the men leave the wharf. Go to Pruett's and have a cup of tea, dear, and calm down."

His condescending words infuriate me.

"No, I'm going on my boat—now!"

Aiden exhales and sets his hat back on his head.

Callum and the other fishermen begin to talk in quiet voices. Then they turn back to me.

"All right, go get Blade's things, but make it fast," Callum says.

I don't wait another second. I hurry toward the boat.

Frank Defoe jumps off his boat onto the wharf road. He stomps toward me, his fishing boots thudding like hammer blows on the wooden planks. Two seagulls standing on the wharf right in his path are fighting over a sugar doughnut, but they take off as Frank nears them, one with the doughnut clamped in his beak as the other pursues him.

Frank stops only a foot from me, eyes simmering with outrage. "Where do you think you're going, little lady?"

"Leave me alone, Frank."

"You're a bold one, you are," he says, his fists clenched at his sides. "Don't listen none too well, either. I guess that's why your husband's dead."

His words slam into my gut like a kick from a horse. I gasp and look away, fighting tears.

Two boat engines start up with a loud rumble. I cut my eyes sideways and see their running lights come on. At least those two captains aren't going to try to stop me.

When the other fishermen hear the other boats getting ready to head out, they start to get anxious. They call out to Frank from the decks of their boats.

"Forget her, Frank. Let's go."

They go into their wheelhouses and I hear their engines start up.

Suddenly seeing her chance, one of the women breaks out of the group in front of the diner and runs toward the wharf. I freeze, unsure what's she got planned. She dodges around Callum and the others at the end of the wharf and races toward me, a cup of coffee with a white plastic lid clutched in one hand.

Frank whirls around and steps in front of her. "What do you think you're doing, Joey?"

"Get out of my way before I plough you down, Frank," Jolene Taylor hollers. "I'm not afraid of you."

Her long, fiery red hair lifts in the air behind her and she's grinning so widely that her white teeth glitter in the glow of the streetlights. She's wearing mannish trousers, a man's turtle green flannel shirt under an unzipped tan jacket and men's black sneakers. She's really flying in those sneakers.

She darts around Frank and runs right up to me, breathless. She holds out the coffee, her emerald green eyes twinkling with mischief. "Here you go, Duska. I'm so sorry about your husband. Good for you, standing up to these morons!"

I accept the coffee. "Thank you, Jolene."

Jolene is a likeable yet quirky character with an infectious grin. Strangely, she's married to one of most unlikeable men in town. Her shirt is open at the collar and I see a whale bone dangling from a black string hanging around her neck.

"You're welcome, love," she says with a wide grin that reveals the gap between her two front teeth, one of which is chipped. "God bless you! And don't let those guys stop you."

Laughing under her breath, she spins around and takes off up the wharf, the men and women on shore glaring bullets at her. Because she dresses mannishly and is what men call "mouthy for a woman," many in town derisively call her Joey. Some behind her back, most to her face. She makes it clear she doesn't care.

She also has the speed and grace of a panther. As she passes the group of fishermen, one of them—her husband, Burke—lifts his leg and kicks her in the backside. He misses.

"Get home, woman!" he yells. The men around Burke all laugh.

Jolene reaches the end of the wharf road, veers left onto Waterfront Street, and races away, shouting over her shoulder. "Go jump in a lake, all of you!" Her flaming red hair lifts in the air again. It looks like a blaze of fire coming out the back of her head.

I turn to Frank, who's still glaring at me.

"Admire her, do ya? We'll see what Burke does to her when he gets home." He grips my elbow. "Last warning: you turn around and follow that fool off the wharf!"

I see an RCMP patrol car turn into the parking lot of the diner. It circles and then stops, facing the wharf. In the light of the streetlamp, I recognize Constable Hayes behind the wheel, the same officer who helped me the day Blade died.

I jut my chin toward the diner. "There's a Mountie parked in Pruett's lot. He's watching us right now. Let me go or I'll scream for help."

Frank stiffens, looks over at the patrol car, and releases my arm. "You'll pay for this, girl."

He strides away on that ominous note. A few seconds later, I hear his wheelhouse door bang shut. I stand there for a moment, my throat bone dry, my heart thundering in my ears.

CHAPTER SIX

I go into the wheelhouse and shut the door behind me. I look around and my eyes flood with hot tears. Blade's foul-weather jacket and overalls hang from a peg on the back wall. His coffee mug sits on the dashboard. Next to it sits his stainless steel coffee thermos. A photo of Blade and I, taken on the beach below our cottage, is tacked to the side wall next to the windshield.

I stand for a few minutes, paralyzed by both despair and anger at those who'd tried to stop me from coming aboard. Though I tried to appear as though their words and actions didn't bother me, in truth they're as scalding as boiling water.

I swipe the tears away from my eyes, gulp in a tremulous breath, and steady myself. Then I remove the photo and place it in the box. I pick up the mug and thermos and set them down in the box along with his jacket and overalls. I add his binoculars, rubber fishing gloves, and black wool cap. He must have removed his hat to work on the engine.

I open the cabinets below the dashboard and find a set of wrenches I gave him for Christmas. I'll give them to my brother.

That's all I want.

I sit on Blade's chair in front of the steering wheel and stare out through the windshield. Water licks against the hull, rocking the boat in its slip, the bowlines creaking. I hear boats leaving the wharf.

A half-hour later, the glorious sunrise unfolds before me. Blazing pinks, lavenders, and oranges streak the eastern sky. I can't appreciate it. Again it strikes me how incongruous it all is when Blade no longer walks this earth. We'd been heartbroken this summer to learn that I was barren, that we'd never have children.

A child together would have been such a comfort now. I'd always have a part of him. A son or daughter to remember him by.

My throat aches, my chest constricts, and I feel so empty inside. I drop my face into my hands and weep.

Later, composed, I step out of the wheelhouse carrying the box of Blade's things. And almost walk right into a young woman who's standing on the deck right outside the wheelhouse.

I jump a little. "Whoa, you scared me."

"Sorry, I was just about to knock on the door when you opened it," she says. "Good morning, Duska."

"Morning. You're Ethan Wade's daughter, aren't you?" I recognize her from seeing her around town with her father and little brother.

"Yes. I'm Larkin Wade."

She's younger and taller than me, around five-seven and slender. She's very pretty with long, strawberry-blond hair, high cheekbones, and eyes the colour of warm toffee. She's dressed in a buttercup yellow dress under a white sweater and tan shoes, She wears a little blush and lipstick but really doesn't need it.

"How'd you get on the wharf?" I ask.

"I waited till most of the men left."

I nod. "What can I do for you?"

She pushes her tan purse up on her arm and draws in a quiet breath. "The reason I'm here is… I imagine you know my dad was murdered just after midnight on the same day your husband died."

Dark circles surround her eyes and her face is etched with fatigue. I figure that, like me, she'd hardly slept after her loss. "Yes, I do."

"I thought as much. It'd be hard not to, with it being a murder and in a town this size." Her voice sounds too high and brittle. "I saw you at the Baptist church the day of their funerals. Dad's was across the road at the Lutheran church but was held an hour after your husband's so people could attend both if they wanted. You were just coming out when I was going in."

"I'm very sorry about your father, Larkin."

"I'm very sorry about your husband."

I look away, my eyes moist, heartsick with grief. She looks away too. Both of us are swept away by the unimaginable tragedy of our losses. I hear her take in a shuddering breath.

"Are you okay?" I ask.

"Yes, no… it's just that… I saw him on the kitchen floor. I had to go in the kitchen to get my brother's asthma medication. They shot him three times, twice in the head. I checked his pulse, but there was none." Tears gleam in her eyes and she swallows audibly before continuing. "I knew it, but I had to check anyway. I wish now I hadn't gone inside. The blood was the colour of black cherries, and the scent filled the room. Like iron. It's burned into my memory. It wakes me up at night."

I clear my throat in a hopeless attempt to get rid of my own aching lump. "I understand. I saw Blade on the stretcher… the injury to his face."

She nods, the horror of it all in her expression. "I have nightmares. Do you?"

I exhale. "Yes. Sometimes the image of him lying on that stretcher comes flooding back, even during the day. I know I'll remember it for the rest of my life. The pain of living with his loss is bad enough, but living with that last image of him is nearly intolerable… I looked at his face and felt something deep in my core die. Like you, I wish I never saw it."

"Yes," she whispers and reaches out and squeezes my hand. I squeeze hers back.

A fishing boat steams away from the wharf and the *Duska Mae* rocks on the waves left in its wake. Like me, Larkin doesn't lose her balance at all. She's clearly used to being on a boat.

Larkin lifts a hand and pushes some loose strands of hair away from one side of her face, tucking it behind her ear. "I didn't come to give you my condolences, though."

"Oh? So why are you here?"

"Mind if we talk inside?"

"Sure." I step back to let her enter, then shut the wheelhouse door behind her. I set the box down on the floor and straighten up to face her.

She studies me for a few seconds. "Have you heard the rumours about why my dad was killed?"

"No, I just heard he was killed. That's it. I've been staying in the house, keeping to myself. Not only because I've been grieving, but because a lot of people in town blame me for Blade's death. I've gone to Martin's for groceries, but people only whisper behind my back. No one speaks to me. I was on our boat helping for a few days before and on the day of the accident, so they think I brought bad luck."

She gives me a small, bitter smile. "Superstitious idiots. It was a catastrophic accident, nothing more. I used to go out on my dad's boat, too. When he needed me. He thought it was foolishness but was careful that no one saw me. Don't pay any attention to their hurtful talk."

I nod but think that's easier said than done.

"I heard people in Pruett's yesterday saying that the bank is taking your boat," she says. "When they saw me come in, they stopped. But then they started whispering about my dad."

I shake my head. "What bothers me most is they don't seem to have any idea how hurtful they can be."

"Bunch of blabbermouths and curtain twitchers. And some of them claim to be Christians, yet it doesn't seem to matter to them if what they're spreading is untrue or unkind."

I raise my brows. "But you're a Christian too?"

Her warm brown eyes hold amusement. "Yes, but I try to never judge anyone, and I refuse to gossip."

I nod, though I've also noticed that gossipers are in the minority.

"So it's true then, about the bank?" she says.

"Yes, it's true. Probably take the house before long too."

"Vultures," she grumbles. "You'd think they'd have the decency to wait until a body is cold in the ground."

I look at her, appalled.

She cringes at what she'd just said, clearly horrified by her own words. "Sorry. I don't know why I said that. Since my dad was murdered, my brain feels like it's on fire. I blurt things without thinking sometimes."

"It's fine." I tap the box on the floor with my foot. "I was just getting some of Blade's things to bring home before the bank takes it."

"When are they going to take it?"

"Soon, but I'm not waiting for them. I'm going to turn over the key before I go home today."

She stands, brow furrowed, and looks me directly in the eye. "Don't."

"Don't what?"

"Don't give the bank the keys."

"Why not?"

"This is the reason I came. I can help you make enough money to keep your boat and house."

I give her a sceptical look. "And how will you help me do that?"

Her stare is intense. "First, I need your word that no matter what your answer is, you'll keep what we talk about to yourself."

I frown. "This sounds illegal."

She cants her head from one side to the other. "Depends how you look at it. To me, we'll just be transporting a product from one businessman to another."

Curious, I lift my eyebrows, wait.

"Swear you won't tell anyone."

"All right," I say. "I swear."

"Good. What do you think is the biggest moneymaker in this town?"

"Fishing."

"Wrong."

I shake my head. I'm in no mood for guessing games. "What then?"

"Rum-running," she says, her tone blunt.

"Right. So?"

The boat bumps against the wharf pylons with a steady, soft thump.

Larkin takes a deep breath. "I'll start by telling you that my dad was a rum-runner."

My jaw drops. "No!"

"Yes. He was killed by gangsters from New York because they thought he stole their product."

I stare at her, stunned. Her dad had been a devout Christian.

"I know, it's shocking, but he was at his wit's end. My mom was sick with cancer for three years. My little brother is a bad asthmatic and needs expensive medication. My dad was overwhelmed with medical bills. He couldn't fish last year because my mom was dying, and he needed to stay home to care for her. After she died, he started fishing again, but the bottom had fallen out of it. You know that yourself."

"Yes."

"Our church helped, but how much could they do realistically when so many others in the congregation were struggling too? My dad was going to lose his boat and house. We'd actually started packing when a friend talked to him about rum-running. After wrestling and praying with it for a few days, and the bank at his throat, he decided to do it just until the fishing improved. In only a few months he made enough to pay off the medical bills and get ahead a little. He was going to stop. But due to oversupply and poor prices, fishing worsened. And he felt sure that the stock market was going to crash this fall. So though he was plagued by guilt and in a constant battle with God over it, he decided to continue a little longer. I babysat my brother while he was gone."

"You knew what he was doing?"

She gives a me a quick, wry smile. "Not at first. I thought he was fishing. But later, I suspected and came right out and asked him. He admitted he was."

"Must has been such a shock."

"I literally had to sit down. He said he was working for the mob, and it was dangerous, but he had no choice. He promised me he'd be careful and nothing would happen to him. And he promised he'd quit as soon as the lobster prices came up again, but…" Her voice cracks and trails off.

"Want a cup of coffee? I brought a thermos."

"Yes, that'd be great, thanks."

I take the thermos out of the box and get a mug from the cupboard below the helm. I fill the mug and pass it to her. Then I set the plastic cup from the thermos on the counter and fill it for myself. I screw the lid back on and put it back into the box.

I take a sip, eyeing her over the rim of the cup. "So mobsters killed your dad?"

She too sips some coffee. "Yes, he'd had some bad luck on his last two runs. He hit a storm the first time and lost thirty tons of liquor, whiskey mostly. They didn't like it but gave him another chance. But about ten days ago, pirates attacked my dad's boat just off the coast of Massachusetts. They beat up him and his crew, stole all the liquor, and sank his boat. Luckily another rum-running boat came along in time to pull him and his three crewmembers out of the water. But this time the gangsters accused him of stealing their liquor and selling it himself. And they came for him."

"That's awful."

"He had a shotgun. But when the gangsters broke into the kitchen where he was hiding, he only gave them a warning shot." She smiles sadly. "My dad used to catch flies in the house and let them back outside. He couldn't kill anyone, not as a Christian."

"Do the gangsters know you were there and witnessed it? I don't want to scare you, but isn't there a saying that the mob never forgets? Will they come back for you and your brother?"

Her face pales but her voice remains steady. "I doubt it. The Mounties kept that fact from the news to protect us. Newspapers reported that we were at our grandparents in Halifax. I think we're fine."

"I hope you're right."

I hear men talking and laughing as they walk by the *Duska Mae*. The side window is open and we both fall silent, waiting for them to pass.

Larkin looks out the window. "That's Brandon Foster and Parker Freeland. You know where they're going?"

"Rum-running?"

"Yes, almost half the fishermen in town are involved in it now." She looks back at me. "But please, don't judge them. It's not that cut and dried. So many fishermen are desperate. They're doing it to hang on to their boats and homes, keep their wives and kids from starving. In times like these, many good people have been forced to rum-run."

"I suppose. But how do they get away with it?"

"They still get their lobster fishing licences and keep their annual registrations up to date so it looks like they're fishing. But of course they're not."

"Right."

"Anyway, that's what I'm here to talk to you about. I have a proposition for you. Come rum-running with me."

I choke a little on the coffee I swallowed. I step back and plop down into Blade's chair in front of the steering wheel, setting my cup down on the dashboard.

"Oh, no, no, no! I'm not going to rum-run. And if you're going to ask me to take this boat out rum-running, don't bother. The engine was destroyed in the explosion."

She watches me with a thoughtful expression. "I know all that, but I know a guy who repairs and installs diesel engines. His name is Fallon Smith. It just so happens he has one to fit your boat. *And* I know, because my dad told me, that Blade told him you have your boat licence. I have mine, too. I don't know any other women in town who have their licences *and* a boat and are desperate enough to do this. Other than us, that is."

"None of that matters, even if I wanted to do this. As I told you, the bank's taking the boat. Blade was having a bad season and he'd already missed two payments. They threatened to repossess the boat if he missed another. So, like I said. I'm going to stop in the bank today and give them the keys."

"No, don't! I'll give you the money to make the two missed payments. I'll have Fallon start replacing the engine tomorrow and you and I can start rum-running within a week. You'll earn enough to keep the boat and your house."

I jerk my head back, eyes wide. "Are you crazy? No, I'm not going to be a rum-runner. And after what happened to your father, you shouldn't either. You want to get killed, too?"

She looks startled and bruised. "No, I'm not crazy, I'm desperate. I'm all my little brother has for family now. I have to raise him. I won't be going to university in Halifax this fall like I'd planned. My dad didn't have life insurance. As I said, my brother's a brittle asthmatic. His medicine and doctors' bills are expensive. Like you, I have a mortgage, insurance, and other bills. I can't manage all that without rum-running."

"How old are you?"

She lifts her chin, eyes fierce. "Eighteen. Old enough to live on my own and be legal guardian for my brother. *I will* be raising Bash, and for that I need to make money. Fast."

"It's common knowledge that rum-runners make a lot of money. Your dad must have had some money saved."

She sighs. "He did, but he hid it at home. After the gangsters shot him, they searched the house and found most of it. He had some stashed in a box in the attic that they didn't find. I'm using it now for Bash's medicine, this month's mortgage payment, and food. I'm offering you the rest for your boat payments and for a new engine. There won't be much left after that."

I wave a hand at her. "I don't want your money. I'm not going to become a criminal just to keep my house and the boat."

She glances out through the window to the wharf, but no one is nearby. Still, she lowers her voice. "Hear me out. It won't be that dangerous. We won't be working for the mob like my dad, and we won't be sailing any farther than ten or fifteen miles offshore. A bootlegger who was a friend of my dad's came to my house to offer me a great deal. He buys his liquor from rum-runners and then trucks the liquor to other bootleggers all around Nova Scotia, who supply the blind pigs."

"Blind pigs?"

"A blind pig is a legit business that appears to be something else—say, like a barber shop—but has secret rooms in the cellar, or in back, where they sell liquor," she explains. "There's lots in Halifax and in a lot of towns. Some businesses, the bigger ones, become secret bars and dance halls at night. The bootleggers sell the liquor to business owners, who usually water it down and sell it to their customers."

"I see." I'm astounded that this young Christian woman would know so much about rum-running and bootlegging.

She reads my expression and chuckles. "My dad explained it all to me. The bootleggers put the liquor in a secret spot close to their customer's mailbox. Flag up means they want their usual bottle of rum or whiskey. They put the flag up at night and leave the payment inside. The bootlegger hides the bottle in the secret spot, takes the cash, and puts the flag down. You'd be shocked to know just how many flags are up at midnight in this town."

I shake my head in wonder. "I had no idea. I don't drink. Neither did Blade."

"Not my dad or me either. Anyway, this bootlegger, I'll call him J.C., told me he only works on land, trucking the liquor. He needs someone to make the ship-to-shore runs. We'll just meet the rum-running boats at sea and bring the liquor back to him on shore. We'll be what's called a transport boat."

"Will you stop saying *we*. I'm not doing this."

"Why not? J.C. told me there are two women who rum-run off the coast of Massachusetts. If they can do it, why can't we?"

"Good for them. As for me, no way."

She gives me an imploring look. "Come on. This is a new boat. It's sleek and fast. We can make the runs so quick that we'd be there and back to shore in no time. And if we're spotted, we can outrun the Mounties and the Coasties. I know you don't have a big or deep enough dock to moor it, but I do. Once the engine is installed, you can sail it over to my dock and tie it up there. That'll be our base."

I'm amazed by her nerve. "How do you know I don't have a dock? You were snooping around my property?"

"Pfff. Snooping? No. Scouting you out for a potential business partner is all."

I give a sardonic snort. "Oh, well, that's all."

We fall silent, sipping our coffees. Outside, the boat groans in its mooring. A man shouts and a car horn beeps twice up on Waterfront Street.

Larkin draws in a soft breath. "Duska, please listen to me. All we have to do is motor out to the rendezvous point south of Three Islands, where we'll meet up with the rum-runners. We transfer the liquor from their boats onto your boat, then sail back to a small cove just up the coast from town where the bootlegger will be waiting for us with his truck. There's a dilapidated wharf at the cove that no one uses anymore. We can dock there to unload the liquor onto the truck. The bootlegger will pay us in cash right on the spot. That's it. Easy work for big money."

I frown. "Why tell me all this? I said no and I mean it."

She tucks her hair, which has fallen loose again, behind her ear. "Why not? It's a lot of money without a lot of risk for us."

"Because it's illegal!" My frown deepens. "How do you, as a Christian, even consider breaking the law? Isn't that hypocritical?"

Her face and neck turn a splotchy bright red. She's embarrassed and stung by my words, but her voice is resolute. "This guy assured me that a lot of his customers buy whiskey and rum from him just for medicinal purposes."

"Oh, come on. You don't really believe that. They can get that at the drugstore."

"Only with a prescription, and most aren't the type to run to the doctor," she says. "Others are too afraid that the news will get out somehow from the doctor's office, and the gossip will be that they're drinking. But many really do just use it as medicine. It's called a hot toddy. They make tea or coffee and then add honey and either rum or whiskey to it. They swear it reduces a fever faster than anything else. It's saved people's lives."

"Well, if that's how you need to justify breaking the law, then fine, but that's still a very small minority of the people who are buying the liquor off this bootlegger. Most are buying it in speakeasies, or those blind pigs, and the others buy it to get drunk at home."

She stares into her coffee mug. "I realize that. My decision isn't an easy one, not at all. But my brother's and my lives have drastically changed. If I don't do this, Bash and I will end up in the poorhouse. It's not just the destitute who live there… it's the insane, and troublemakers too. That's not safe for a little boy. So I don't think you or anyone else has the right to judge me."

Her voice is so raw and broken that it stops me from rebuking her too harshly.

"I'm not judging," I say, more tenderly. "But why not just get a job?"

"Where? In a bookstore, like you, and then still lose the house? There aren't any jobs in this town, other than fishing, and that's hit rock bottom. As I said, my dad watched the economy carefully. He was sure there's going to be a stock market crash in the fall and a depression will follow. That's part of the reason he was saving most of his rum-running money. If he was right, things are going to get worse, especially for single women."

"Larkin, think about what you might lose if you follow through with this. What will happen to your brother if you get caught? What if the cops raid these illegal underground establishments? They'll trace it back to the bootlegger and then back to you. You'll still go to jail, and your brother will still end up in foster care."

"Of course I've thought about that. I've weighed the risks. If I do this and don't get caught, I'll make enough money to keep the house, and save up enough for Bash and I to live on for years, even with a depression. I may even be able to pay off the mortgage. Then I'll never lose Bash. It won't be forever. A year at the most. I promised my dad that I would always look after Bash. It was the last thing I said to him. I've prayed about it, and God hasn't opened any other doors for me. I have to do this, but I need your fast boat and your help."

"I understand, but still… it's a ludicrous idea. Two women out on the ocean alone? You know the storms we get here, and how violent the sea gets. And what about the fishermen? They won't allow women to fish. What do you think will happen if they find out we… ah, you're transporting liquor?"

She shrugs. "I have to risk it."

"I'm sorry, Larkin, but my answer is still no."

She looks out the window to the wharf for a few seconds. Then she finishes her coffee and sets it down next to mine on the dashboard. She reaches out and squeezes my shoulder.

"Thanks for the coffee and for hearing me out. But at least think about it some more and let me know what you decide by end of day tomorrow. If it's a yes, I'll have Fallon over here in…"

I hold a hand up to stop her, but she continues.

"…no time. Once he has the new engine installed, I'll have him paint it grey. The red and white paint is too bright. It'll stand out too much."

"Changing the colour of a boat is bad luck," I say.

"You don't believe that." She points out of the windshield to the harbour. "So once he's done all that, you sail it over to my place. We'll go out at night under the cover of darkness. No one comes around my place because the cove is cut off at both ends by jagged high rocks. Steer wide of them and come in right down the centre of the cove. I've only got two neighbours, both of whom live at the entrance to my lane. They don't even face the water, so they won't see you come in, and no one will see us leaving or coming back in from sea."

I roll my eyes. "And once it's moored at your dock, I sneak out late at night, drive over to your place in my truck, and then we head out to sea to begin our new careers as rum-runners?"

She smiles. "Transporters. Listen, you'll need warm clothing. I've taken in my dad's denim overalls, and I'm going to wear his heavy fishing jacket and boots. You should do the same with your husband's fishing clothes. Once we move more into spring, the nights will be warmer and we can wear lighter clothing."

"Larkin, stop. I'm not going."

"Fine, but whether you decide to join me or not, I'll be going out alone."

"You'll be going out alone?" I echo in a whisper. "In what? Aren't you scared?"

"Terrified. That's why I'm asking you to go with me. If you don't, I'll take my dad's old dory and motor out. I can meet the rum-runners offshore and motor back by myself."

I gape at her, incredulous. "You're going to sail that far out in a dory alone? That's crazy. Dories are notoriously tippy. You could capsize or fall overboard in rough seas. The waves out there can reach six feet or more and can be unpredictable. When Blade fished in his dory, he said that a wave of three feet coming at him sideways could flip him over, even on a calm day. Or it could swamp and he'd sink to the sea bottom."

"I know. I should be able to power through the waves."

"What if a storm comes up without warning? The waves can grow as big as a house. And the winds? They can throw you right out of the boat."

"I'll always listen carefully to the weather reports. Besides, I won't be that far offshore."

"Still, what if your motor dies and you have to row? You'll be exhausted in no time at all. Then the waves will pull you so far out into the Atlantic that you'll never be seen again."

"I have a good motor. Besides, the men have gone out in dories for years, like your Blade. If they can do it, I can too."

I'm taken aback. She's an arrestingly beautiful young woman and so thin and small-boned that she appears fragile, vulnerable. "That's true, but Blade was six feet and two hundred pounds. He was as strong as an ox. You don't look like—"

"I'm not fragile, not by any means," she cuts me off, a trace of anger in her voice. "People often underestimate me. Please don't be one of them."

"Sorry."

"I know the danger. I have no choice."

I see now that though she appears delicate and vulnerable, she's nothing of the sort. Rather, she's bold, strong-minded, and resilient. I understand that she's going to do this one way or the other. But I still can't help feeling astonished at her bravery.

"Please sleep on it tonight," Larkin says.

"For the last time, *I am not going with you.*" It comes out more harshly than I intended. She looks tired and a bit deflated, so I soften my voice. "I'm sorry, Larkin, I just can't. No matter how you dress it up, you're breaking the law."

She stiffens a little. "And I'm sorry you feel that way."

She walks past me out of the wheelhouse, shutting the door behind her.

CHAPTER SEVEN

I leave a moment later and walk to the truck holding the boat keys. I set the box on the passenger side seat and shut the door. I then start toward the bank but stop to study the downtown for a moment. For some reason I can't really explain, I pocket the keys, open the door, and climb in the truck.

When I pull into my driveway later, I see a black sedan parked in the yard. It's Blade's parents, his dad behind the wheel and his mom in the passenger seat. I get out and walk over to their vehicle carrying the box of Blade's things.

But before I reach them, Blade's mom gets out and walks around the back to meet me.

"Good morning, Elsie," I say.

She's wearing a black dress, shoes, coat, and hat. And they're not mourning clothes for Blade. That's just her normal cheery attire. Her face is the colour of creamy porridge. Her expression, always stern, is now also bitter.

I glance over at the car and see Blade's dad, Edmund, staring straight out through the windshield. His window is down.

I like Edmund. He's a nice, funny man and I've always felt closer to him than Elsie.

"Good morning, Edmund," I call out.

He turns to look at me, his face red with anger. His eyes are as cold and shiny as river stones. Without a word, he faces forward again and rolls up the window. The effect is like a punch to my heart.

"I heard you were on the wharf earlier. Went on Blade's boat," Elsie says in a cold tone. "Took a whole bunch of stuff that doesn't belong to you."

"Who told you that?"

"Doesn't matter."

I shift the box in my arms and tilt it down so she can see inside. "I only collected some of Blade's things before the bank takes it. It all belongs to me."

She eyes the items and then shifts her icy gaze to me again. "Still, you shouldn't have done that. Callum could have gotten that for you. Who knows who you've jinxed now."

"I went early, thought the fishermen wouldn't be on the wharf then."

"Well, they were there, weren't they? And that still didn't stop you, did it? Why didn't you turn around and go home? You'd think you would have learned your lesson after killing my son."

I go still. "Elsie, I didn't kill—"

"Yes, you did. You've always been selfish, Duska, but now you're a murderer too." Her hazel eyes are filled with condemnation. There's a spot of white spit in the corner of her mouth.

The force of her words has cut me terribly, as if she's thrown stones at my face. But I refuse to let her see that she's hurt me. I look away and try not to cry.

She sees, though, and gives me a cruel smile. "A little late to cry now, isn't it?"

"Elsie, please, it wasn't—"

"Don't you dare tell me it wasn't intentional. You just keep pushing it. Ever since you married my son and moved to this town, you've done what you like without a care for anyone else."

I stiffen. "That's not true."

"Yes, it is. Blade would have never let you on his boat unless you forced him to do it. He knew better."

"I didn't force him into doing anything of the sort. Blade didn't believe in that foolishness."

"Liar. Now you have the nerve to stand there feeling sorry for yourself."

I've had enough. "What do you want, Elsie?"

"I don't imagine you make enough at the bookstore to keep up the payments on the house, do you?"

"No, I don't."

"So the bank will be taking it as well as the boat?"

"In another month, two at the most, yes."

She glares knives at me. "Then go back to New Brunswick. Go back to your family, Duska. Pack up and leave. There's nothing for you here. There's *no one, no family* for you in Whaleback Cove."

The hiss of venom in her words shocks me, and I flinch, stung.

She glowers for a few more seconds, then walks around the car and gets into the passenger side. Her door slams shut like a gunshot.

The motor starts up and I watch them drive away, unable to move, the sting of her hateful words burning into my flesh.

Seconds later, an RCMP cruiser turns into my driveway and parks beside my truck. Constable Hayes climbs out and shuts the door.

He walks over to me, removing his hat. "Good day, Mrs. Doucette."

"Hello, Constable," I say quietly, for though he seems a kind man I'm in no mood for conversation.

"I hope you don't mind my showing up unannounced like this," he says with an apologetic smile. "I wanted to see how you were doing. I saw you on the wharf earlier with the fishermen. Are you okay?"

"I'm fine," I say, though I'm not at all. The sympathy in his eyes is about to undo me. "I really need to get in."

I turn sideways a little, wanting to leave before I start crying in front of him.

"Of course. Goodbye, Mrs. Doucette." He pulls a card out from his shirt pocket and hands it to me. "If you need anything, please call the detachment and ask for me."

I accept the card, surprised but also thankful for his thoughtfulness. "Thank you."

He smiles and then turns and walks to his car.

I go inside and sit heavily on a chair at the kitchen table, Elsie's words ringing over and over in my mind. I understand that she's suffering from the loss of her oldest son, but I believe the loss of a husband is much worse than the loss of an adult married son.

I sit there for a long time in my chilly, silent house, staring at the box of Blade's things on the tabletop. Outside, the sky is cloudy and the ocean is grey. Tree branches thrash in the wind as a buoy bell clangs mournfully out in the bay.

Glancing around the room, I see that it's filled with memories of Blade, with the echo of his voice and laughter. This was our first home. It will destroy me to lose it.

A swath of weak sunlight breaks through the clouds and streams through the window, falling across the table where the box sits. I reach in and take his wool hat out of the box and set it down on the table. A rush of sorrow engulfs me. I pick up the hat again, bury my face in it, and weep, my sobs reverberating through the house. My entire body aches for my Blade. The pain is unrelenting. I feel so lost, so hopeless, like I'm tumbling down a dark, bottomless hole.

Later, tears spent, I get up and walk into the living room. I stand in the silence, looking out the window at the dark green pickup Blade affectionately called Bouncing Betsy. A cold draft slides out from the hallway, freezing my feet.

I look into the fridge for something to make for lunch. I stare inside for a while, then shut the door again. Having no appetite, I make a cup of tea and sit back down at the table. I drink it while staring out the window, without seeing anything.

At five, still not hungry, I go into my bedroom. I climb in under the blankets fully dressed, for it seems too much for me to even summon the strength to change into my nightgown. I lay on my side, pick up Blade's pillow, and hold it against my face. I breathe in deeply, smelling his shampoo and aftershave just to get a scent of him.

After an hour, I get up and walk over to the window and open it a few inches. The briny tang of the sea wafts in. The wind is strong and pushes the waves high up on the beach with a recurring thud.

Wiping tears from my eyes, I look up as a few dark clouds drift across the sky. They sprinkle a light rain and it's like the sky is crying with me.

I look over to Blade's boat shed, where he kept his fishing gear. A wave of anger fills my body, supplanting the feeling of hopelessness. Both Blade and I had trusted God to provide, and where had it gotten us? In deep debt to the bank. Now Blade is dead and I'm going to lose both the boat and the house. And his family has disowned me and wants me to leave town.

Meanwhile, the rum-runners are all still alive and making a killing. I feel a cold, heavy stone settle in my heart.

I close my eyes in the forlorn silence of the house and think, *It's not right. It's not fair.*

I open them again and look out at the sea, so dark now that it looks black. I'm seriously beginning to consider Larkin's offer.

CHAPTER EIGHT

The next morning, I make a fried egg with toast and eat my breakfast on the back deck. I'm still not hungry, but I'm going to eat anyway. Often I bring my Bible out, but not today. Instead I picked it up from my nightstand and slid it into the drawer earlier. Though deep sorrow and regret fill me, I just cannot read its passages or pray this morning.

The day is getting warm and the sun glitters off the water. I feel different. Still empty, but with a new feeling of resolve. I have to go on without Blade. It's what he would want. And I won't give Elsie and the others in Whaleback Cove the satisfaction of driving me out of town.

Later, I jump in the truck and drive with the window down, the warm breeze on my face. The sky is a cloudless blue and the morning smells of wildflowers blooming on both sides of the road.

Ten minutes later, I pull up in front of the Wade home. It's a two-story with brown cedar shingles, a buttercup yellow door, and matching shutters. The door looks brand new and I remember Larkin telling me that the gangsters kicked it in. There's a wide, white front porch that runs the length of the house with two white painted rocking chairs on it.

I climb out, straighten up, and survey the property. There's a garden shed to my left and, down from that, near the shore, a boathouse. I can see the ocean beyond the back yard, and a long dock. Sunlight slices between the branches of trees on the east side. Closest to the house, a large birch has clam and scallop shells hanging from its branches; they tinkle in the breeze. My mom did the same thing on an elm tree in our back yard when I was a child. I always loved the sound coming through my open window during the summers.

It's a gorgeous day without a hint of rain. The sun's shining and the air laden with the invigorating scents of pine and spruce, wild rose bushes and salt. The bright, cozy-looking home and view of the ocean seems inconsistent with the violence that happened here only a week ago.

I go up onto the porch and knock on the door. I hear footsteps and then Larkin opens it.

Her face lights up. "Good morning, Duska."

"Morning."

"It's good to see you. What brings you out here?"

"I wanted to talk to you. My phone's a party line, so I didn't want to call you first. You know Phyllis McFadden is always on it eavesdropping."

She laughs. "Yes, then she hustles over to Pruett's and spreads what she heard. Nothing's private in this town." Larkin steps back to allow my entrance. "Come on in. Let's talk in the kitchen."

I follow her inside. The house is as bright inside as outside and smells of apple pie and the faint trace of cleaning products. I hear the notes of the hymn *Yes, Jesus Loves Us* coming from the parlour. As I pass by, I glance in and see a little brown-haired boy and young blond woman sitting on a bench in front of a piano. I recognize the boy from seeing him around town. It's Larkin's brother, Bash. He plays while the woman nods her head in encouragement.

I step into the kitchen which, like mine, opens out onto the back porch. There's a large wood-burning cook stove and an oak table with six chairs. I'm surprised by the cleanliness, remembering that Ethan Wade was shot here. I smell apple pies baking in the oven and hear the snap and crackle of burning wood.

She sees me looking around and her eyes fill with grief and pain. "Yes, it happened here," she says in a quiet, wretched voice. "There was blood everywhere—on the walls, the ceiling, the kitchen counter. My best friend, Sadie Sheehan… she's the woman teaching Bash piano… I don't know how she did it, but she cleaned it all up."

I feel a tightening in my throat as images of Blade lying dead on the stretcher flood back. I nod in empathy.

"What shatters me is how he died," Larkin says. "Being alone. I keep wondering, did he die instantly? Or did he lie here in pain, slowly bleeding to death while Bash and I hid in the woods? Were we his last thoughts?"

I see the unmitigated grief in her eyes. I reach out and rest my hand on hers. "You had to stay in the woods to protect yourselves. That's what your dad wanted."

"Yes, but still. I can't help wondering if there wasn't something I could have done to scare off the mobsters."

"You and Bash would have been killed too."

She sniffs, wipes at her left eye. "I guess. So what did you want to talk about?"

"I'm considering your offer."

Her face brightens and she points to the table. "Have a seat. Want a coffee? I just made a pot."

"Sure," I say, sitting down. "I do have a few questions first."

"Of course. I'm happy to answer them." She goes to the stove, lifts a coffee pot, and pours two mugs of coffee. She sets the pot back down and carries the mugs over to the table, putting one down in front of me. "Milk and sugar?"

"Thanks, no. Just black." I pick up the mug, take a sip, and hold it in both hands.

She sits down across from me. "Fire away."

"First, the *Duska Mae* is fast, but so are the RCMP and Coast Guard boats."

"Your boat is faster. We can elude them."

"If they're close and spot us, we may not escape. And if they do catch us, they'll board the boat and find the liquor. It'll be game over for us."

She sips from her own cup, looking at me over the rim. "Which is why we'll need hidden compartments in your hold. Fallon can build them after he's finished with the engine. Cops will never find them. Thing is, the bootlegger, his name is Jean-Claude Boudreau—"

"Jean-Claude Boudreau? He owns a seafood distribution company, doesn't he?"

She nods. "Yes, he does, but he sells more liquor than fish these days."

"Right, I've seen his truck around."

"He lives outside town on Calm Waters Road. Anyway, he wants the bottles of liquor kept in burlocks. They'll protect the bottles and save a lot of room when we store them in the compartments. He brings in high-quality liquor for his customers, so he's fussy about how they're handled. With burlocks, we'll be able to carry a lot more than if we were hiding crates."

I frown. "What's a burlock?"

She sips her coffee and sets it down. "It's a large burlap bag. An American rum-runner created them and most rum-runners use them. The bag holds six forty-ounce bottles stored in a triangle formation. Then they stuff straw around the bottles and sew the bag up snug. Even if the bags move around in heavy seas, or if they're dropped, they almost never break. Also, if it looks like the Mounties or Coasties are gonna catch us, we can chuck them overboard and they'll sink to the seabed."

"And then the bootlegger shoots us for tossing his liquor," I say with a wry tone.

She ignores that. "As I mentioned before, your boat is too bright. There's grey paint in my dad's boat shed. I'll have Fallon paint the boat once he's done replacing the engine and building those hidden compartments in the hold."

"In the hold?"

"Yes, he'll build the compartments in the walls and floor of the hold. They'll be wide and deep enough to store a hundred gallons of liquor each. He'll use wooden boards to cover the compartments, but they'll be removable so we can stow and remove the liquor easily. Then over that, a second set of planks. We'll keep lobster traps on the deck. With them, the winch, and the snatch block, it'll look like we're fishing."

"Fishing at night?" I scoff.

"We have to go out under the veil of darkness. If we get stopped, we'll just say the town's fishermen threatened to ram us if they see us out there. That's why we fish at night. The Mounties are aware of how the fishermen are around here. It'll work."

I'm dubious. "You said we'd meet the rum-runners south of Three Islands. That's not the fishing grounds. If the Mounties or Coast Guard see us, they'll instantly suspect we're doing something illegal."

"That's one of the spots. There's three rendezvous points, and two are close to the fishing grounds. We can say we have to dock at my place instead of the wharf. It'll just look like we're either on our way out to the grounds or on our way back to my place. If we're careful, I think we'll spot them before they spot us. We can evade them."

"Okay, but some local fishermen who rum-run also go out in the middle of the night. You know what will happen if they see us."

"Yes. But again, Duska, that's why I need you and your fast boat. If it happens, we can outrun them."

I drink some coffee, then set it down, tapping my fingers on the tabletop while I ponder all this. Shafts of sunlight slash through the window and across the table.

After a moment, I look at Larkin. "And this guy is okay with me working for him even though we've never met?"

She nods. "Yes, he's fine with it. He knows about Blade's accident."

I feel my throat close at the mention of Blade's name. I look out the window to the bright, sunny sky, fighting back tears.

She watches me. "You okay?"

"Yes." I take a breath and look back at her. "Where do we get our fuel?"

"Jean-Claude has a guy not far up the coast who will sell us fuel. He'll pay us each a hundred dollars a month, and a hundred dollars for every load we successfully bring ashore. I'd like to bring in three, maybe four loads a week."

I do the math in my head and widen my eyes. "That's seventeen a month each. That's a lot of money."

"It is. And we're just small ducks in a big pond. It's nothing compared to what some of the town's fishermen and others along the south shore are making."

I shake my head in wonder. Even in his best seasons, Blade never made even a quarter of this, not after paying for diesel, gear, traps, and wages for his helper. I'd be making a pile of money with only a small expense for fuel and oil.

"It's your deal with this rum-runner," I point out. "You're not going to take more of the profit than me?"

"No. You're taking the same risk as I am. Even more, since it's your boat. So equal pay. And we'll share the cost of your fuel and whatever else the boat needs."

I look out the window, pondering it all, ignoring the voice of the Holy Spirit and murmurs of my conscience.

"It sounds tempting, but I'm still worried about what happens if we hit a storm and lose the liquor, or pirates rob us. We could get killed by the mob like your dad."

"My dad worked for mobsters in New York. He travelled from St. Pierre and Miquelon to the U.S. east coast. He worked twelve miles offshore. We'll be working for this local guy close to home."

"Still, he works for the mob."

"The Boston mob. Technically we're not doing anything illegal. We're not buying or selling. We're simply transferring liquor from one person out at sea and bringing it back to another onshore. Jean-Claude is the one buying the liquor from the mob and reselling it. That's contraband booze. He's cheating the government out of taxes. If he's caught, he'll be charged with tax evasion. But that's his risk, not ours."

I give her a sceptical look. "It has to be illegal to transport the liquor."

She shrugs. "Maybe. Anyway, the mob won't bother us and Jean-Claude's a good guy. He's not known to be violent, and he assures me that he knows the risks… that once in a while we may lose a load. He said we won't get paid if that happens, and if it happens too often we're done working for him. But he promised me he'd never hurt us."

I'm still dubious. "And you trust the word of a bootlegger?"

The piano music stops and I hear the murmur of Bash and Sadie's voices.

Larkin gives me a solemn nod. "I trust *this* bootlegger. He and my dad were friends. He offered me the work to help out. I only wish my dad had worked for him. He'd be alive right now."

"Maybe," I say, unconvinced.

"You'll see when you meet him. He's—" She pauses and gestures with a sharp tilt of her head behind me.

I turn around and see her brother walking into the room. He's slender like Larkin but has a little button nose, while hers is long and thin. He has doe-like brown eyes. I've seen him in town before, but only from afar. Up close, he's a cute little boy.

"Hi, Bash," I say with a smile. "I'm Duska."

He smiles shyly back. "Hi."

"Great job playing the piano."

His smile broadens.

"What's up, little guy?" Larkin asks.

"I'm hungry. Can I have a slice of pie now?"

I hear the wheezing in his voice and remember that he has asthma.

Larkin gets up and goes to the cupboard. "They're not ready yet. How about some cookies and milk?"

"Okay."

She goes to the fridge and pours a glass of milk for him. She hands it to him along with two cookies from a ceramic jar on the counter.

"Thank you," he says.

She looks at me and holds up the jar, grins. "Sorry, I'm a terrible host. I offered you coffee but nothing else. Would you like a molasses cookie?"

I smile back. "No, thanks."

Bash goes back into the living room. He seems like a well-mannered child and has the same friendly manner as his sister. But he's clearly a sick little boy. I can also tell that he and Larkin are very close, probably more so now that they've lost their father so soon after losing their mother. I understand better now why Larkin is so desperate.

"Who's going to watch Bash for you?" I ask.

"Sadie. She'll come and stay with him. I'll introduce you once they're done." She points out the window to the road. "Sadie lives in that white house with the red shutters at the entrance to my lane. She's my best friend. She'd never tell a soul."

"I don't like anyone else knowing what we're doing."

"Too late. Anyway, I need her whether you join me or not. Don't worry. Sadie's completely trustworthy. I've thought everything through very, very carefully."

I see that the youthful innocence on her face hides an iron will and a mature, sharp intellect.

"How will we know when to go out and meet the rum-running boat?"

"Jean-Claude has a sister who lives in town. Her son will come over here with a message from Jean-Claude with instructions… what night, which rendezvous site, and the time we're to meet them. We flash a light at the rum-runners when we're out at the rendezvous, and they'll flash back. Same thing with Jean-Claude at Schooner Cove, where he'll be waiting for us."

I bite the corner of my lip, watching her. "It all sounds so perilous."

Her tone is grave. "It'll be risky. It's certainly not an endeavour for the frail or faint-hearted. But then you don't strike me as either."

I feel unexpectedly warmed by the compliment, but inwardly I'm not so sure.

She reaches out and squeezes my hand. "We'll need to be extraordinarily brave and bold if we're going to keep the doubt and fear at bay. I believe that describes us. And if we stay strong, alert, and smart out there, no one is going to stop us."

I nod, still a bit uncertain, for it's not all about safety and the risk of being caught. It's the tidal wave of guilt I feel knowing that I'll be disobeying God. And Blade would be so disappointed, so saddened, if he knew what I was about to do.

"All right. I'll go to the bookstore now and tell Sophie I need some time off." I let out a breath. "I just hope I won't regret this."

Larkin squeezes my hand again, her gentle, reassuring eyes on my face. "Don't worry. It'll go smoothly. Remember, we may be the first women in Nova Scotia to go rum-running, but we aren't the only women. There are two off the eastern seaboard. They've been at it for a while and have been successful. If they can do it, we can too."

I push my chair back and stand. "I guess I'll see you once all the work is done on the boat."

"I'll contact Fallon right away so he can start. I'll tell him to leave some traps on the deck." She stands, smiles gratefully, and then reaches out and hugs me. "Thank you, Duska. You won't regret this."

I return the embrace and she walks me to the front door, opening it for me. We step outside into the warm sunshine.

Once I get the engine running, I get behind the wheel. I give Larkin a wave and drive away, my heart filled with uncertainty, my stomach roiling with anxiety.

CHAPTER NINE

A week later, the boat's ready. The new engine's been installed and the hull is painted grey. The hidden compartments have been built into the hold. Fallon also painted the new name on the bow and stern, in bold white, after I asked him. I smile to myself as I admire his handiwork. *Bad Reputations.* I hope the name maddens Doreen Jolly and all the other dour-faced, judgemental people in town.

It's a warm and beautiful spring day, but I'm too grief-stricken to appreciate it. Midmorning, when I was sure the fishermen were gone, I walked from my house to the wharf. I thanked and paid Fallon with the cash Larkin gave me for the work. Now I'm in the wheelhouse, getting ready to sail over to Larkin's place.

Suddenly I hear thumping on my deck and angry voices. I go out and see Johnny Defoe on my deck, and Billy and Eric Stoker standing on the wharf in front of my boat. I'm surprised. I thought everyone had left long ago.

I also notice Jolene Taylor standing atop stacks of lobster traps, grinning down at the men.

"Hey! Get off my boat!" I shout at Johnny.

He ignores me and grabs the gaff off the back wall of the wheelhouse, where it was hanging from a hook. He dashes over to the traps and starts swinging it at Jolene, the same way he would to hook a buoy.

Billy and Eric laugh and encourage him on.

Jolene scrambles up the traps to get onto the highest ones in the stack. They're tied but still wobble from her weight. She's wearing black trousers, a white wool sweater, and black sneakers. Her ruddy hair hangs loose on her shoulders.

"Jolene! No, stop!" I say. "Don't climb any higher. That stack you're on isn't secured."

She looks down at me and grins.

Laughing, Johnny reaches up and tries to snag her sneaker with the gaff. She leaps back and the whole stack wobbles dangerously.

Billy and Eric throw their heads back and howl with laughter.

"Johnny, stop that," I shout, furious. Moving in front of him and grabbing the gaff with my hands, I yank it from his grip. "Get off the boat!"

He laughs, dodges around me, and reaches up with his arms and tries to grab Jolene by the ankle.

I wave the gaff at him. "Try that again and I'll stick this hook right in your eyes."

His eyes narrow. "You wouldn't dare."

"Try me."

"Calm down, woman. I wasn't going to hook her. I was just giving her something to hang on to so she wouldn't fall and break her stupid neck."

"Sure, you were. Get off my boat. I mean it."

He smirks. "It's the bank's boat from what I've heard."

I wave the gaff closer to his face. "Get off now."

"Fine, but you girls have two minutes to get off the wharf, or I'll be back to throw you both into the harbour." He brushes past me and jumps over the washboard to the wharf road, joining his buddies.

I look up at Jolene. She's standing on the highest stack, both her feet planted on traps, her arms spread out for balance.

"Jolene, come on down now, carefully as you can."

She grins at me. Quick and agile as a cat, she climbs down and jumps the last couple of traps to the deck beside me.

"What happened anyway?" I ask. "Why did you climb up there?"

"I was outside Pruett's and saw you. I was coming over to say hello when those idiots saw me on the wharf and chased me. I made it to your boat, but Billy jumped on the deck. So up I went."

"That was dangerous."

"Nah, I have good balance and Johnny's too chicken to climb up after me."

She possesses bold courage. Her face, true to her vivid red hair, is freckled across her cheeks and nose. Her vibrant green eyes tease a playful spirit. She has an impish grin and innocent, childlike manner. She looks like she's easy prey for the bullies in this town, but clearly she's nothing of the sort.

"Oh, Jolene, afraid or not, don't do anything like that again. You could get hurt."

She scowls, wounded. "I didn't climb up because I was scared. I'm not afraid of them. I run as fast as a jaguar. I could have taken off at any time and they wouldn't have caught me. I was just having some fun with them."

"Still…"

She puts her hands on her skinny hips and jerks her chin toward Johnny and his two buddies. "They won't let women on the wharf because they're just afraid that if we start fishing, we'll outfish them."

"Probably true."

She's quiet for a moment, considering this. Finally, she nods briskly. "I'm right, and my husband is the worst of the bunch. As for the others, ha! They won't stop women from going out, but they won't help us, either. They would never stand up to Frank or his pals."

I hang the gaff on the hook. "Well, you're not afraid of them. But most of the women are, and I suppose a lot of the men."

She nods, and we're quiet for a moment.

Jolene smiles and points to the bow. "You aren't afraid of them either. I love the new name."

I smile back, then pick up a container of lubricant, open the lid to the wooden gearbox, and set it down inside next to a jug of oil and metal toolbox. Also in the box are stacks of coiled line.

I shut the lid, turn, and face her. "But I am a little afraid of them, Jolene. I just don't let it stop me from doing what I need to do."

"Glad to hear it. Listen, the next time you need help with anything, on the boat or anything else, just ask me. I think we're a lot alike."

"What about Burke?"

"What about him?"

"You'll ruin your reputation hanging around me."

She laughs. "I'm not worried about that either. I'm not interested in winning a popularity contest. Trust me, my reputation was shot years ago. I've long been a misfit in this town."

"All right then. There is something you can do right now to help me."

"Name it."

"Would you unmoor the lines and throw them on the boat for me while I start the engine? I'm moving the boat."

"Really? I heard the bank was taking it."

"No."

"You sold it?"

"No again."

"Ha, you're hiding it from the bank, aren't you? Good, I hate banks."

"No, I'm just moving it to another dock."

"I'm happy to help." She punches me on the arm before walking over to the nearest bollard and lifting the bow line.

I go into the wheelhouse and stand at the helm. The waves roll beneath the boat and thump softly against the pilings. I draw a breath, turn the key, and the engine settles into a quiet purr.

Through the open wheelhouse door, I see Jolene toss the last line onto the deck.

"Bon voyage, Duska!" she yells with unmistakable admiration.

"Goodbye, and thanks again."

"Anytime!" Grinning, she gives me a thumbs up and strides away down the wharf.

Gulls swarm over the wharf. A buoy clangs from the harbour mouth.

I wipe my damp palms on my trousers and stand straighter. I throttle forward and ease the boat away from the wharf. Pushing the throttle, I motor out of the harbour as a small herd of seals, the pups barking, follow. I'm trembling a little and my pulse thumps in my throat. Yet, surprisingly, I'm as excited as I am fearful.

CHAPTER TEN

The following evening, with the sky growing a lush purple, I go into the kitchen and add wood to the stove. I turn down the damper so it'll burn slower and then walk to the front door. I'm wearing one of Blade's flannel shirts, a wool sweater, and long johns under a pair of Blade's denim overalls I shortened and took in at the waist.

I pull on Blade's fishing coat; it's too big but will keep me warm. I tuck my long, light brown hair up under Blade's black cap and pull on cotton gloves, sliding the rubber fishing gloves in my coat pocket. Lastly, I slip my feet into my knee-high rain boots that, along with the two pairs of wool socks, should keep my feet warm.

Then, smelling Blade's aftershave, I go still. It smells like the sea, cloves, and cinnamon. A fresh spicy tang I always loved. My heart squeezes painfully as I lean my face into the collar of his coat and breathe deeply.

"Oh Blade, how can I live without you?" I whisper in a broken voice.

Once I pull myself together, I leave the house, making my way to the truck. I hear the tide rushing in and wail of the foghorn on Redemption Island. The wind moans in the tops of the trees around the property. An icy chill stubbornly clings to the night air though it's spring. T.S. Elliot is right; April truly is the cruellest month.

I open the door but pause to look out to sea. The moon is hidden behind clouds in a charcoal sky. Darkness falls like a blanket over the ocean. Far out, green buoy lights flash, but nothing else. The vast blackness makes me uneasy. I draw in a deep breath and climb in behind the wheel of the truck.

I drive through the quiet streets of town. Yellowish-white fog slithers over the road like long, fat pythons. The street and sidewalks are empty, and the windows of the businesses and houses are dark.

When I leave town, Waterfront Street becomes the Oceanside Highway, winding around the coastline all the way to the larger town of Thunder Cove thirty miles south. After two miles, I turn right onto Whitecap Lane and steer down the rutted dirt road to Larkin's house, the last of only three on the road. I pull into her driveway and park next to her father's car.

All the windows are dark except for a dim yellow light in one of the front windows. As I get out, I hear the surf rushing up the shore below her house.

Larkin must have been watching for me, because the front door opens and she pokes her head out. "Hi, come on in. I was just having a coffee before we head out. I need it to keep me alert. You want one?"

"Yes, sure."

"Let's be quiet. Bash is upstairs sleeping. Sadie's in the bedroom next to his."

We stand at the kitchen counter and gulp our coffees down. Larkin's wearing a pair of her father's denim overalls, a red flannel long-sleeved shirt, and over that a heavy sweater. We set our cups in the sink and then Larkin pulls on her dad's fishing coat and black wool cap, her hair tucked up under it. I see a pair of black rubber fishing gloves sticking out of her coat pocket.

Out at sea, in the dark of night, with no lights, we'll sail almost unseen. In the moonlight or illumination of shore lights, our silhouettes will make it look from shore like we're fishing. And if the RCMP spots us and shines a light on us, they'll think we're men. Even if they realize we're women, it won't matter. I've taken over Blade's fishing licence and territory. The lobster traps marked with Blade's registration numbers, and orange buoys, are now registered to me. We've also kept his fishing gear on the deck. If they stop us, we'll look like legitimate fisherwomen.

Larkin says goodbye to Sadie and we leave the house to walk down the dock. There's Blade's boat, rocking on the water in the moonlight. I freeze. Despite the new name and colour, seeing Blade's boat, the stern stacked with traps, is like being hit in the chest with a sledgehammer. It's all I can do to stay standing. A lone tear slips down my cheek. It's hard to breathe.

Larkin reaches out and wipes it away with her fingertip. "You okay?"

I take in a deep breath. "Yes."

"Let's pray first."

I frown. "A bit hypocritical, isn't it?"

"We can still ask Him to keep us safe as far as the sailing goes."

I nod.

Holding hands, we bow our heads and ask God to watch over us. When we're done, I manage a silent prayer asking Him to forgive us. My heart is a storm of guilt, excitement, and fear. Of the three, guilt is the strongest.

"All set?" Larkin asks.

"Yes."

We jump over the rail onto the deck. My petrified heart bangs in my chest. I can't believe I'm going to do this.

The sea billows with steel-grey night fog that shrouds the boat. Dew drips from the lobster traps onto the deck and the boat groans at its mooring, as if it can't wait to get going.

Larkin unmoors us while I go into the wheelhouse. I step up to the helm and with shaky hands turn the key. The engine turns over and runs smoothly. Larkin enters the wheelhouse, shutting the door behind her. She stands beside me at the helm and arches an eyebrow at me.

Smiling, she gives a silent nod, her teeth glinting white in the moonlight shining into the dark cabin.

I ease the throttle ahead and carefully steer the boat away from the dock. Seagulls follow us, wheeling above the deck where the bait bucket sits.

"Wow, we're really doing this," Larkin says, white puffs of her breath spiralling in the cold air. "I'm both scared and excited."

"I feel the same way." I gaze out the windshield to the fog-wreathed water and add, "Let's be careful."

I throttle forward, heading into the open sea, my heart about to burst. I grip the steering wheel with white-knuckled hands.

The bow knifes easily through the waves as I steer through the fog bank, only able to see about a hundred yards ahead. I watch for Coast Guard or Mountie boats that might be lurking in the darkness or following us at a distance. Larkin alternately keeps an eye out for boats and shines a flashlight at a map as she guides me in the right direction.

Once we're in deeper water, the fog thins out and I push the throttle. We roar out to sea, the bow lifting and then smacking back down on the water. The deep rumble of the engine drowns out our voices.

Clouds cover the moon, making the night tarry black. Like us, the rum-runners run without lights and we have to watch diligently for them.

The water is velvety black. On the horizon, the lights of a big cargo ship glow as it sails past. I hold the throttle in my right hand and the steering wheel in my left, my heart racing with the thrill and terror.

The seas are mild tonight and we make good time without seeing any boats in the vicinity. Once at the rendezvous site, I ease off the throttle and cut the engine.

Larkin goes out onto the deck and drops the anchor over the side. I go outside too, watching as the clouds scud away, revealing a half-moon that casts a shaft of silver light over the wide expanse of the open Atlantic. We'd be easy to spot under that moonlight.

We stand at the starboard side deck rail, the boat rocking on the waves. It's a windless night, the air fresh but very cold.

I inhale and feel the chill of the air in my nose. When I exhale, white plumes spiral into the night air. I shuffle my feet on the deck to keep my toes from freezing. The swells lap gently against the hull and I keep my eye on the water, knowing that the ocean can be deceptively tranquil.

"I hear a boat," Larkin says.

I listen, ears straining, muscles rigid, but detect only the light thump of waves against the hull. "I don't hear anything."

"It's approaching from the south."

I look south, ears peeled. And then, in the near distance, I hear the low throb of its diesel engine advancing. But still can't see it. It keeps coming.

Before the boat reaches us, its idles down to a low rumble. In the moonlight, I make out the silhouette of a long, slender boat gliding on the waves. It's so slender that it's hard to see with the naked eye.

Larkin points her flashlight, then turns it on and shuts it off. Seconds later, a light flashes once, back at her. Larkin turns the flashlight on and off three more times; the opposing light blinks three times back.

"That's them," she says. "They'll come over now."

I watch the dark shape of a grey boat take shape. The name *Nachtleiter* is painted in white lettering on the stern. Two men dressed in dark clothing standing on the port side are holding onto the wooden rail. Their voices, speaking German, carry over to us.

The younger man turns on a flashlight and runs the beam over our faces. Then he moves it away and rakes the deck and wheelhouse of our boat.

"Gut," he says to the other man and clicks off the light.

The older, stockier man grunts and then leans down, picking up a coil of rope from the deck. He tosses it to Larkin but misses her outstretched arms and it falls into the water.

"Verdammt," he curses and yanks the line back up.

He pulls his left arm back farther before tossing it over the railing again. This time she catches it and ties it securely to the stern railing. The man tosses another rope to me, and because our boats are close now I'm able to catch it on the first try and tie it to the bow.

The hulls of both boats rub together, making a grating, metallic squeak that carries across the water.

"Damen, attention," says the older man in a gruff voice. "We must work in the dark and be as quiet as possible. We'll lower down the burlocks in wooden crates. There's seven burlocks in each crate. Take the burlocks out of the crate and stow them in your hold. Then we'll haul the empty crate back up and fill it again. Handle them with care and stow them snugly. You pay for any you break."

"Understood," Larkin says.

She lifts her arms to grab the crate as the men lower it to us. I open the hatch to the hold and climb down the short ladder a few rungs and then stop. Larkin carries the crate over to the open hatch door and sets it down on the deck. We work as noiselessly as possible as she lifts the burlocks out one by one and then passes them down to me where I stand on the ladder waiting. I take a burlock and climb to the bottom of the hold and place it carefully in a hidden compartment in the port wall. I stow them from the port to the starboard wall, working my way from stern to bow. Then I start placing them in the hull under the false floorboard. It's just my imagination, but it seems like I can feel the boat sink slightly under the weight of the burlocks.

Once I'm done, I climb back up to the deck and secure the hatch cover.

"That's all we can take," Larkin calls up to the men.

"Schoen," the gruff-sounding man says. He pulls a small flashlight from his coat pocket, puts it in his mouth, and grips it with his lips. He then pulls a notebook and pencil from his coat pocket and holds it in the flashlight's beam. He writes something, then puts the pencil back in his pocket. He removes the flashlight from his mouth, clicks it off, and slides it back into his pocket. "Alles fertig."

"Watch out for the Mounties," warns the second man, a teenager with thick blond hair sticking out from under his grey cap. He has a milder German accent. "They're out and about tonight."

That gives us pause.

"Thanks for the warning," Larkin says after a few seconds. "We will."

"Auf Wiedersehen." The teenager offers a quick wave and smile.

"Auf Wiedersehen," we say, untying the lines and throwing them back up to the men.

The older man begins coiling the line up while the younger opens the door to the wheelhouse and calls in to the captain. "Alles fertig, Papa."

Their engine starts up with a loud rumble in the night air and the boat eases away. It makes a slow turn, then roars off, picking up speed as it races south. Waves rise in its wake and rock our boat. Cold sea spray splashes up and slaps us in the face.

I wipe my face with the sleeve of my coat. My toes and fingers are so cold that they're cramping up. "I'm freezing. Let's go in."

Larkin nods and we both hurry into the warmth of the wheelhouse.

I start the engine. "They didn't care about me being here with you."

Larkin shakes her head, raising her voice over the rumble. "None of their business. Jean-Claude filled me in. That's Gunther Reinhardt's boat from Lunenburg. He's of German descent. *Nachtleiter* means *Night Glider* in English. The older man is Gunther's brother. The boy is Gunther's son. They work for Jean-Claude as contact boats just like us. Jean-Claude buys the liquor from gangsters in Boston. He pays Gunther to pick up the liquor from another boat off the coast of Massachusetts and then bring it here to us. Jean-Claude pays us to meet up with Gunther and then bring the liquor ashore to him. Gunther's brother was recording in his notepad how much liquor they offloaded. The mob keeps meticulous records."

"Jean-Claude sells that much liquor?"

"Yes. Over the past few years, it's become a very lucrative business." Larkin cants her head. "But not for much longer. There's talk that prohibition is going to end within a year."

I nod, having read about that in the town newspaper. The government is going to concede defeat to the rum-runners and gangsters.

"Let's head to Schooner Cove now," she says. "Jean-Claude's waiting."

Soot-black clouds move across the moon again as I steer the boat in thick darkness toward Schooner Cove. I have mixed emotions. I'm surprised and thankful at how smoothly the first part of the mission went, but guilt for disobeying God once again blankets me. I push the guilt away, since we're in greater danger now with the liquor on the boat. If we're spotted now, we're done for. I'm so frightened that my throat is bone dry and my heart pounds violently. I push the throttle forward even more and speed toward Schooner Cove.

As we get closer to land, warm yellow lights glow in some of the windows of the houses that dot the coastline. It's almost three-thirty. Must be fishermen up early and getting ready for another day at sea.

I still can't relax. The Mounties and Coast Guard boats could be hiding in the shadows close to shore, ready to pounce.

When we reach the cove, I pull back on the throttle and idle the engine as low as it will go without stalling about a hundred yards offshore. "This good?"

"Perfect." Larkin goes out onto the deck and stands at the bow, pulling her flashlight out of her jacket pocket. She aims it at the shore, turning it on and off three times.

My eyes comb the beach. I make out three dark shapes, standing near the water's edge. Seconds later, a light blinks back three times.

Larkin comes back inside the cabin, her face flushed from the cold. "That's Jean-Claude. Let's go in."

I steer toward the beach and soon see three men standing at the water's edge, close to a long and narrow dock. To the left of the dock, about fifty feet behind the men, is a five-ton truck with a canopy over the bed. Behind the truck, set back on the lawn above the embankment, I see a dark cottage.

I carefully ease the boat up beside the dock and Larkin ties it up. I cut the engine and join her. We proceed down the dock and stop in front of the men on the beach. I shine my flashlight on Larkin and myself so they know for sure that it's us. Then I shine it up to the cottage. It leans to one side, like it's about to collapse. The windows are dark at the back and one is boarded up. It's clearly been abandoned for many years.

I move my light onto the three men. One is short, has thick grey hair and a moustache, and looks to be in his fifties. This must be Jean-Claude. He has a huge tattoo of a crab on his neck, greenish-grey and brown in colour. I recognize it as a horseshoe crab, common to the waters off Nova Scotia.

The other two men are in their teens or early twenties. They're wearing tan ball hats on their heads with a logo that reads "Boudreau & Sons Seafood." They're tall and thin but look strong.

Jean-Claude raises a hand, a curt motion in the dark, as though to say, *Move the light out of his face*. I do so but keep the light on, pointing it to the ground.

The older man doesn't introduce his two companions, but they both resemble him. They must be his sons. They constantly look out to the water, then back to a narrow dirt lane on one side of the cottage, no doubt watching for approaching boats or vehicles.

Jean-Claude looks at Larkin. "Any problems?"

She shakes her head. "No, it went smoothly."

"Bon." His eyes slide from Larkin to me and remain on me. He's about five-seven in height and slender, but he has large hands and thick fingers like a gorilla.

"This is the friend I spoke to you about, Duska Doucette," Larkin says. "Her husband was Blade Doucette."

He's quiet for a moment, rubbing his cheek with his fingertips while studying me. "Oui. I'm sorry about your loss. Was a terrible accident."

Once again, the gut-wrenching shock of Blade's grisly death overcomes me. It hurts to swallow.

"Doucette? Parlez-vous Francais?"

"No, my husband did," I reply. "I know a few words, but that's it."

He nods. "I agreed to you working for me only because I trust Larkin. But I have to ask you dis: if you get caught, can you keep your mout shut?"

"I can."

"You'll go to jail," he warns. "Maybe for a long time."

I give him a bold stare. "I know the risks. I've accepted them."

"It's a hard ting to take a boat out to sea when da weather bad. You'll get tossed around, maybe flipped right out of your boat. You fall in, or your boat sink, don't matter you can swim like a dolphin, you'll die of hypothermia."

"I can do it," I assure him. "I grew up on my dad's fishing boat. And my husband took me out often. Both let me steer, even in rough seas."

He observes me for a time. "I tink you two girls are tougher den a lot of men I know."

Larkin and I exchange smiles.

"Bon. Let's get to work."

Larkin and I lead the two young men down the dock. We jump back aboard while they wait. I open the hatch and go down into the hold. I open the hidden compartments, starting with the starboard side, and take out the burlocks one by one, passing them up to Larkin, who then carries them out. The men carry the burlocks up to the truck, where Jean-Claude waits on the open tailgate and stacks them in the truck bed.

Larkin and I work steadily, the muscles in our arms straining, until the hold's empty. We then walk back to the beach and join Jean-Claude at the truck. Like the logo on their hats, I see that the sign on the side of the truck reads "Boudreau

& Sons Seafood." I look inside and see large wooden crates with the same name printed in white lettering. They're stacked three high, filling the entire bed. I wonder if any actually have seafood in them.

Jean-Claude notices me looking. "Crates in front hold lobster. Booze in back ones. If I get stopped, I'm hoping the cops will only open the front ones."

I nod.

He pulls a notebook and pen from his coat pocket and records numbers in it. He then puts the notebook and pencil away and jumps down from the truck. He shuts the tailgate while the young men walk around to the passenger door and climb into the cab.

Jean-Claude hands each of us a yellow envelope thick with bills. "Bien joue, mon cheres."

"Thank you," Larkin and I say simultaneously.

He lifts his brows. "So Wednesday night you meet up wit da *Night Glider* again. I'll send da nephew with instructions. After you offload booze, meet me here, same time."

Larkin nods. "All right."

"Bon." He turns and climbs in behind the wheel of the truck.

We watch Jean-Claude and his two helpers drive away. We then leap aboard the boat and go into the wheelhouse. A moment later, we're racing across the waves in the direction of Larkin's place, the thick envelope of cash stuffed in our coat pockets.

Larkin takes hers out and counts the bills. "Two hundred dollars!" She raises her eyebrows and smiles. "Duska, we did it."

I smile back in wonder. "That we did."

An hour later, I'm driving home, the smell of salt on my skin. Salmon pink streaks of dawn are filling the sky. I pull into my driveway and hustle out of the truck and into the house. Only then does my heartbeat return to normal, and my stomach unclench.

Though I found the whole endeavour petrifying, it was also undeniably exhilarating. I still wrestle with guilt, but I'm relieved that I'll be able to make the mortgage and boat payments on May 1. I'll also be able to pay my utility bills, buy groceries, and have some money leftover.

I put the cash in the lockbox under the loose plank in the floor of the closet and go straight to bed. Within seconds, I fall into a heavy sleep, the first since Blade died.

CHAPTER ELEVEN

April 11, 1929

Jolene Taylor sits on the kitchen chair in the darkness, shattered, vacant-eyed, perfectly still. She turns her head and glances down to the right. Sees him sprawled on the floor below the stove, not moving. She shudders and draws in a breath.

Standing, Jolene picks up her suitcase and walks to the front door. It opens with a squeal that screeches through the quiet house like a watchman's trumpet. She freezes, heart thrashing in her chest.

Nothing.

She goes out and walks to the end of the driveway, where she takes one last look at their home. It sits silent and dark as death itself. Even the chill night air is unnervingly quiet.

She draws in a deep breath to calm her nerves, then buttons her coat up to the collar and turns toward town. Two voices are speaking in her head. One says, *Oh Jolene, what have you done? You need to help him.* But the second whispers, *Run, Jolene, run while you can.*

She flees, sprinting down the dark, vacant road. Alternately, she looks ahead and then behind her for headlights. It's nearly 3:00 a.m. and she has a couple of hours before any fishermen will be up, their vehicles beginning to appear on the road.

Still, she has to be careful. The Mounties will be patrolling the roads in and out of Whaleback Cove. They'll wonder why she, a young married woman, is out and carrying a suitcase in the dead of night.

Jolene jogs down the tree-lined road in the stillness. Shadows lie waist-high along the road, which snakes for a few miles from her house to the southern edge of town. The half-moon shines just brightly enough for her to make out the road in the dark, cool night. The only sound is the scrape and rustle of branches when the wind stirs the trees. And her own footsteps on the road, of course.

A fox steps out of the woods and onto the roadway, startling her so badly that she jumps about a foot in the air. They both stand still, staring at each other. After a moment, though, the fox simply trots across the road and disappears into the woods on the other side.

She runs faster, wanting to make good time before daylight, and then hears an approaching car. She dashes into the ditch and splashes through the cold water. Clambering up the bank into the woods, she ducks behind a thick bush and peers around it. Headlights illuminate the road as the vehicle nears and then speeds past. She scrambles back out onto the road, watching the red taillights fade and then disappear around a turn; the sound of its engine dies away into the night.

She pushes forward. There's the steady buzz of insects from the bushes and the croaks of frogs from the ditch. But no more vehicles or wildlife appear.

Soon she reaches town. Here, closer to the ocean, the fog thickens, twisting over the road like white ribbons. But the wind coming off the water is pushing east, away from town. She walks along Waterfront Street as a dog barks at her from the front yard of a house. It doesn't approach. The dark streets and sidewalks are quiet and empty.

She's wearing brown men's trousers, a regular habit which her husband Burke thinks is disgraceful. She receives a lot of rude comments from townspeople for doing so, but she doesn't care. Under one of Burke's plaid flannel shirts, she's wearing a long-sleeved red cotton shirt. Over that, a green sweater and a black fleece-lined jacket. On her feet she wears black socks and tennis shoes. She's tucked her long red hair up under Burke's wool hat.

She's packed a loaf of bread, the leftover chicken she baked for their Sunday dinner earlier today, as well as a block of cheddar cheese, six gingersnap cookies, five apples, and coffee. It's all in the suitcase, stored alongside the clothing and personal items she'd been packing for the past few months. Also in the case is her wallet with the four dollars she's been secretly saving.

The suitcase is heavy, but she's strong for her size, and even more strong-willed. That, and her inner fear of being caught, pushes her on. It's not all she needs, but it's all she managed to find as she ran through the bedroom and kitchen, adding things in unorganized panic.

Jolene hears a vehicle approach and ducks into an alley between the drugstore and the hardware store. She watches from the shadows as an RCMP patrol car drives past and then turns left onto a residential street.

She leaves the alley and pushes on, soon leaving the business strip. Not long after that, she reaches the southern edge of town, where Waterfront Street becomes the Oceanside Highway. She relaxes a little. There are a few homes here, but only one has a faint yellow light in a window.

She's anxious to reach her great-aunt Beulah's cottage, about five miles from town. It sits at the end of a dirt lane called Schooner Lane, off the right side of the highway along the ocean. The cottage faces a sheltered inlet called Schooner Cove and features a magnificent view of the Atlantic. The cottage is the lone home on the lane and hasn't been used in more than two decades. Beulah was a spinster and left the cottage to a great-nephew who lives in New York City now. He's never done a thing to the property, and only visited once since Beulah died, only staying long enough to lock the place up. Jolene only went once as a child, but she heard her parents talk about it. It must still be there, vacant and in such rough shape that no one would expect a person to hide out inside. She recalls that it has a big woodstove and a pump; her aunt had severe arthritis and couldn't carry a pail of water from the well.

More important, Burke doesn't know about the property. In fact, no one seems to know about it. She'll be safe there for a while, even when Burke comes after her.

But of course in a town this size, he'd find her before too long.

Jolene picks up her pace, and she sings to herself as she walks, falling back on her favourite hymn, "Be Thou My Vision." But she notices there's a peculiar empty pitch to her voice.

CHAPTER TWELVE

Jolene reaches Schooner Lane an hour later. There's no sign out front, but she knows to turn right onto a narrow, rutted dirt lane that's overgrown with grass and weeds. She dashes down the long, dark road to the end. Branches of pine and oak grow on both sides, reaching out over the road like the arms of ghouls. Thick brush grows, too, but she figures a car could, if the driver was careful to avoid the holes, make its way to the cottage, barring some scratches.

She stops in the weedy driveway and studies the cottage. She trembles, but not from the damp sea air. She's woozy with hope. She's done it. She's escaped.

The cedar shingled walls are weather faded grey, the windowsills peeling with black rot showing underneath. The roof is bowed; in fact, the whole structure leans precariously to one side. When the wind rises, she hears the cottage groan. It looks unsafe to live in, but she has no other choice.

She steps up on to the front porch and tries the doorknob. It's locked. She tries the two front windows, but they too are locked. Walking down the porch steps, she slips around the side of the cottage and climbs the back steps to another rickety porch.

The back door is also locked.

There's a window on each side of the door, one boarded up, the other not. She sets her suitcase down and pushes it up. It gives a little, but then jams. The cottage is so badly tilted that the window has shifted and won't slide easily. Using two hands, she pushes as hard as she can; finally it gives and slides all the way up.

She's about to climb over the sill when she suddenly freezes, a leg raised in the air. Voices are coming from the beach, below the house. She holds her breath and listens.

Heart thumping, she slips down the steps and across the high grass and weeds of the back lawn. Where the back lawn surrenders to the embankment, there is a cluster of skinny juniper and pine trees. She creeps over, crouches down behind them, and peers down to the beach.

In the moonlight she sees the dock extending about a hundred feet into the water. She hears the growl of a diesel engine and sees a fishing boat slowly approach. To the left, on the light sand that stays dry even at high tide, sits a big truck at the end of a narrow lane. Beside the canopied truck, outlined in the moonlight, stand three men—one short, the other two thin and tall. The words "Boudreau & Sons Seafood" is printed in white lettering on the truck's side. She recognizes the name. Someone named Boudreau owns a seafood distribution company.

But why is he parked on her great-aunt's property? she wonders.

The boat pulls up next to the dock. As Jolene watches, a slender figure comes out of the wheelhouse and jumps onto the dock, tying the boat's bow and stern lines. Its engine dies and another thin figure emerges to join the first. The two of them—young men, she figures—walk down the dock and to the other three on the beach. Then darkness falls over the ground as clouds obscure the moon. One of the men from the boat turns on a flashlight, shining it on himself first and then on his companion. He shines it briefly on the cottage, and then on the three men standing across from him.

Jolene gasps in surprised recognition. Those aren't men; they're women. One is Larkin Wade, a young woman whose father was recently murdered. Talk is that he was involved in rum-running for the mob and his death had something to do with that.

And the second is Duska Doucette! The men must be Boudreau and his sons.

The clouds slip away from the moon and once again light up the beach. Jolene sees Boudreau walk over to the truck, open the tailgate, and pull the canopy back. She can't quite make out what happens next, but it looks like the women unload sacks from the boat and deliver them to the waiting men, who then load them into the truck. Their boots crunch on the sand and seashells.

An hour later, they're finished. The young men shut the tailgate and jump into the cab. Boudreau hands the women white envelopes and then gets behind the wheel; the truck grinds into gear and slowly drives up off the beach and up the narrow lane past the cottage. The truck is high enough off the ground that Jolene realizes it can easily manoeuvre down the weedy, overgrown driveway.

Hearing the women's voices, Jolene turns to see them walk down the dock to the boat, their rubber boots thumping on the wooden planks. Duska leaps over the railing onto the deck and disappears into the wheelhouse. The engine starts with a low rumble, then Larkin unmoors the lines and jumps aboard. She coils and stows the lines.

The boat backs up, idling away from the wharf, and turns to face the bay. They roar away, the sound carrying across the water and fading off into the distance.

Jolene walks down the embankment to the beach. The wind has grown stronger and gusts on the water, thrusting up swells topped with whitecaps. She stands at the water's edge and gazes out to sea. The tide rushes in and she leaps back before it soaks her shoes.

She walks to the end of the weather-beaten dock, its old posts grey and cracked in places. Though many of the planks have been replaced recently, the ones that haven't sag under her weight, groaning a little. But it's been repaired enough to use while still appearing unusable to anyone who sees it from the water.

The incoming tide hisses as it rolls over pebbles up the beach. Jolene's mind reels from her discovery. Then, as the sun begins to creep up the horizon, she walks back to the cottage, feeling a bloom of hope in her heart.

CHAPTER THIRTEEN

I'm standing at the stove stirring a pot of leftover chicken soup when I hear the creak of footsteps cross the front porch boards. Then there's two light raps on the door. I slide the pot over to the cool side of the stove and go to the door.

A young man stands on the step, face turned away. He's slender, about five-four, wearing a navy blue wool hat, brown trousers, knee-high rubber boots, and a black jacket.

"Hello?" I say.

He looks at me, revealing vibrant emerald-green eyes. He pulls off his hat and shakes loose his long, thick, fiery red hair.

My eyes widen. It's Jolene Taylor! And she has a swollen lip.

She glances nervously over her shoulder to the road before facing me again. "Hi, Duska. May I come in?"

"Of course." I step back to let her in and then shut the door behind her. "What's up?"

"I need to talk to you," she whispers, her eyes darting first into the living room on her right and then the guest bedroom on her left. "Are we alone?"

"Yes, it's just me." I feel a twist of raw pain in my heart. The house is so quiet without Blade. Sometimes I wander from room to room, feeling lost here without him. I keep having to tell myself that he's gone; though it frightens me, I must carry on.

"Hey, you okay?" Jolene asks. "You look like you went a million miles away there."

I let out a soft breath. "Yes, let's talk in the kitchen. Want a coffee?"

"Sure."

I lead her into the kitchen. I fill two mugs from the coffee pot warming on the stove, setting one down in front of her. "Sugar or cream?"

"No, I like it black as oil, and hot enough to burn your lips, thanks."

I carry my own mug over and join her at the table. I sip my coffee, eyeing her over the rim. "So how can I help you?"

"What were you and Larkin Wade up to last night at Schooner Cove?"

I set my mug down and look at her, too stunned to speak.

She places her hat on the table and smiles. "I saw you, Larkin, and three men at Schooner Cove around four o'clock. You tied up your husband's boat at the old dock there."

It feels like all the air has been drained from the room. My heart stutters for a few seconds. "So?"

"Sooo, the other day when we met on the wharf you told me you were taking the boat to another dock. I'm guessing that was Larkin's place. She has a nice dock. Am I right?"

"Not necessarily."

"Ha! I see right through you. Anyway, it doesn't really matter where you sailed. What matters is that last night I saw you and Larkin offloading sacks from your boat to the men's truck."

I fight to keep the shock I feel from my face.

Jolene sees anyway and chuckles. "Yup, you're busted."

Mind reeling, I take a slow, deep breath. "Busted? Why would you say that?"

"I know what you were doing."

The room goes still. I can't believe this. "We were just offloading lobsters."

She snorts. "Lobsters, sure."

"It's true. Larkin and I are lobster fishing at night. We sell them to the guy who owns the truck, and he then sells them to restaurants in Halifax."

"Nope. That's not what you're doing."

I fight to keep panic from my face. "It is. Larkin got her dad's lobster fishing licence transferred to her name. I transferred Blade's into mine. But as you well know, if the town fishermen see what we're doing, they'll sink us. So we fish at night and sell our catch to the guy we met on the beach."

"Nice try, but I was less than a hundred feet from the truck. That wasn't lobster you were unloading. That Boudreau guy is a bootlegger and you guys are rum-running." She says it with a lingering note of awe in her voice.

My ears are on fire. "Wrong. We're fishing and you simply saw us selling our catch."

Jolene laughs. "Oh, for pity's sake, stop it. You're a terrible liar. You should see your face. It's as red as a boiled lobster. *And* I was close enough to see that you were carrying canvas bags from your boat to the truck. They're called burlocks and they hold bottles of liquor protected by hay."

My entire face is flaming. "How do you know what a burlock is?"

She grins. "I make it my business to know a lot of things. A lot of the resorts, restaurants, and seaside inns in this province have bootlegged liquor hidden in a cupboard for their special guests. You pick up the liquor at sea and transport it back to Boudreau, and he sells it to these businesses. Maybe he sells lobsters to them too, just to look more legit, but that's not what you were loading onto his truck. It was liquor."

A chill finger of fear slides down my back. *One trip out and we're caught already. And here Larkin and I thought we'd done so well. What does Jolene want?*

Jolene folds her arms over her chest and stares at me with quiet intensity. I'm unnerved and don't know what to say. I'm don't know if she's harmless or a troublemaker.

We're silent for a long moment, eyeing each other.

A gust of wind rises up and a tree branch scrapes across the window, making the hair on my neck stand up.

"Fine, so what do you want?" I ask in resignation. "Money, I suppose, or you'll go to the Mounties and tell them everything?"

She looks mortally offended. "No! I can't believe you'd even think that. I'd never rat on you guys to the cops. I want to join you two in rum-running."

"We're not rum-running. We're simply transporting liquor from one businessman to another."

Jolene bursts out laughing and hoots. "Dress it up all you want if it makes you feel better, but you girls are transporting the demon rum!"

I wait until she stops laughing, then arch an eyebrow. "Why were you down at Schooner Cove in the middle of the night?"

"You're changing the subject."

"Partly," I admit. "But I am very curious about what you were doing there, and why you're disguised as a man."

"I've always dressed like this."

"Yes, but you've never hidden your hair, so there's no mistaking you for a woman. You've got it tucked up under a hat like you want to hide it, and you're wearing a man's coat too. And you were clearly nervous on my doorstep. You kept looking back to the road, like someone was chasing you. In fact, even now your eyes keep flitting to the windows and back door."

She gives me a tight smile. "All right, I'll tell you. But only if you swear to keep it to yourself. Because if you don't, my life is in danger."

I'm taken aback. "Whatever it is, it can't be that dire. Here, in Whaleback Cove?"

"I'm serious. To some, living in this seaside town is paradise. To others, like me, and I'm sure like you, since Blade's death, it's a small-town hell."

I know most people in town think Jolene peculiar and their talk about her is unkind. I nod in understanding. "All right, you have my word. I won't tell anyone."

"The old cottage at the end of Schooner Lane and the dock you're using belonged to my great-aunt, Beulah. She left it to her nephew years ago, but he lives in New York and never used it. He just let it go to ruin. I'm staying there for now."

I frown. "I saw it from the beach. It looks like it's about to collapse. Is it even habitable?"

"It's in rough shape. The roof leaks in some spots. The ceilings in the bedrooms look like they bleed water when it rains. But the kitchen and living room are in decent enough shape to live in. There's a large woodstove in the kitchen that heats the place up good, and a water pump in the sink. I sleep on a cot in the kitchen close to the stove for heat. Also, the back door is off the kitchen, in case I need to leave in a hurry."

I raise my eyebrows. Leave in case the whole roof begins leaking badly, or in case the place starts to come down on her head?

She continues, "There's a good three-inch layer of dust across everything. Some of the wallpaper is coming off, and there were spots of black mould on the walls of the rooms with leaking ceilings. I found some bleach this morning and cleaned the mould. I tore off the peeling wallpaper and cleaned the place up. The outhouse is in surprisingly good shape There are oil lamps and lots of quilts and blankets. They smell like old potato sacks, but I'll wash them and hang them out in the sunlight. The place will do me for a while."

I'm now completely puzzled. Jolene and her husband have a house on Dover Road on the western edge of town. "But why? You're married and have a nice place."

Jolene gazes miserably into her coffee. "I left Burke. I've been planning to do it for some time. We weren't married more than a week before he started smacking me around."

I recall Blade saying once that he thought Burke treated Jolene badly. And now I notice the fat lip, so I believe her. I'm thankful that Blade always treated me with love, as an equal, and respected my opinion on all matters before we made a mutually agreed upon decision.

"I left him after he hit me on Sunday night." She pauses and draws a shaky breath. "This time was worse than ever before. I've never seen him in such a rage."

I wait for her to go on.

"Sunday night, after he hit me, I ran upstairs to our bedroom and locked the door. That really set him off. He kicked it open and grabbed me and dragged me down the hallway to the bathroom. He started running the water in the tub. He said he was going to drown me and make it look like an accident, like I'd fallen against the tap and knocked myself out and drowned." A visible shudder runs through her.

"No!" I gasp, appalled.

"I don't know if he really would have, but the look in his eyes terrified me. I fought hard and broke free, then ran out of the bathroom and down the stairway to the kitchen, intending to go out the back door. But he caught up to me there. I grabbed a frying pan off the stove and clobbered him over the head with it... I knocked him right into next week."

I can't keep the shock from my face. "Is he okay?"

"Don't know," she says in a careless tone. "He was lying flat on his back on the kitchen floor. I saw blood pooling around his head."

I repeat, mortified. "You saw blood pooling around his head?"

"Yes."

I blink in astonishment.

"Why are you looking at me like I'm a serial killer? I just bopped him on the head. What'd you expect to do? Let him kill me?"

"Did you at least check his pulse before you left?"

Her expression is remorseless. "I did not."

"And you haven't been back since then?"

"Nope."

I wince. "I hope he isn't dead."

She shrugs. "I don't care."

"Jolene."

She eyes me with a strangely bright gaze. "What? Better him than me."

I let out a quiet breath. "So you're hiding out in this cottage in case the cops are looking for you?"

"Them and Burke. If he's dead, then the cops are looking for me. If he's alive, then he wouldn't have gone to the cops; he'll come after me." Then she adds, "I don't know what he'll do to me if he finds me, but it won't be good."

I open my mouth and shut it again. A heavy silence hangs in the kitchen.

A seagull swoops past the kitchen window with a harsh shriek that gives both of us a start.

Jolene smiles. "We're both edgy, it seems."

"So this happened last evening? My soul, Jolene. He could very well be laying in your house dead or badly hurt. We need to call the police now."

"No, we don't. His parents were coming over for lunch today." She glances at her watch. "It's one-thirty. They'll have found him by now if he didn't wake up last night himself."

"Then you should call the Mounties and tell them what happened before they do," I tell her. "You need to explain to them that it was self-defence."

She snorts. "I called the cops twice before. All they did was take him aside and speak to him about being more patient with me. After that, they scolded me, said I needed to try harder to be a more loving and obedient wife."

"But why would you marry a guy like that?"

She lets out a rueful sigh. "He wasn't like that during the six months we dated. As I said, it started soon after we married."

"Did you talk to your pastor?"

"I did. And he spoke to Burke. It made things worse. I went back to Pastor Browne, and he and two deacons spoke to Burke. He only got angrier, more violent. Burke is a weed among the tares."

"I'm sorry, Jolene."

"Yeah, so after that I stopped trying. I never shed another tear."

"Why didn't you just leave? What about family, your parents, can't they help you?"

Her eyes fill with despair. "My parents died during the Great August Gale, on August 24 in '26. Do you remember that?"

"Yes, of course. I was living in New Brunswick then, but it was big news. It was a Category 2 hurricane. Did so much damage, it's hard to forget. But didn't it hit further up around the southwestern shore?"

Jolene twists her hands together. "Yes, it did. They were visiting my mom's sister and brother-in-law just outside Yarmouth when it struck. There were two witnesses, a young couple up on the shore who saw my parents and aunt and uncle watching the waves on the beach. A massive wave surged in so fast that my mom and aunt got swept out. They kept trying to stand and get back to safety, but then another would come right behind it and knock them down again. Each time, they got swept farther out. My dad and uncle ran out to help, but the waves were too powerful. That young couple could only watch as all four were swept away. None of their bodies were ever found."

"That's horrible. I'm so sorry, Jolene."

She swallows and I see in her eyes a shadow of hurt that goes deep. It may never heal. "I have no siblings or cousins, no family I could turn to for help. No friends. Burke made sure of that. I think that's partly why I married him. I was so lonely, I probably ignored the red flags."

"What about his parents? Can you go to them?"

"No way!" she howls. "That hateful woman and that creepy old man? His mom doesn't like me and his dad has always made my skin crawl."

I lift a brow at that.

"What? It's true. And speaking of in-laws, I don't see Blade's parents or siblings here helping. Everyone knows they blame you for his accident."

I feel my face flush. "Yes," I admit, unable to mask the hurt from showing on my face.

Though I wasn't close to Callum or Blade's mom, I'd always liked his dad and sister, Faith. I missed their presence in my life. I can handle the hate and accusations of the townspeople, but the family's blame and rejection guts me.

"Right, so I stayed with Burke and played the role of the good wife," Jolene continues. "But I kept a suitcase with clothes and personal items—toothpaste, toothbrush, hairbrush—hidden in the back of my closet. And I started saving a secret stash. He controls our finances, so I'd sneak change out of his pants pockets, nickels and dimes and quarters. I couldn't risk taking any bills out of his wallet. He'd know."

"It would take forever to get enough to leave."

Jolene grins. "It did. So I started taking it from our tithing envelope. On Saturday night, he'd put in our monthly tithe, lick the envelope closed, then set it on his Bible. I waited till he was in the shower on Sunday morning, then steamed it open and took out a dollar bill. I did that twice and hid it in a shoebox. One Sunday after that, the pastor gave a sermon on holding back on tithing and the whole time he was looking at Burke. Honestly, I could hardly keep from laughing out loud."

I can't hold back a small smile.

Jolene looks out the kitchen window and bites the inside of her cheek. She sighs. "But it felt like stealing from God."

I reach out and squeeze her forearm. "I'm sure God understands. But you said if Burke is alive, he's going to come for you. Is there any way at all he can find out about the cottage? If he wasn't hurt badly, he could already be on his way there."

"No. The nephew changed his name when he was eighteen and left home. He led what the rest of the family considered to be a wicked lifestyle. Other than my great-aunt, they wanted nothing to do with him. She put the title in his new name and everyone else who knew is dead now. I can't see how anyone would be able to connect that property to me. I'm safe there. It's just walking around I need to be careful about. I don't think my disguise will work against Burke. He knows me too well. So I'll try not to go out in the daytime unless I absolutely have to, and I'll make sure it's in a spot where there's lots of people around. He won't try to grab me in public. And if he does, I'll scream so loud they'll hear me in Halifax."

"You came here in daylight," I say. "He could have seen you."

"I walked along the shore, almost all the way into town. In the few places where it's all rocky, I had to wade through the water. I found rubber boots in a closet in the cottage, thank goodness. When the water was too deep, though, I did have to go up onto the road. Even then, I crossed over to the wooded side where I was hidden in the trees."

"Still, you walked through town, and then down my lane."

"I was careful. I walked behind businesses when I could, and when I couldn't, I kept a constant eye out. Nobody gave me a second look. Besides, this was important. I had to risk it."

We both fall silent again, the only sound being the creaking of the house as the wind whips off the water and hits the back wall.

"Should you be lighting a fire in the woodstove and the fireplace? Aren't you worried someone will see the smoke?" I ask.

"Nah. The cottage is down at the end of a long weedy lane. The trees hide it from the road. No one comes around there." She tilts her head and grins. "Other than you guys, I mean."

"So you risked being seen just to come and tell me that you saw us last night?"

"I risked it because I want to go rum-running with you and Larkin."

My jaw drops. "Oh, Jolene, no."

"I have less than four dollars to my name, and I'm running out of food. I need to make some real money quick, so I can leave town. I'm thinking of leaving the province. It's my only hope of escaping Burke for good. If I stay here, he'll find me."

"Do you know anyone in another province?"

"No, I haven't even been to Halifax, and that's only six hours away," she says with a rueful tone. "Working with you girls is perfect because I can go out at night when no one will see me, and I'll make a lot of money in a short time. Everyone knows there's big money in rum-running."

I give her a sympathetic look. "I'm sorry, Jolene, but I have to say no."

"Duska, please, I'm desperate. If I go back to Burke, the least he'd do is lock me in a room."

"I wish I could, truly, but I can't."

She bristles. "Why not?"

"Number one, I don't know this Boudreau that well. Larkin's dad was friends with him. Number two, Larkin and I have sworn to him that we won't tell anyone what we're doing."

"You didn't tell me," she counters. "I saw you guys. Tell him that."

I blow out a breath. "No way. I'm not sure how he'd react. He seems like a good guy, but still, he could get violent."

"Then let me come down to the dock tonight and talk to him. I'll explain to him that I saw you but would never tell the cops. I only want to join you."

"Don't do that," I caution her. "That could turn out badly for you."

She waves off my words. "I doubt this guy will hurt me if I'm only asking for a job. If Larkin's dad knew him, and she feels safe working for him, he's likely not violent."

"Maybe, maybe not."

"So when are you going out again?"

"I have no idea."

"Yes, you do. Tell me."

"I honestly don't. Larkin gets the messages and then tells me."

"Fine. Then I'll walk down to the beach every night until I find you there and talk to this Boudreau myself."

"Jolene, listen to me! Do not do that! None of us really knows if he's dangerous or not."

"Pfff, I'll bet my life he's not."

I shake my head. "Don't say that. This isn't some adventure, some game. It's dead serious."

Her normally impish green eyes turn fierce. "I understand that. It's the same for me with Burke. It's dead serious. I have to get out of town. I have no other options."

"There must be another option, Jolene."

"No, there isn't. I'll come down there every night. I swear I will."

Feeling desperately sorry for her and seeing such despair in her face, I relent a little. "Go outside and wait. I need a few minutes to think it over. If it's yes, we'll drive over to Larkin's and talk about it. If it's a no, I'll drive you back to the cottage and you'll have to swear to forget everything."

She drains her coffee and sets the mug on the table. "Okay, and thank you, Duska."

"Don't thank me yet. I can't promise anything. If Larkin says no, it's no."

Jolene pushes her chair back, stands, and grins in triumph. "She won't say no."

She tucks her hair up inside her hat and pulls it down low over her forehead. Sliding on her gloves, she then nods once and leaves the house.

I sit for a time, thinking it over. Jolene isn't as naïve as I first thought. That childlike twinkle in her eyes and mischievous smile are misleading. Though she can be slightly reckless, I know that she's quick, strong, and brave. I like her, and I believe she's in danger. With a third person helping us, we could work much faster, cutting the risk of us getting caught. It strikes me that Jolene would be a good fit for our operation.

But Jean-Claude made it clear: no one else was to know about this.

Five minutes later, I go outside and stand on the porch. Jolene looks up from leaning on the front bumper of my truck.

I nod.

She claps her hands together and grins again. "I knew you'd say yes!"

I hold up my hand, palm out. "I've only decided to talk it over with Larkin."

"Duska, I don't know whether to hug you or kiss you."

"Do *not* kiss me."

Her grin only broadens.

"After we talk to Larkin, I'll drive you back to the cottage," I say. "But first we'll stop in town. No one should recognize you with the hat on, at least if you slouch down in the seat. I'll run into Martin's for food and whatever else you need."

"That'd be wonderful, thanks. I need milk, fruit, meat, and ice for the ancient icebox. Coffee and matches. I used the last of what I found in the cupboards this morning. I have my money on me."

"Keep it. I'll get it this time."

"Thank you, Duska, that's so kind of you. Can you grab me a chicken and some cans of beans, too, then? I can bake the chicken and make soup. That's it… oh wait, and can you get some chocolate bars? Let's see… and a couple bags of candy, any kind. I'm a fiend for sweets."

I pause for a few seconds. "Sure."

"So whose idea was it to start rum-running anyway, yours or Larkin's? What a great idea! Woohoo, I can hardly wait!" She lets loose an unholy shout of glee, then lopes around to the passenger side of the truck and leaps into the cab.

CHAPTER FOURTEEN

The next night, I stand at the living room window watching a dramatic sunset, blood-red and deep purple, without appreciating it. A cold weight sits in my stomach like a stone. It's the fear of being caught, and the deep shame I feel before my heavenly Father. I'm torn between wanting to stop and wanting to continue. Rum-running distracts me from my grief, but then my sorrow flares again when I wake up in the morning. The heavy guilt dogs me like a storm cloud. I feel like I've sold my soul to the devil.

A thermos of coffee and a ham sandwich rest on the floor next to my boots. I pace the house as the minutes tick by.

I'm going, I think.

No, I'm not going. I have to quit, I think only a second later.

My stomach is upset. I could throw up.

Finally, at ten o'clock, I step out of the house into darkness. It's a cold, damp evening and the temperature is falling below freezing. A wall of night fog rolls in off the water, wetting my face and hair. A thin layer of ice covers everything. The tide is retreating and the air is heavy with the odour of seaweed and shells left on the beach.

I start the truck and drive out to Schooner Cove to pick up Jolene. Feeling sleepy, I roll the window down a crack and drive with the smell of the ocean blowing cold in my face.

Larkin has agreed to allow Jolene to join us tonight, but once we arrive at the rendezvous sight Jolene will have to go down into the hold so she doesn't see anyone. Not yet. The final say will come from Jean-Claude—later. If he says no, we'll pay Jolene for one night's work, but that'll be it. We're both nervous about his reaction but have decided to risk helping her out.

I bump down the long weedy drive, bouncing in my seat. When I pull up in front of the cottage, I see the dark silhouette of someone sitting on the front steps. My heart wobbles. Has Burke found her already?

But then the person stands and I see that it's Jolene, dressed in a dark trousers and coat, her hair tucked up under her wool hat. She vaults off the steps and races to the truck, grinning broadly. She rips the door open and leaps in beside me.

"What took you so long? I thought you'd never get here!" She slams the passenger door so hard that my ears ring. "Whoopee! Let's go!"

I shake my head and drive away. What a nut. But a loveable one...

Jolene is excited on the drive over but frequently looks out the back window for any sign of headlights.

"Worried Burke might be following us?" I ask, glancing up at the rearview mirror. The road is dark and empty behind us.

"Just being careful. You know, I found a baseball bat in the cottage. I think I'll start bringing it in the truck from now on."

"You will not!"

"Fine," she says, but in a tone that implies she will.

"I've been keeping my ears open in town and reading the newspaper," I tell her. "But I haven't heard anything yet."

She grunts. "I'm sure he's fine, with his thick skull."

We reach Larkin's place without incident. Larkin leads us into the kitchen, motioning upstairs where Bash and Sadie are sleeping. We'll need to talk quietly.

I also notice that she looks troubled.

"What's up?" I ask. "I thought you agreed to Jolene coming along."

"It's not Jolene. I heard that the Mounties caught Dietrich Schumer's boat, the *Intrepid*, from Mahone Bay. His engine quit on him and they found over a thousand cases of liquor on board. He and his three crewmembers are in jail right now."

I sigh deeply. "Shoot."

"Yeah, that's the second boat the Mounties have seized this week. They're bound to be out there patrolling again tonight. We need to be extra vigilant. And we need an escape plan in case they spot us. Someplace closer than here, somewhere we can hide until it's safe to go meet with Jean-Claude."

"I know," I say. "Skeleton Island. It's an uninhabited island halfway between Three Islands and Schooner Cove."

Jolene frowns. "That island has nothing but rocks, trees, and snakes. There's no shoreline. It's earned its name. We'd never be able to get your boat close enough."

"It's not all rocky shoreline," I explain, holding up a finger. "Blade took me out there once. We found a spot on the northeast side where we could bring the boat in. We only found it by accident, when we had engine trouble, and the boat drifted into this small hidden cove. There's no reef or rocks. We could back in under the canopy of overhanging tree branches and anchor in the shallow water. We'll be hidden good. If we think they're going to find us, we could unload all the liquor and hide it on the island. Come back for it another time."

Larkin's brow is knitted in thought. "Could work. And Jean-Claude would like the idea of us hiding the liquor before we're caught."

"Agreed then," Jolene says.

"Are you ready?" Larkin asks her.

"Are you kidding? I haven't slept a wink since you told me I could come. Let's go!" She punches Larkin, and then me, on the arm. It's like getting smacked with a hammer.

She takes off out the back door and Larkin and I, rubbing our arms, follow her down to the dock where the *Bad Reputations* is rocking on the water.

I board and go straight into the wheelhouse. Larkin lifts the bow lines from the bollards as Jolene lifts the stern lines. They toss them onto the deck and jump in after them.

I stand at the helm and start the engine. Larkin and Jolene then come inside and stand on my right. Jolene is so excited that she's bouncing on her toes. Her eyes are as big and round as silver dollars.

She sees me looking at her and nudges me in the side. "What are you waiting for? Go!"

I ease the throttle forward and reverse direction. Once safely clear of the dock, I turn the boat and slice through the swells toward the open sea.

Only five miles out, Larkin raises a hand and points east to the horizon. "A boat!" she shouts. "Kill the engine! It can't be the rum-runners. It's coming from the wrong direction."

I stop the engine and we pitch from side to side, our eyes on the boat's dark silhouette. The temperature is below zero now and the bracing wind blows from the north. There's sea frost and fog shrouds the sea.

The waves move us away from the advancing boat and I have to squint. I can't see it clearly.

Larkin lifts Blade's binoculars from the dashboard and points them out through the windshield to the ship. "Uh-oh. It looks like a Coast Guard cutter. Headed right toward us."

"Should we try for Skeleton Island?" I ask.

"Hold on." Larkin follows the boat with the binoculars. "Yes, it's the Coasties. Oh, wait, it's veering away now. Heading east. But let's stay here for a few minutes to be safe."

Five minutes later, the cutter is barely visible and Larkin gives the okay.

"We just dodged the Coast Guard." Jolene pumps a fist in the air. "Yes!"

"We were just lucky," I say.

"Still." She laughs, slapping a hand on her thigh. "I haven't had this much fun in my life. Have you?"

Larkin and I exchange smiles, both thinking that our brave friend has the heart of a lion.

I motor south. We soon reach the rendezvous site and I kill the engine while Jolene and Larkin go out and throw the anchor overboard. We have to fight to keep our balance on the slick deck. The wind off the sea cuts right through our layers of clothing. It's bone-chilling and we stand shivering, teeth chattering, as we scan the water for approaching boats. The moon pours a silvery sheen of light across the dark ocean.

To the west, in the distance, the yellow lights of an ocean liner sail past.

Suddenly, the wind increases and the seas grow rough. The five-foot rolling waves are topped with whitecaps, cresting and crashing into each other. At times the water spills over the side of the boat.

Soon our clothing is soaked. Our lips are blue, our faces and hands white and bloodless, even with two pairs of gloves and scarves pulled up over our mouths and noses. None of it fazes Jolene, though. Wet and cold, she stands with the salt air cutting into her. She keeps scanning the sea without complaint.

Minutes later, we hear the low rumble of an engine. Soon after, we see the shape of a boat emerge from the darkness.

Larkin scans the boat with binoculars. "That's them, the *Night Glider*."

She hands me the binoculars and pulls out the flashlight from her coat pocket. She gives the signal and they signal back.

"Okay, down in the hold, Jolene."

The rum-runners pull up beside us and the transfer goes smoothly. Soon we're back in the wheelhouse and motoring to Schooner Cove. As we near the cove, the fog grows heavier. Through it, though, I can make out Jean-Claude's truck shrouded in grey mist.

"Let me do the talking," Larkin tells Jolene.

"Sure," Jolene says, but to me her tone implies otherwise.

I manoeuvre the boat alongside the dock and we tie up. The three of us then walk down the dock.

I grab Jolene's arm and stop her for a second. "Jolene, let Larkin handle this."

"Of course. What are you so worried about?" she says with an innocent look, pulling her arm free.

On the beach, Jean Claude is furious. "I tot I told you no one else."

"I apologize, Jean-Claude," Larkin says. "This is Jolene Taylor from town. She'd like to work with us if that's okay with you. Larkin and I can vouch for her."

He rubs his jaw and scowls. "I don't like dis. She been to the rendezvous site, seen the rum-runners and dere boat, her."

"No, she stayed in the hold and didn't see anything, don't worry," Larkin says.

"She see me and my boys! She know too much. She's a danger to us now."

"She already saw us all on the beach the other night," Larkin explains. "So I didn't think it mattered. She's staying in the cottage right behind you."

He glances back over his shoulder. "I checked it out. No one's been inside that place for years. It falling down."

"She's hasn't been there long," Larkin says. "She could have gone to the cops the other night, but she didn't. Instead she came to us and asked to join. You can trust her."

His eyes darken. "You saw us?"

Jolene nods. "Yes."

"I know her, and I trust her with my life, Jean-Claude," I put in fast.

"Yes," Larkin adds. "Jolene's a Walters from town. Her family goes way back."

The air around us turns quiet as he stares hard at the sea, breathing through his nose.

A seagull suddenly shrieks; the noise is as startling as a burst of laughter at a wake. Larkin and I jump.

"Believe me, Jean-Claude," she assures him. "I'd die before I ever told the cops. I just want a job."

He turns to her, and Jolene, fearless, holds his gaze. "Are you related to old Jimmy Walters?"

"Was. He died a few years ago. He was my grandfather's brother."

"I knew old Jimmy." Jean-Claude grins. "A big man, no? Give you his last nickel. Lost at sea during a winter squall a few years ago, wasn't he?"

Jolene nods. "Yes."

Jean-Claude goes quiet, then looks away for a moment. He moves his eyes back to Jolene. "Who owns the cottage?"

"My great-aunt owned it before leaving it to her great-nephew. He lives in New York and let it go to ruin."

"So he don't know you living dere?"

"No. But even so, he wouldn't care. And I'm careful. I won't get caught there."

Jean-Claude nods, his lips pressed in a thin line.

"You can trust me, Jean Claude," Jolene says. "I'm not a blabbermouth, and I'm not about to start now. I'm tough as nails, a hard worker, and I don't scare easy."

He's quiet for so long that I think he isn't going to respond. But finally he turns and narrows his eyes at Larkin and me. "Bon, she can stay. But don't bring no one else. I mean it. You tree girl is it. Too many peoples knowing about this isn't good for any of us. You bring anyone else and you're done working for me, understand?"

Larkin and I nod in unison. Jolene looks as pleased as punch.

"Bon. You girls help Louis and Andre get da booze off your boat before da cops catch us here talking."

"Merci, beaucoup, Jean-Claude!" Jolene jauntily punches him on the arm before strutting across the sand toward the dock and Jean-Claude's sons. "Come on, girls, let's give these two lazy bums a hand. If we leave it to them, summer will be here before we're done."

I see Jean Claude's body stiffen. "What did you just call dem?"

Larkin and I exchange mortified looks.

Jolene stops but doesn't turn around. "Lazy bums, why?"

Oh no, I think. I want to give Jolene a warning look, but she has her back to me too.

Jean-Claude puts his hands on his hips. "Dos two *lazy bums* are my *sons*."

"Are they?" Jolene says audaciously, without a backward glance. "Well, sons or not, they're slower than molasses in January."

"You got some mout, you."

"I know it," Jolene says.

Jean-Claude watches as she strolls away, chuckling under his breath.

CHAPTER FIFTEEN

Constable Asher Hayes sits in his patrol car off the highway. His engine and lights are off and he's parked in the shadows of the towering trees that line both sides of the old logging road. He's been here late at night all week, watching for drunk drivers and speeders. His side window is open a few inches; even this far from the water, the briny scent of the sea wafts in.

He looks out through the windshield to the road and sees headlights approaching from the left. When the vehicle speeds past, he's surprised to see that it's Blade Doucette's truck, the fisherman who died when his boat engine exploded.

Hayes couldn't make out the driver clear enough to know who was behind the wheel, though.

If it is Mrs. Doucette, what is she doing out at 4:00 a.m.? he asks himself.

He starts the engine, shifts into first, and pulls out onto the highway, speeding after the truck. When he gets close, he slows and stays far enough back so the driver won't notice him.

The truck moves through town, heading in the direction of the Doucettes' home. Whoever it is, they're driving too fast, but he decides not to pull them over, curious about why they'd be out so late.

At times the truck is smothered by the dense rising fog and Hayes has to accelerate not to lose it. About a mile outside town, the driver turns onto Rowboat Lane. He follows the truck down a dark, narrow lane, but slowly. Then the truck's brake lights flash and it turns into the Doucette driveway.

Hayes pulls over, staying far enough back that he can see the house through the trees without being spotted. The truck's headlights go off and the driver gets out, going up the steps and unlocking the door. Under the porchlight, he can see that it's Mrs. Doucette. She looks to be wearing dark men's clothing and rubber boots. When she steps inside, a light goes on in the home. It goes out soon after, casting the yard in silent darkness.

He leans ahead and looks out at the patches of dark sky showing through the pine branches. He drums his fingers on the steering wheel, thinking.

Then he shakes his head, chuckling under his breath. What did he think she was up to anyway? She seems a fine young woman.

I've been a cop too long, he thinks. *Getting too suspicious. Likely overreacting. Must be a good reason for this.*

But strangely, his mind can't let go of what he's seen. It hits him that Mrs. Doucette was dressed not so much in men's clothing as in men's fishing clothes. And if she's fishing, which seems ludicrous, why is she doing it in the middle of the night.

Then he remembers that the town fishermen don't like women on the wharf, let alone out fishing lobster. That could explain a lot.

But it doesn't explain everything. Where did she keep her boat?

Hayes sees a thicker shroud of fog roll in off the water and soon feels it on his face, wetting his hair as it drifts through his open side window. He rolls it up, makes a U-turn, and drives away.

While patrolling the town's streets, he can't let the puzzle go.

He also can't let go of thoughts of Duska Doucette herself. Realizing that he's drawn to her sends heat rising to his face. His attraction is foolish and reckless. And, he reminds himself, she's only just lost her husband. He recalls the depth of her suffering and the grief he saw on her face the day her husband died and he stayed with her. And the morning he dropped in to check on her after that confrontation with the fishermen on the wharf. The grief that he still sees…

What are you evening thinking? he asks himself. *Idiot.*

He decides to keep an eye out for Duska at night. After all, he's only doing his job as a police officer, making sure she's safe. Nothing else.

CHAPTER SIXTEEN

Over the next few days, we make two more trips without any problems. Then, on a Wednesday night, our fifth trip, all three of us are in the boat at the rendezvous point. We've motored out through cold, heavy rain thundering on the wheelhouse roof and slashing against the windshield. Soon after arriving, the rain suddenly stopped, but the wind kept blowing. Rain drips off the railings and the roof of the wheelhouse onto the deck. Our faces are raw from the frigid bite of the spray it kicks up.

We're a little early, because I know the way to our rendezvous site by heart now and we made good time. We bob on the water, shuffling our feet to stay warm. I'm in the stern, Jolene's at the bow, and Larkin is moving between the port and starboard sides. We're studying the sea, anxious for any sign of approaching vessels.

Clouds, heavy with more rain, scud across the moon, blotting out the light. Everything's black, as dark as a grave.

I know we'll hear a boat before ever seeing it, so I hold my breath and listen. Still nothing. They're late, which makes me uneasy. My hands and feet grow numb and I make a mental note to wear another pair of wool socks and two liners inside my rubber gloves next time.

Then I hear the low thrum of an engine approaching from the south. It eases off to a low idle.

"Boat," I say, my breath billowing into the air.

Blade's binoculars hang from my neck. I lift them, point them toward the sound, and peer through the lens.

Larkin comes up beside me. "Can you make it out?"

I scan the sea. There's a dark shape steaming across the waves. "Not yet."

Jolene comes up on my other side. "Sounds like it's coming toward us."

"That engine sounds more powerful than the *Night Glider*'s," Larkin says, sounding worried.

Jean-Claude did warn us that the Coast Guard and RCMP boats have been out more heavily the past few nights.

Suddenly, a ship bursts from the dark. I hear a loud click and a brilliant spotlight hits us, illuminating us on the deck. The boat churns toward us, bouncing over a wave.

I squint against the blinding light, my blood whooshing in my ears. "Mounties! In the wheelhouse, quick!"

The RCMP boat's engine screams as it throttles toward us. I hurry toward the wheelhouse door and yank it open—but when I look back at Jolene, she's standing brazenly in the spotlight, shaking a fist at them.

That woman is going to give me a heart attack.

"Jolene, no!" I shout.

"I'll get her." Larkin scrambles over, grabs Jolene's arm, and hauls her into the wheelhouse, banging the door shut behind them.

I start the engine and ram the throttle forward hard. The bow lifts off the water, scaring me, but I don't ease off. We tear away across the water, heading northwest.

"Skeleton Island, or your place?" I ask Larkin.

"My place. It's closer."

Jolene cracks the door an inch and looks out. "They're gaining on us! Faster, faster!"

I drive so fast that the bow lifts into the air again and smashes down with a violent bang that shakes me right to the spine. The wind, filled with icy salt, rushes over the boat.

Suddenly, the skies open again and horizontal rain slashes at the windshield, blurring my vision so I can barely see. White-topped waves rise to six feet as icy water washes over the deck.

I'm so afraid, my blood surging so hard, that I shake even though the wheelhouse is warm. I push the throttle forward even more and the boat bounces even harder. The vibration goes right through to our bones. We all groan and hang onto the dashboard as tight as we can.

"Look out again," I tell Jolene. "See where they are."

Jolene starts for the door just as the boat lifts high in the air. She loses her balance and falls on the deck.

"Are you okay?" Larkin asks.

"Yup." Jolene crawls over to the door. With her hands on the wall, she stands to her feet and cracks the door. A cold rush of wind and rain tears into the wheelhouse, lifting my hat off the dashboard where I lay it earlier. It drops to the floor. "They're behind us, but not as close. I think we're pulling away."

"Good," I say, glad I don't have to open the throttle anymore. I'm already pushing the engine as much as I dare.

Minutes later, Jolene looks out again. "We lost them. Way to go, Duska!"

I blow out a breath, thinking that we might have evaded the authorities, but we didn't meet up with the rum-runners. I'm not sure how Jean-Claude is going to feel about that.

I continue for another few miles alongside the coastline until we reach Larkin's cove. I ease the boat alongside the dock and cut the engine. Jolene goes out to tie us up and then comes back in the wheelhouse.

She looks at us, her eyes dancing with delight. She claps and laughs. "Holy Hannah, girls, that was some exciting! I've never had so much fun in my whole life."

Jolene's exuberance is contagious and Larkin and I can't help smiling. I'm surprised to find that, like Jolene, I found the adrenaline rush of the chase exciting. I'd never stand on the deck shaking my fist at the cops, but still, I can't deny that it gave me a thrill.

We all grab our thermoses and get off the boat. We run up the dock and over the lawn through the heavy rain coming down on us like a waterfall.

We go into the house through the back door, kicking off our boots and shedding our coats in the hallway, and then enter the kitchen. We stand by the woodstove, soaked, rubbing our hands briskly over the burners to bring back feeling in our numb fingers.

"That was too close," Larkin whispers, not wanting to wake Bash and Sadie. "Think it was an RCMP boat?"

I nod.

"Could have been pirates," Jolene says merrily.

Larkin and I give her a look.

Jolene grins. "What?"

Nothing scares the woman.

"At least with our hair up under our hats, and our men's clothing, we looked like men," I point out.

Larkin winces. "I hate to tell you, but my hair came loose from under my hat. It was hanging down my back. I meant to tuck it back up, but the boat came up on us so fast that I didn't have time."

"Hm. Well, I guess we'll find out soon if they recognized us, and who they were," Jolene says.

We glance out of the room toward the front door, as though someone were out there waiting to arrest us right now.

"I don't think you two should go home tonight," Larkin says. "Stay here until the morning just to be safe."

I agree. "Good idea. Even if they didn't recognize us, they might have patrol cars watching the roads. If the RCMP see Jolene and I driving home now, they might suspect it was us."

"One of you can sleep in the guest room. The other can take the couch in the living room. I'll gather up a pillow and some blankets for whoever's taking the couch."

"What about the rum-runners, and Jean-Claude?" I ask. "They're still waiting for us."

"No," Larkin replies. "They'll wait a half-hour past our meeting time. If we don't show up by then, they'll know something went wrong and leave. Jean-Claude will contact me through his nephew with instructions for what happens next. Probably we'll just go back out tomorrow night and try again."

I nod, relieved. "Good."

"I'll get the bedding. I'm going to have a cup of hot milk before bed. You two want one, or a coffee? It'd keep me awake, but I'll put on a pot if that's what you want."

"Nothing for me, thanks," I say. "I'm exhausted. I'm going right to bed."

"I'll have a coffee," Jolene says. "As strong as you can make it. I drink it all day and right up until I go to bed... and still sleep like a coma victim. A tornado wouldn't wake me."

I look at her wonderingly. "No..."

She grins. "Oh, yes, been like that since I started drinking it at thirteen." She looks at Larkin. "Got any chili flakes?"

"Huh?" says Larkin.

"I like mine with a sprinkle of chili flakes. Gives it a nice kick. My dad drank it like that and got me hooked on it. I love it."

"Um, sorry, no chili flakes."

"What a shame. All right, just black then."

Larkin glances at me as she heads for the staircase. She silently mouths, "Chili flakes?"

I just smile back and then go into the guest bedroom. I collapse onto the bed fully dressed and pull the quilt over me. Though it's not my own bed, I fall instantly into a deep sleep.

CHAPTER SEVENTEEN

On Saturday morning, I wake at eleven-fifty tired to the bone. I stumble across the room to the open window, lean on the sills, and lean out. The warm sea breeze caresses my face and carries the scent into the room. The impenetrable fog that shrouded the property last night has been burned away, leaving behind a flawless blue sky. With the change of seasons, the ocean is turning aqua green and sparkles. A gull glides past the window, the breeze carrying it almost gracefully out over the water.

I slept late because I was too wired from rum-running last night to fall asleep right away. I was happy, though, that we gotten back to Larkin's earlier than ever before. The first few nights I found the darkness and fog a bit disorienting, but now I'm used to it and can navigate the route in good time. And we three have established a routine which makes the work faster.

I step over to my closet and lift the loose plank in the floor. I pull out the metal lockbox, open it, and count the cash inside. Over six hundred dollars. And this is after paying the mortgage, boat payment, and other bills. I made extra this week, because we went back out on Thursday night to make up for Wednesday's miss, and then again last night. If we keep this up, I'll be able to pay off both the mortgage and the boat. The thought thrills me, for both carry such strong memories of Blade.

But only minutes later, I look into the mirror on my bathroom wall and my joy dies. Two sad, guilt-stricken eyes look back at me. I'm engulfed by the impossible sorrow and great shame of what I've done. It comes on me whenever I think of my heavenly Father. It happens whenever I think of Burke. I've stopped reading my Bible and I've stopped praying. How can I and then head out to sea as a rum-runner, as if I weren't doing anything wrong in God's eyes?

I have few good days, more bad days. Yet I can't seem to make myself quit. Heartsick, I put on my blue flannel housecoat over my pyjamas, then slide my feet into slippers and go downstairs to the kitchen. I stir the embers, add wood, and put the coffee pot on to boil. I put bacon fat in a cast-iron skillet and, once it melts, set it aside. I'll fry some eggs when the coffee is ready.

I then go out to the front door and step outside to grab the newspaper.

My heart lurches. Frank Defoe is standing to my left, smoking a cigarette and looking into the living room window with his back to me. When he hears the door open, he languidly turns to face me. He drops the cigarette on the step and grinds it out with his boot. My porch and steps are painted white, and he deliberately drags his boot across the wooden plank so the crushed cigarette leaves an ugly black streak and bits of burnt tobacco.

Still groggy, he's caught me off-guard. I should have looked out first, unable to believe that I didn't hear his truck tires crunching on the shell-lined driveway or the sound of his footsteps on the porch. Usually both sounds carry into the house, even over the surf.

I clasp the collar of my housecoat and take in a quiet breath. "Morning, Frank."

He's doesn't even have the decency to look embarrassed about being caught looking through my window. "Morning. I knocked but you must not have heard me."

"I didn't, no."

He clears his throat and spits on the grassy lawn. Then he turns back to me with an unreadable smile. "Lazy as a housecat, aren't you? Sleeping till noon?"

I shrug, feigning casualness.

He has cold dark eyes, a narrow pointy nose, and a thinly trimmed moustache. His skin is leathery brown and deeply lined, weathered from years of fishing in the harsh sun and sea. He has a cigarette tucked behind his ear, a habit of his.

"How can I help you, Frank?"

He stares at me, and his expression makes my heart rap in my ears. "I saw Fallon Smith putting in a new engine on Blade's boat a couple of weeks ago. When he was done with that, I saw him carrying some wooden boards into the hold, heard some hammering. It's got a new name… *Bad Reputations*."

My stomach drops, but I fight to keep my voice calm. "So?"

"*So* what's going on?"

"Why do you ask?" I bend over to pick up the newspaper without looking up.

"I thought the bank was taking it."

"I've decided to keep it. I hired Fallon because it needed a new engine and some repairs."

He fingers his moustache, his eyes narrow and calculating. He's known around town as a sly, vindictive man who quickly takes offense if he's made to look foolish. I need to be very careful.

"What are you up to, girl?"

I feign a nonchalant yawn. "Nothing. Going to sell it."

"That so? Then why were you and two others on it out at sea Wednesday night? I put my spotlight on you. When you took off, I saw the name on the stern." He scratches his cheek with a fingertip. "*And* I recognized one of the two other people onboard with you. It was the Wade girl. So answer my question. What's going on?"

Razor-sharp shock rushes through me. It feels like I've fallen into through ice into a pond of icy water. It was Frank who chased us.

I wait for the hammering of my heart to abate. "What do you mean, Frank?"

His eyes rake me with suspicion. "You know exactly what I mean. What are you girls up to?"

"We're lobster fishing."

He gives a cynical laugh. "Lobster fishing?"

"Yes."

"I don't believe you. No women have the stamina to fish lobster."

"We do."

"I didn't see many traps on the deck."

"We'd already set most of them. We were on our way back in when you saw us."

"At two in the morning?"

"Yes."

His eyes darken. "Don't say."

The wind picks up a little and shakes the branches of the trees, peppering the deck with pine needles. I watch two squirrels fight over a pinecone; one grabs it and scurries back up the trunk with the other chasing him.

I turn back to Frank, fighting to keep my thoughts straight. "When else can we go fishing, Frank, but at night? You'd harass and drive us away."

He smiles with mean eyes. "Harass you? We'd sink you. Why fish lobster, and this late in the season? You won't make enough to pay for the new engine and repairs."

I turn my eyes to the trees to suppress my rising panic. "The insurance paid for the new engine and repairs." I'm aware of how unconvincing this sounds, so I add another lie. "And we're hoping to fish mackerel and herring once the lobster season ends. We can make a living at that."

He takes the cigarette from his ear and puts it between his lips, but he doesn't light it. "Thing is, not many are fishing these days. There's no money in it, so I think you're lying."

The sun beats down on my head. My pulse throbs so hard behind my eye that it hurts.

I squint a little. "It's more than I made working in the bookstore. And Larkin can't find a job in this town, so it pays plenty for her. We have to do it to keep the banks from taking our homes."

"Bill Tucker won't buy your lobster, so who is?"

"A guy we know. He sells them to restaurants and inns all over. And we sell some to friends and family. We're not getting rich, but we're making a modest living."

He scowls. "What guy?"

"You don't need to know that."

"If you're only lobster fishing, why'd you take off when I hit you with the spotlight?"

"Larkin's father was murdered by gangsters involved in rum-running. She was sure it was them and was out of her mind with terror. So I took off."

His stare is unnerving as he mulls that over. "Who's the third person with you? Looked like a young guy, but then you and that Wade girl were dressed like men too. That's disgusting."

"We can't exactly wear dresses while fishing, Frank."

He goes still, angry. "Who's the third person?"

"She's a cousin of Larkin's from Halifax." I have to protect Jolene in case Burke's been asking around town about her.

"Where are you docking your boat? Must be at the Wades' place."

I shrug.

"Who's the ringleader of your little gang?"

"Gang? We're just three women fishing lobster, Frank."

"Doesn't that Wade girl have her little brother to raise now? She should be minding her house and brother, not out at sea fishing. Same thing goes for you. You should be at home keeping your house."

"We do all that and fish lobster besides."

He spits on my deck again. "Then I guess you'd better watch your backs while you're out there, because no fishermen in town will be happy to hear about this."

My heart drums in my chest. He's going to tell them.

We fall silent, an electric pulse of tension between us.

The sun's really heating up the air. Overhead, the birds around my property sing gaily and a gentle breeze blows off the water. Yet a chill runs through me as I hold Frank's gaze.

He eyes me sceptically for a few more seconds, then pokes me hard in the arm. "You listen to me. If you girls are fishing in my territory, there'll be hell to pay."

I garner my courage. "Your territory? You don't even fish. Everyone knows that you're rum-running now."

His voice turns venomous. "You listen to me. If I catch you out there again, I'll ram your boat, and then I'll blast holes in it. And when you're all in the sea, I'll just stand there and watch you girls drown. That's a promise."

Goosebumps rise on my arms. Shaken by the viciousness of his threats, I have to look away and compose myself.

He seems amused by the fear he's triggered in me. With a final smile, he stomps down the steps and over to his pickup truck. He starts the engine, backs up, and drives down the lane so fast that dust clouds kick up behind his bumper.

I watch his truck drive away, my face cold, my legs shaking.

CHAPTER EIGHTEEN

That night, we gather in Larkin's kitchen, enjoying a piece of her delicious blueberry pie and a coffee before heading out. Tonight Bash is staying at Sadie's.

It's a cool evening, and a mist of fog blankets everything. While we eat, we discuss Frank's visit.

But we go silent when we hear a car turn into the driveway. Its headlights sweep into the room and we listen for the sound of the engine shutting off and the door opening. Then we hear bootsteps on the porch, and two knocks on the door.

"Might be Frank," I say. "He's going to stop us from going out."

"I hope it is," Jolene growls as she rises from her chair. "He doesn't scare me. Threatening us like that. I'll knock him from here to Sunday."

"Jolene, is there anything you're afraid of?" I ask.

"Maybe snakes." She grins. "Just not the two-legged kind. Let me get the door."

Larkin lays her hand on Jolene's arm to stop her. "No, let him knock. I'm not expecting anyone this time of night, and he'll go away eventually." She pulls her arm back. "But I don't get it. What does it matter to Frank if we're lobster fishing? I mean, he's rum-running."

"It doesn't have to make sense," Jolene says. "Frank was born mean."

We hear two more raps, harder.

Larkin pushes her plate of unfinished pie away. "Shoot. He's not leaving. Nothing ruins a delicious piece of pie quite like Frank showing up unexpectedly at your door."

Jolene shakes her head and stuffs a big forkful of pie into her mouth. "Won't stop me."

"I'll get it. You guys stay here," Larkin says.

She grabs a housecoat from where it's draped over a chair, puts it on over her green flannel shirt and brown trousers, and ties the belt around her waist. She holds the collar of the housecoat to her throat and heads to the door.

We hear her let someone in, and then a man's voice. Seconds later, there's footsteps as they walk down the hallway.

"Please come into the kitchen," Larkin says.

I look up as they enter the room. It's Constable Hayes! I gulp in a breath.

Larkin crosses the room and stands with her back against the counter, looking nervous.

The constable follows her in, stopping in front of the table where Jolene and I sit. He removes his hat and holds it with one hand at his side. His eyes slide around the room before coming back to us.

"Good evening, ladies."

"Good evening, Constable Hayes," Larkin manages a smile, while Jolene and I only nod. "Please have a seat. Would you like a cup of coffee?"

"No, thank you, and I'll stand."

A slightly stricken expression comes over Larkin. "Is this about my dad?"

He shakes his head, his expression sympathetic. "I'm afraid not. There's nothing new to report on your father's murder."

Larkin goes quiet, looks away.

The constable's eyes linger on the loose men's trousers and flannel shirt she's wearing under the housecoat. He moves his eyes back to me and Jolene, taking in our own men's clothing. His seems to be mulling that over but doesn't say anything.

His gaze settles on me. His eyes are an arresting grey-blue, deep and warm. His face is gentle, concerned.

"Mrs. Doucette, how are you?"

"I'm fine, thank you." I drop my eyes down fast.

"I noticed your husband's boat tied up at the dock out back," he says. "I'd heard the bank was taking it."

I lift my head, surprised that he recognized the boat with the new paint, and that he knows about my business with the bank. My hands shake and coffee spills over the rim of my mug. I'm embarrassed and set the mug down on the table, hiding my hands in my lap.

He tilts his head in apology. "Sorry, I was in Pruett's a few days after your husband's accident and overheard talk that the bank was repossessing his boat."

The room goes silent, pulsing with tension.

Jolene huffs out a disgusted breath. "It's mind-numbing just how many blabbermouths live in this town. They have nothing better to do than sit in Pruett's, stuff their gobs, and spread gossip."

Hayes turns his attention to Jolene, studying her for a moment. "Are you Jolene Taylor?"

Jolene stiffens in her chair. "Excuse me?"

His eyes are questioning but his voice gentle. "Are you Mrs. Jolene Taylor? Your husband is Burke Taylor?"

Jolene blinks and takes a moment to answer. "Was."

He looks surprised. "You're divorced?"

Jolene takes a sip of her coffee and swallows. "Separated, soon to be divorced."

He frowns. "I wasn't aware of that. Well, Mrs. Taylor, you're the reason I'm here. I have some bad news. Your husband was found unconscious on the kitchen floor of your home at noon on Monday. Apparently, his parents found him lying there with a head wound. They took him to the town hospital. Luckily, it wasn't too serious. He suffered a concussion and needed thirty stitches, then was released to his mother's care the same day. However, he is confined to bed for the next ten days."

Jolene snorts. "Do tell."

Hayes observes her more closely. I notice a steely flint in his eyes. His gaze changes from warm and kind to cool. They can also be cold as ice.

"Do you know anything about that?" he asks. "How he came to be injured?"

Jolene picks up her mug and takes a sip. Her hands are steady. "I do not."

I cut my eyes sideways to Larkin and see her picking nervously at a thread on her housecoat. I catch her eye and give her a reassuring look. He's not here to arrest us for rum-running. And at least we now know that Burke's alive.

"When was the last time you saw your husband?" Hayes asks.

Jolene shrugs, remarkably nonplussed. "I left over a week ago, but I can't remember the exact day or time. Why?"

"We're trying to pinpoint when exactly your husband had his accident. Your mother-in-law said you both attended church Sunday morning, April 14, but missed evening services. So did you leave that afternoon on Sunday?"

"No."

"After supper then, or that evening?"

Jolene squints her eyes, thinking, or fake-thinking. I'd bet on the latter.

A gust of wind slams into a side wall and the house gives an awful groan.

"Mmm..." she says breezily, taking her good old time. "It was after supper."

He raises a brow. "What time exactly?"

"I didn't notice the time."

"Where was your husband?" he says, his voice soft but insistent. "Did you speak to him before you left?"

She lets out a bitter snort. "Not likely. He was drunk as a skunk and passed out on the couch in the living room."

Hayes goes quiet. The four of us fall into an uneasy silence. Through the open window, we listen to the sound of waves rolling onto the beach.

After a moment, Hayes speaks. "Your husband says he doesn't remember anything, although the doctors think he will regain some memory in time. In fact, it was your mother-in-law who reported you missing."

"Well, clearly I'm not missing. I left. And I have no idea how he got hurt."

"Or when?"

"Or when."

He raises his eyes from the notepad where he's writing this all down. "As I said, his parents say they last spoke to him at the morning church service. No one saw or spoke to either of you after that. They found him the following day, Monday, April 15. So it does appear he fell sometime on the fourteenth, either that afternoon or that evening."

"Goodness," she says. It sounds so flat.

A much cooler silence falls over the room as another gust of wind howls around the house.

He watches her, waiting. I can see that he's wondering if she is really that indifferent. Jolene holds his gaze, her expression impassive, not backing down an inch.

He sighs. "Mrs. Taylor, did you—"

"I'm not Mrs. Taylor anymore. I'm going by my maiden name now. Walters. Call me Jolene or Miss Walters."

"Ah... Miss Walters, were you there when it happened? And if so, why did you leave your husband so badly injured?"

Jolene's face darkens. She closes down.

"Miss Taylor?" he prods.

She glares back at him. "I told you. I wasn't there when it happened, so I couldn't have left him injured. Burke's a heavy drinker, and when he does drink he falls down a lot. I'm sure he just drank too much, took a tumble, and cracked his head on something... after I left."

Hayes rubs the bridge of his nose. "Your mother-in-law claims that your husband is a teetotaller, and it's you who drinks. That you buy contraband liquor and keep it hidden down in the cellar. She also claims that you have a bad temper, which gets worse when you drink."

Jolene puts a hand on her hip, furious. "She did? Why, that lying old bat."

He gives Jolene a long, steady look. "Mrs. Taylor seems genuinely concerned about you."

Jolene blurts a harsh laugh. "Sure she is."

"She asked me, if I did find you, to tell you she would like you to stay with them until your husband is fully recovered. He's quite dizzy and nauseous and can't walk more than a few steps without help. She'd like you to help care for him."

"She wants me to stay with them, in that snake pit? Well, you can tell her I'm never going back to live with her or her wife-beating son."

Now his eyes become even more steely. "Are you claiming he abused you? If so, I'll take your statement and press charges."

"No thanks. I did that once and nothing happened to him. But for me, things got a whole lot worse."

"Then we can start by taking out a restraining order on him."

"Wonderful. I'll wave it at him the next time he tries to hit me."

Hayes pauses. "Ma'am, I promise you I'll see that he leaves you alone."

Jolene taps her fingers on her lips. "Constable, you're new here, aren't you?"

"Yes, I was recently posted from Fredericton."

"Right. Then here's some facts for you. My husband's father, Rolf Taylor, is the mayor of this town. His uncle is a bigshot politician in Ottawa. Your detachment commander is close friends with both. They're all golfing buddies. Nothing will happen to Burke, just like before, so thank you, but the answer is no."

Hayes is silent for a time, looking deeply troubled by this news. "Miss Walters, I will see that charges are filed against your husband."

"Constable, I'm sure you mean well, but the night I left my husband, he filled up the bathtub and told me he was going to drown me in it and make it look like an accident. So, trust me, I am entirely sure."

He stares at her for a long time without blinking, then speaks in a careful, measured voice. "That's attempted murder. You need to press charges against him. I'll follow through with this. You have my word."

Jolene looks pained. "My word against his. The best thing for me was to leave him. Now it's best for me to stay gone."

I see his chest rise and then fall again, as he takes a long, deep breath, and then lets it out. "All right. But if you change your mind, please call the detachment, and ask for me."

"Right," she says with a cynical tone. "So are you here to force me to go back?"

He looks taken aback. "No, I'm here in response to a missing persons report, and to inform you that your husband was injured. You clearly are fine, and you're an adult. You claim to have no knowledge of what happened to your husband, and we have no evidence that a crime occurred. What you do now is your decision."

Jolene nods. "Good, then you can tell Burke that I'm never going back to him. If I did, I might as well start planning my funeral. Do you understand?"

He's quiet for a few seconds, absorbing this. Then he says, in a softer voice, "I do."

"One thing, though," Jolene says. "How did you know who I was, and how did you find me?"

"Your mother-in-law gave me a photo of you. And then yesterday I saw you walking along the Oceanfront Highway. You took your hat off briefly, and your hair was hanging down your back. It's a very distinctive colour."

Jolene frowns. "What's that supposed to mean?"

"Nothing. It's a beautiful colour. My mother has the same shade."

Jolene's face brightens. "Thank you."

He allows a faint smile. "When you heard me coming up behind you, you quickly put your hat back on and tucked your hair up into it. But I recognized you. Then, about fifteen minutes ago, I saw you and Mrs. Doucette driving along Waterfront Street in her truck. You had on the same blue hat. I knew it was you and followed you here."

Jolene bites her lower lip, clearly troubled by that.

He understands her concern. "I'll let your ex-husband know that you're safe and well but will not be returning home. I won't tell him where you are. Do you think he'll come after you once he's back up on his feet?"

"Yes."

"Then I'll keep an eye out for him. If I see him around town, would you like a heads up?"

"I would, yes."

"Where are you staying?"

"Do you have to know?"

"If your husband is as violent as you claim, and if you believe he'll come looking for you, then it's imperative that I know so I can warn you. You can trust me."

"Or you can just tell me and I'll let Jolene know," I offer fast. I'm worried he might come around the cottage when we're on the beach loading liquor into Jean-Claude's truck. "You know where I live."

He turns to me and I take notice of his dark brown wavy hair, high cheekbones, and lean but strong look. Our eyes meet and I look away, disconcerted, for I find him a handsome man.

He smiles. "Yes, I remember. But I think I should know in case Mr. Taylor does find her and she needs help."

Jolene huffs out a breath. "Fine, I'm staying at a cottage on Schooner Lane. That's off the Oceanside Highway, on the right, about five miles outside town."

He nods. "Does your husband know about the cottage?"

Jolene shakes her head. "No. I've only told Larkin and Duska."

"Good," he says but doesn't write that in his notes.

Jolene crosses her arms over her chest. "We're done then?"

He puts his hat back on. "Yes, we are. Good evening, ladies." But his eyes are on me.

"I'll show you out, Constable." Larkin leads him out of the kitchen.

When Larkin comes back into the kitchen, she purses her lips and breathes out in relief. "Thank goodness. I thought he was here to arrest us for rum-running."

I nod and look at Jolene. "And it's good to know that Burke's alive and they don't suspect you of hitting him."

"Yes," Jolene says.

But later, as Larkin and I are in the wheelhouse getting ready to head out to sea, Jolene stays out on the deck. Larkin and I have retreated into silence, but not Jolene. She's agitated. She paces from the stern to the bow, shaking her head and cursing Burke one minute, humming tunelessly under her breath the next.

CHAPTER NINETEEN

Hayes drives away from the Wade home feeling saddened and disturbed. Filled up the tub and threatened to drown her? If Jolene Taylor is telling the truth, and his cop's sense tells him she is, then her husband is a very bad character. He's heard the rumours about Burke Taylor, and in his six years on the force he's learned that if it walks like a duck and quacks like a duck, it's a duck.

What he finds most disturbing is Jolene's claim that she reported her husband but it did no good because the detachment commander was close friends with her father-in-law, the town mayor. He purses his lips and blows out a soft breath. If it's true, it's deeply unsettling.

And what a curious trio the three women are. A teenage daughter of a homicide victim, a young widow, and a young wife fleeing an abusive spouse, who, despite her denials, may have assaulted him before she fled. And why were the women wearing men's clothing, and, he had the feeling, going out at 10:00 p.m.? Whatever Mrs. Doucette had been doing out the other night, her two friends seemed to be involved in it too.

If they're only fishing, why that fearful expression on Miss Wade's face when she opened the door and saw me on the step?

An escalating sense of unease fills him. The look on her face lasted too long. It's not the normal reaction most people feel when a cop comes to their door.

He drives further down the lane before pulling over onto the shoulder. Then he walks back in the darkness to the Wade home. He makes his way through the trees that grow along the south side of the house and stands there in the shadows. He eyes the boat tied up at the dock. It's Mrs. Doucette's husband's sleek fishing boat, repainted and renamed. There's a stack of lobster traps in the stern and two barrels against the wall of the wheelhouse. The tide laps against the hull and a gust of wind off the water shakes the trees.

Soon he hears the back door open and the women's voices. He moves up a few feet to a big pine and cranes his head around it to get a better look. Larkin emerges first, followed by Duska and Jolene. Jolene keeps looking behind her, as though she's worried someone is sneaking up on them in the dark.

The women jump aboard and Duska and Larkin go into the wheelhouse while Jolene stays out on the deck. Seconds later, the engine roars to life. The boat eases away from the wharf and motors away. Without running lights.

As it heads out to sea, he lets out a dismal sigh. They may be sailing out to deep water without lights to avoid being spotted by the town's fishermen, but the fishermen wouldn't be out at this time of night. Running without lights is something rum-runners would do to avoid being seen by the authorities.

Yet it's hard for him to believe these young women are involved in rum-running. He shakes his head and smiles a little for even considering it. The odds are that they're fishing. It's a tough, dangerous occupation and they have the added pressure of going out in the dead of night to avoid being harassed. He can't help admiring them for their courage.

Still, the cop in him has to be sure. And one way to be sure, he decides, is to come back in a few hours to see when they get back in, and whether the boat is empty of traps.

———   •   ———

At 3:00 a.m., Hayes returns and parks his car on the side of the lane.

The house is dark and silent. He gets out, cuts around the side of the structure, sticking close to the woods, and approaches the dock. The sea is still calm, the waves lapping gently onto the beach. He walks to the end, stares out to the ocean, and then down into the translucent black water, pondering everything.

Thirty minutes later, he hears the low growl of a boat engine approaching from the south. He hurries back off the dock and over to the woods, watching from the shadows. Predawn fog is rolling in, making it hard to see and filling the air with the rich scents of salt and damp earth.

As the rumble of the diesel engine increases, he lifts his binoculars. He spies the dark silhouette of a boat glide through the fog and into the cove. It heads straight for the dock. It's the *Bad Reputations*.

The wheelhouse light comes on and he sees Duska is at the helm and Larkin's on the stern deck.

The boat slows to an idle and eases up beside the dock. Larkin leaps over the railing and ties the boat. Then the engine shuts off and the wheelhouse door opens. The two women hurry up the dock, across the lawn, and into the house.

He scans the boat. If they were setting traps, then why is the boat still loaded with so many contraptions? And if they were pulling up traps, where is the catch? Who are they selling to without the fishermen in town knowing?

And where is Jolene Walters?

He focuses on the barrels. One for bait, the other to hold their catch. He wonders how long lobsters can live in a barrel of seawater.

Still, if they are fishing, he understands that they need to make a living. Once more, he can't help admiring their pluck. Going out on the Atlantic is perilous, even for the biggest and strongest fishermen. These three women are all slender, even delicate.

But he realizes now that this is a false impression, for they're clearly strong and capable.

He rubs his forehead in frustration. Despite his admiration, he can't shake his gut intuition that something is off. There's a chance, however slight, that they may be involved in something illegal. And in a small seaside village like this one, the most popular illegal activity is rum-running.

He makes his way back to the car with a heavy heart, deciding to keep a closer eye on them.

CHAPTER TWENTY

On the boat, the bristling sea air kept me alert. But in the truck on my way home, with the heater blasting, I'm dazed with fatigue and don't pay attention to my speed. With the dense fog, the headlights barely light up the road and I don't see the RCMP cruiser parked on the shoulder in time to slow down. After I zip past it, I look up into the rearview mirror and see its headlights snap on. It pulls onto the highway and accelerates after me with its emergency lights flashing.

My heart wobbles. Shoot! I ease off the gas and pull over, telling myself to stay calm and stick to the plan. If he asks what I'm doing out this late, I'll tell him I'm getting back from lobster fishing.

I look into the side mirror and watch as the driver's side door opens and the officer gets out. He shuts the door and walks toward the truck. I have a quick, sinking sensation in my gut.

It's Hayes.

Was he waiting for me? Larkin, Jolene, and I left the house shortly after he did. He saw our clothing, which must have struck him as odd. Did he then watch us board the boat and head out to sea? Did he see us coming back in? Did he wait out here for me to drive by?

Hayes steps up in front of my closed window and shines his flashlight at me. The blinding light stabs at me. I hold up my left hand to shield my eyes.

He lowers his flashlight and raps his knuckles on the window. "Roll the window down please, ma'am."

My hands are shaking. I take a deep breath, steel myself, and then roll it down. In the glow of his headlights, I can see his face clearly.

"Good evening, Mrs. Doucette," he says. "Late to be out on the roads, isn't it?"

His gentle manner puts one at ease, but I know from past experience that it can change fast. I tell myself to stay sharp.

"Yes, it is," I say, my voice slightly strained. "I was lobster fishing. I just got back in and I'm heading home."

He nods, like he already knew this. "Fishing at night? Why?"

"Because this superstitious little town wouldn't allow it. Some of the fishermen are capable of violence, so we go at night."

"By *we*, do you mean Miss Wade and Miss Walters?"

"Yes."

His expression turns thoughtful. "I saw you on this same road at this same time a couple of nights ago and wondered what you were doing. There's nothing open at this time of night." He points the beam of his flashlight at my trousers and jacket. "That explains your clothing."

The wind hisses through the wall of spruce trees lining both sides of the road. He looks up at the trees just as an owl hoots a warning. I flinch and he doesn't; he just coolly fastens me with a level gaze.

"Do you sell your catch to Bill Tucker?"

"No, he'd never buy from us. We sell to a friend who owns a seafood distribution company. He sells to restaurants, inns, and grocery stores around the province."

He raises his eyebrows. "And you meet up with him in the middle of the night?"

No wonder he doesn't miss much, I think, wary and annoyed.

"No. We keep the lobsters in a barrel of seawater on the boat. That keeps them alive for a few days until we can meet him."

"I see. And who is this friend that buys your catch?"

"Jean-Claude Boudreau," I say quietly.

He looks me right in the eyes. "The thing is, two nights ago our patrol boat spotted three people on a grey fishing boat, in an area where rum-runners are known to meet up with the contacts who ferry their product to shore. They spotted another boat in the distance, one that seemed to be leaving the same area. They believe they came very close to intercepting rum-runners offloading their liquor. And I noticed that your husband's boat has been repainted grey."

It feels like a steel clamp has gripped my heart. I sit there, immobilized.

"Would you please step out of the vehicle?" he says. "I'd like to have a look through it."

"Yes, of course." My voice sounds forced and unnatural.

He opens the door for me and I step out, my hands clammy, my skull humming. I stand there in all my glory, the salty diesel stench of my clothing permeating the air around us. I shouldn't be embarrassed, for it only supports my story, yet that's exactly how I feel.

"Please step to the back of the truck, Mrs. Doucette."

I stand at the back end while he searches the cab. The seat groans as he leans on it. Over this, I hear the wind blowing through the trees, and in the distance the roar of the sea crashing into shore.

He backs out of the cab, then closes the driver's door. He walks around the front of the truck to the passenger side and searches there. I hear him open the glovebox and rifle through it. The passenger door shuts.

He comes around to the back, opens the tailgate, and shines the beam of the flashlight around the bed. It reveals a coil of rope and a metal toolbox that belonged to Blade. Thankfully, that's all there is.

The wind has picked up now and the powerful gusts make the trees creak. Their branches sway in a wild dance.

Hayes looks at me, his expression kind. "Mind if I look through the toolbox?"

"No, go ahead."

"Thank you."

He seems impossibly gentle and patient. I find that I like him and reach down and pinch my thigh as hard as I can.

He's a cop, I tell myself. *Smarten up!*

He reaches over the side of the truck and pulls the toolbox toward him. He opens it and finds nothing but tools. He closes it again, then steps back and shuts the tailgate as well. He faces me and clicks off his flashlight.

The way he stands, regarding me in curious silence, is unsettling. I'm sure nothing gets by him. I avert my gaze to the trees over his shoulder.

"That's all then," he says, sounding troubled. "Good night, Mrs. Doucette."

"Good night." I step toward the driver's door, when he calls out again.

"Mrs. Doucette?"

I turn around. "Yes?"

He smiles. "You were driving a little fast. Please slow down."

To my horror, I feel my heart tumble in my chest. That shy, tender smile again. Flustered, I drop my eyes to the ground.

"I will."

I open the door, jump in, and close it fast. As I drive away, I flick my eyes to the rearview mirror. He's standing in the road, swathed in eerie white fog, watching me.

I'm sure now that he was waiting for me. And I'm not sure he believed my story.

What's even more disconcerting is how much I'm drawn to him, the catch in my throat I feel whenever our eyes meet. And the way his eyes soften and linger on mine, I think that it's mutual.

It strikes me that grief has made me foolish. It's not the warmth of affection I see in his eyes. It's just pity for a young widow. I tell myself to wise up.

It's maddening, for I wish he was cold and harsh so I'd dislike him. I'll have to be even more careful. What if he follows me out to Jolene's, or follows us to Larkin's. He might watch us head out to sea, then radio the RCMP patrol boat, or the Coast Guard…

I steer down the highway toward home, my mind reeling.

———•———

Hayes stands for a moment, wondering why he can't shake the feeling that Duska lied about the fishing.

What are they really up to? he asks himself. *Why does she feel the need to do so?*

One answer, of course, is that they've resorted to rum-running, that the *Bad Reputations* is the boat spotted by the patrol the other night.

He walks back to the car, tosses his hat on the passenger seat, and climbs in behind the wheel. He sits for a moment, thinking it all over, and lets out a long, heavy sigh. He feels a sudden wrench of sadness that Duska might be breaking the law.

With my job, people lie to me all the time. So why does it bother me so much? Am I developing feelings for Duska?

The thought dismays him greatly, as does the realization that he may one day have to arrest her. But to be attracted to her? He shakes his head, thinking he's lost his mind. Her eyes are shadowed with grief, and her smiles, though alluring, are so sad, so rare. Even if he can't seem to stop staring at her, even if he finds her beautiful and charming…

No. What am I thinking?

As much as he wants her story to be true, he can't let his feelings distract him from doing his duty as a police officer. And he can't let it destroy his testimony as a Christian. He gives his chin a brisk rub with the heel of his hand, as if to erase his attraction for her.

Attributing his emotions to exhaustion, he starts the engine and drives. He's been on night shift all week and hasn't been sleeping well. Heck, it's no wonder he's not thinking clearly. Even his brain is tired.

He drives back to town, telling himself to forget these three women. They're respectable young Christians. No way would they be involved in rum-running.

They're fishing, that's all. And they have enough to worry about with all the other fishermen. They don't need me on their backs too.

And as for Duska, he's probably just lonely. He tells himself to forget her… in that way.

I need to forget her. I must forget her.

But then, only a minute later, she's back on his mind… in that way.

A blanket of despair falls over him at the realization that it's beyond him to let these women continue with whatever they're doing. And stifling his attraction seems impossible.

CHAPTER TWENTY-ONE

On Sunday morning, I awake at nine. I was exhausted last night and went to bed at 8:00 p.m. I slept like the dead for thirteen hours.

I stretch, yawn, tumble out of bed, and pad to the bathroom. When done, I go into the kitchen, pour cereal and milk into a bowl and take it onto the back porch with a mug of coffee. Holding my breakfast, I watch sunlight glint off the water. It rained hard the night before, but now the sky is a cloudless crystalline blue. The air is filled with birdsong and smells of clean earth and the sea.

Later, I jump in the truck and drive through the warm sunshine, following the coastline road into town. Lupins are out now and fill the ditches on both sides. And as the summer approaches, I notice that the colour of the sea is changing to a vivid aqua-blue. The temperature is rising fast.

Despite an altogether gorgeous spring morning, none of it lightens the heaviness in my heart.

I'm meeting Larkin and Bash at their church. Jolene's staying in the cottage to keep out of sight. We decided on Larkin's church, because I'm not ready yet to attend mine. My pastor is a good man, and Sophie and a few others in the congregation would defend me, but I just can't face Blade's family. Larkin likes her pastor, and he and the congregation support her and Bash.

And though all the pastors in town preach against rum-running, Larkin's pastor does so kindly, with a deep understanding and concern for the members of his congregation involved in it.

I pull into the hard-packed dirt lot and park next to Larkin, where she and Bash sit waiting. I climb out and join them as they get out of the car.

Larkin smiles. "Morning, Duska,"

"Morning you two," I say, smiling back.

Bash tugs on Larkin's arm. "Can I go in now? Sheamus is waiting for me."

"Sure, go ahead." Larkin looks at me. "You ready?"

I give her a slightly nervous nod.

"Don't worry." She squeezes my hand. "This is a good church. Good people."

As we walk towards the entrance, I spot Constable Hayes standing by the front doors.

He's here?

At once, my heart quickens. He looks smart in black dress pants, a white long-sleeved dress shirt, and a red and white striped tie. Out of uniform, I almost don't recognize him.

"You never told me Hayes goes to your church," I say.

"I didn't remember." She shrugs. "I only saw him once and it was a few weeks ago."

Hayes walks over to us, smiling. "Good morning, Mrs. Doucette, Miss Wade. A beautiful day."

Blood rushes to my face. "It is," I mumble, feeling unsettled by his presence. Even more unsettling is how glad I am that I'm wearing my nicest sapphire dress with tan dress shoes.

"I didn't realize you attend this church," I say.

"Oh yes, my parents are Lutheran. It's just my third time, though. Depends on my shifts. I don't get many Sundays free." He hesitated. "I didn't notice you before either."

"It's my first time. It's Larkin's church. I find it too hard to go back to the Baptists." My voice trembles as I think of the many happy Sundays Blade and I spent at the little white church across the road.

He watches me for a moment. "I understand."

There's a warmth in his eyes that nearly does me in. I look away, tears threatening.

His face falls. "I'm sorry. I've upset you."

I draw in a breath. His eyes are striking, an electric grey-blue that captivate and hold me. "No, it's fine."

He stands about five-eleven and weighs about one-seventy. He has short brown hair and a chiselled jaw. And he smells good. An orange and clove scent that's spicy but not overpowering. It must be his aftershave.

Larkin glances at him, and then me. Her eyes widen.

"Are you ladies still fishing lobster?" he asks, clearly wanting to change the subject.

I nod half-heartedly. Lying doesn't come easily to me, and certainly not in front of a church.

"Please excuse me, Constable, but I sing in the choir." Larkin gives me a contrite look and then ducks inside.

"Lobster fishing…" His expression unchanged, his eyes probe mine. "That's a hard way to make a living. Especially with the price so low right now."

"It is, yes."

Hidden somewhere in the trees, a blue jay gives a loud jeer, as if laughing at my continued lies. It feels like there's a chunk of ice in my stomach.

"I'd better get inside."

He smiles. "Me too. It was nice talking to you."

"Hmmm…"

When I sit in the last pew at the back, the choir is singing "Fare Thee Well." Some parishioners turn to look at me as I enter, but they only nod and smile in greeting.

Hayes is sitting two pews up but across the aisle on the right. To my surprise, he's sitting with a young and attractive brunette. Unconsciously, my heart takes a dive into the pit of my stomach. Irritated with myself, I slip my hand under the Bible on my lap and pinch my thigh, hard enough to leave a bruise.

During the sermon, I steal a glimpse at him. To my horror, Hayes glances back over his shoulder and our eyes meet. He turns his head to face the front and I see the back of his neck redden. Embarrassed to be caught looking at me, or annoyed because he caught me in the act?

Blazing mortification sweeps over me. What am I thinking? He doesn't wear a wedding ring, so this brunette must be his girlfriend. Even a spark of friendship with him is dangerous, though. He's a cop, and a sharp one.

I grip my Bible and focus on the pastor's words. The sermon is about disobeying God, specifically how some crimes, like rum-running, contribute to alcohol addiction, family break-ups, drunk driving, and death. The pastor seems to be looking right at Larkin and me.

By now Larkin has come back to the pew, the choir having finished. I feel her stiffen beside me. I understand. The pastor's words have pierced my heart too. I'm always battling the guilt these days, but right now it's positively crushing. The hot prick of tears threaten and I drop my eyes to the floor.

When it's over, I take a deep, shuddering breath and stride down the aisle, past the pastor and his wife at the front door. I don't shake their hands. I just have to get out, down the steps, and get to the parking lot. I stand there, my pulse pounding.

Raising my hand to shield my eyes from the scorching glare of the noon sun, I wait for Larkin.

A few minutes later, she joins me.

"You flew out of there," she says.

I let out a sigh of despair. "The sermon got to me."

She nods. "Me too."

Hayes and the brunette emerge from the church and walk over to a grey sedan, throwing their heads back in laughter. My heart lurches as they get in and drive away.

"What's wrong?" Larkin asks.

"Nothing."

"Your face is all red."

"It is? The day is getting hot."

A slow smile spreads across her face. "That's his sister. She's up visiting from Moncton."

"How do you know that?"

"I heard them talking to Pastor Woods. Also, noticed the New Brunswick plate."

My heart lifts. "Oh."

"Feel better?" She chuckles and gives me a gentle nudge in the side.

"About what?" I say, though I'm astonished to realize that I do feel relieved. "Want to pick up fish and chips from Pruett's and bring it to Jolene's?"

"Sure."

"All right. Just let me collect Bash."

"Ah, Larkin… I like your church. Pastor Woods and everyone are nice. But I can't come back here. I can't sit there like a hypocrite when I know I'm breaking the law."

Larkin swallows. "I know. I find it difficult too. I can't wait until we're done."

"Me too. I'll come back to church… when it's over."

"I understand. I want to keep bringing Bash, though."

"Of course."

She grins. "And I'll keep my eyes on someone for you."

"Oh, be quiet."

CHAPTER TWENTY-TWO

It's a sunny warm morning. The sky is cerulean blue. The buds on the birch and poplar trees are beginning to leaf out. There's a gentle breeze off the pristine blue water laden with the scent of salt. I make a bowl of porridge and pour a cup of coffee and take it out to the back porch.

When I'm finished, I walk barefoot down to the beach, where the incoming tide is pushing up yellow ribbons of seaweed. I step into the surf up to my knees and stare out to sea. The waves slap, clean and cool, against my legs.

Normally, the ocean calms me. But not today. I'm plagued by guilt. It's like a splinter I can't remove. I also feel more and more unsettled by what's going on with Constable Hayes. I fear he's on to us. Even more disturbing, I've been thinking about him too much. I fear that I like him—too much. That though I tried willing myself not to look at him yesterday at church, my eyes seemed to dart in his direction unbidden.

What did it mean to like a man in this way so soon after Blade's death? Liking him when he's a cop and I'm a criminal?

I'm coming completely undone.

Wanting to get out of the too-quiet house, and distance myself from these troubled thoughts, I drive over to Jolene's place. She's the only one, with her infectious manner and quick wit, who can get me out of this mood.

I gather some pickles, strawberry jam, and wax beans I canned in the fall. I add some potatoes, carrots, and peas from the root cellar. With Blade gone, I have too much anyway.

I park in front of the cottage and walk to the front porch, the cardboard box of food tucked under my arm.

"I'm around back, Duska," Jolene calls out.

I walk around to the back of the house to find Jolene lounging on an old wooden lawn chair on the back porch, enjoying the sunshine. She's barefoot, wearing tan trousers rolled up past her knees and a sleeveless white cotton top. Her lanky legs are stretched out and her slender arms are draped over the armrests, her head tilted back to face the sky. A glass of iced tea sits on a little wooden stand next to her chair.

"Good afternoon, Jolene."

"What's so good about it?" she says without looking at me.

I stop in my tracks. "What? Something happen?"

She turns her head and chuckles. "No, just kidding. It's a gorgeous afternoon."

"How'd you know it was me?"

"I know the sound of your truck. I made it a point to recognize the sounds of Larkin's and your vehicles. Your muffler is a bit loud. Might have a small hole in it. If anyone else drives up, I'll hide fast."

"That's smart." I set the box down next to the chair. "I brought you some bottled jam, pickles, and veggies."

She eyes the box and smiles. "That's wonderful. Thanks so much."

I sit down in the chair next to hers. "Where'd you find these chairs?"

"In the garden shed. The canvas was rotten on all but these two." She picks up the iced tea and sips from it. "I only wish I'd been smart enough to leave Burke and move in here sooner. Living by the sea has a soothing effect on me."

I watch a seagull dive into the froth, then rise again with a mussel clasped in its beak.

"I know what you mean. I've always found it calming, and yet invigorating. I never want to live anywhere else."

She stares happily out to the sea. "It's so mesmerizing. I could sit here for hours looking at the water. In fact, I've been having second thoughts about leaving town." She sets her glass down on the table and sits up. "I might buy this cottage from my great-aunt's nephew. I could make him a decent offer. He'd likely be glad to get rid of it. I could fix it up… once I'm legally divorced from Burke, I mean."

I lift a brow. "Do you think Burke will leave you alone?"

"I don't know. I'm hoping he will once we're divorced. And though I don't trust the cops in this town, Hayes seems different. I think he'll keep Burke away from me. Besides, I have you and Larkin now. I'm seriously thinking of staying put."

I can see that she needs Larkin and me for reasons she may not be able to fully understand. But then, we all need each other.

She waves her hand at the property. "Look at this place. A white sand beach, wild rose bushes on all sides, filling the air with their lovely scent… and no neighbours. It's a slice of heaven."

"The cottage is in rough shape, though. Might cost more to fix it up than to buy something else."

"Maybe, but I love it here. And if I don't use the money I've saved to run away, I'll have it to pay for the repairs."

"I'd love it if you stayed. Larkin would too."

She beams at me, then reaches out and squeezes my hand. "I've never really had friends before. Not like you and Larkin. Hey, want an iced tea? I chipped off some pieces from the chunk in the fridge and made a jug."

"Sure."

Jolene goes inside and returns a minute later with the tea.

I drink some, and it's good. Tart, but not too tart.

I set the glass down on the floor. "Not to be a Debbie Downer, but prohibition in Nova Scotia is likely going to end in another year. Are you sure you'll have enough saved to renovate this place?"

Before she can respond, we hear the sound of a vehicle turning into the driveway.

"Expecting anyone?" I ask.

Jolene sits up at once. "No, and that's not Larkin's car."

We hear the engine shut off, a door open and shut.

I jump to my feet. "In the house, quick!"

"No, wait." Jolene holds up a hand. "If we don't answer, they'll leave. I'll peek around the side of the house and see who it is."

"But my truck is in the driveway," I whisper.

"So? Doesn't mean you're in the cottage."

I disagree, but stop, ears pealed. We hear footsteps on the front porch and then someone knocks on the door.

We wait silently.

There are two more knocks, and after a moment we detect the thumps of someone going back down the steps.

"They're leaving," Jolene whispers.

Suddenly, Constable Hayes walks around the corner of the house, the sun in his eyes. He puts his hand up to shield them from the bright sunshine.

"Hello, ladies," he says. But his eyes are on me, his smile shy.

I feel a warm tug in my heart, and once again I'm needled by guilt.

"Hi," I stammer.

He's dressed in black trousers, a short-sleeved pale-yellow shirt, and brown brogans that look well-worn. He's off-duty.

"Splendid day," he remarks.

"It is." I will my voice to remain steady, for my pulse to stabilize.

"I thought you were on the night shift," Jolene blurts. "Don't you ever sleep?"

"I'm off today and then go on the day shift tomorrow. We work one week of days, one week of nights."

I'm relieved, because that means he won't be watching for us at night this week.

He turns to me, his blue eyes gentle. "Mrs. Doucette, how are you?"

The gentleness in his eyes and tenderness in his voice nearly does me in. I only nod, my throat tight.

"Are you here about Burke?" Jolene asks.

He pulls his eyes back to her. "Yes, I am. I saw him in town an hour ago. He was with another man who was driving a new, dark red coupe."

Jolene grimaces. "That's Burke's car. What did the other guy look like?"

"Husky build, short blond hair, early twenties."

"That's his cousin, Clint. He's a scallop fisherman. Burke works for him."

Hayes nods. "They drove around town, and then out on the Oceanside Highway. I stayed behind them as they drove right past your lane. Then I followed them back to town. They parked and went into Pruett's. I wanted to let you know."

"Last week, after we spoke, did you tell him I'm not coming back home?"

"I did."

"How did he take it?'

"He seemed mostly surprised and sad."

Jolene snorts. "He's faking. He's smart enough not to let on that he's furious and is going to come after me."

Hayes tilts his head to one side. "In fact, he started crying."

Jolene slaps a hand on her thigh. "Oh, that's rich. What an actor!" she says between gales of laughter. "I hope you didn't fall for that."

I stare in mortification at Jolene, but she ignores me. And by the way Hayes eyes her, I can tell that he's not sure who to believe.

"Well, thanks for letting me know," Jolene says once she's stopped laughing. "It was kind of you to come out on your day off."

He stares at her in silence for a time, then nods. "You're welcome. I know you told me he's not aware of this cottage, but what if one of you are followed?" He turns to me and lifts a brow. "Perhaps you should stay with Mrs. Doucette for a little while. You shouldn't be alone, and she lives closer to town."

"Yes, of course," I say to her. "And I have a phone."

Jolene shoots me a dark look. "No."

"Why not?" I ask.

She turns her head and stares at the trees lining the side of the yard.

"You don't have a phone and you're isolated here," says Hayes. "Please consider Mrs. Doucette's offer."

She replies while still pretending to be fascinated by the trees. "I don't want to put Duska in danger. This is my problem, not hers. Besides, I'm impossible to live with. I'm perpetually thin-skinned, argumentative, and unreasonable. She might end up strangling me before Burke ever finds me."

Hayes laughs and I look at him in surprise. It's a warm laugh, unexpected from a police officer. Then the realization that I like it too much strikes me like a thunderbolt. It seems appalling to me, so soon after losing Blade.

I lose the smile and clamp my lips together.

"I doubt if all that is true." He pulls a card out of his shirt pocket and hands it to Jolene. "Take this. The detachment phone number is on there. If you need help, call and ask for me."

Jolene takes the card. "Thank you."

"Your dock's been repaired," he says suddenly.

I follow his gaze to the dock and my heart stutters. Only he would notice the minor fixes. It's nothing more than a few new planks and posts.

"Yes, some of it," Jolene says with a breezy expression. "The owner is thinking of selling this place. He thought repairing the dock would help sell it faster."

"Water looks deep," he muses. "Like a big boat could easily moor there."

Jolene shrugs. "No idea."

He slides his eyes from the dock to Jolene, and then to me, his brow furrowed. His eyes linger on mine. I feel a blast of heat rise to my face.

Jolene watches him for a moment and then looks sideways at me. My expression is dark, but she just grins and waggles her eyebrow gaily.

I could just choke her.

"Right. Good day then, ladies." He turns and walks back around the side of the house.

We hear the car door open and shut, and then the engine starts up.

"So Burke's looking for me," Jolene remarks after the sound of the engine fades.

"Yes, so come to my place."

"No. I'm not going to put you in danger. Anyway, I'm done hiding from Burke."

"What?"

"I'm done wearing the hat and jacket. It's too hot for that now. I have to face him sooner or later. It'd be best if I do meet him in town. He wouldn't dare try to kidnap me in broad daylight. Not with you there."

"What happens if he sees us in town and follows us out here?"

"I'll be extra vigilant. I'll look around and behind me all the time." She smiles. "You keep a sharp eye out when you drive out here too."

"I will."

"I found an old baseball bat in the kitchen closet. When I go to bed, I keep it under the blankets with me. If he does track me down and tries to break in, I'll crack him over the head with it even harder than the last time."

"Not a good idea. Besides, he could take it and then use it on you."

"I won't let him. No way is that man ever going to lay a hand on me again."

I give her a doubtful look.

"I'm staying here, Duska. And one day soon I'm going to buy this place. I'm going to live here and Burke isn't going to stop me."

I nod but don't share her certainty. "What if Hayes comes back around some night when we're on the beach with Jean-Claude?"

"I had the same thought. I think one of us should stand at the end of the lane by the highway. At the first sight of headlights coming down the road, they run back and warn us. There's an old unused lane on the other side of the house where Jean-Claude could hide the truck, and of course we can all hide in the cottage."

"Good idea."

"It'll be all right, Duska."

We sit back against the chairs and sip our iced teas.

A herd of brown wrens suddenly erupt from the trees overhead and fly off. I watch them until they're out of sight, my heart filled with uneasiness.

CHAPTER TWENTY-THREE

Two nights later, at 10:00 p.m., I'm about to leave to pick up Jolene when I hear a car engine coming down Rowboat Lane. I freeze in the hallway, listening. I hear the crunch of shells as the car slows and then turns into my driveway. I look toward the front of the house as a beam of headlights sweeps through the living room. As I hurry in, I lift the window curtain an inch, just enough to peer outside.

A car is stopped in front of the house, engine idling, exhaust trailing from its pipe. It looks new and its paint glitters under the moonlight. I can see the dark shapes of a driver and a passenger in the front seat.

The passenger rolls the window down and sticks his head out, scanning my house. I can't make out his features, but I can see what looks like a white bandage tied around his forehead.

I leap back from the window. It has to be Burke!

If so, there's something deeply unnerving in the fact that he's come to my house. I wasn't a friend of Jolene's until recently, so someone must have seen Jolene in my truck and told him. But the fact that he's here also means he doesn't know where Jolene is staying.

The passenger walks onto my property and stands in the shadows of the trees that grow along the front lawn. Then he comes up the steps and bangs on the door.

Under the yellow glow of the porchlight, I recognize Burke.

He hammers on the door hard a few times before finally giving up and going back down the steps. He steals around to the back of the house, though, and I hear him come up onto the back porch. The floorboards creak and I see his dark shape skulk past the kitchen window.

Seconds later, there's a knock at the door. I wait, and after a time he goes back down.

Then he's out front again, getting into the car. As I watch, the car moves to the end of the lane, makes a U-turn, and proceeds slowly past my place again. I watch until the red taillights disappear. Then I wait another half-hour, making sure he doesn't return, before leaving.

As I drive out onto the highway, keeping a nervous eye on the rearview mirror, I head for Schooner Cove. No one follows me.

"Shoot!" Jolene says in the truck after I pick her up. "You're sure it was Burke?"

"Positive."

Jolene looks sour with displeasure. "Who was driving?"

"I couldn't see him that well, only that he was heavyset. Likely Clint."

"Yes." Her eyes are smouldering. "The nerve! Burke had better not come around your place again. If he does, I'll brain him even harder than ever." She sees my startled expression. "What?"

"You don't mean that?"

"I most certainly do."

"Jolene."

She stares out the windshield, her mood dark. "I have to protect myself."

"You can call Constable Hayes. He'll warn Burke to stay away."

She nods, but in a way that means she won't.

"It's not safe for you to stay at the cottage alone anymore," I point out.

"It's safer than anywhere else. He came to your place, not the cottage, so I was right by staying put. I'm more worried about him coming back to your place."

"He does and I'll bop him on the head with a pot."

Jolene throws her head back and hoots. "You would not!"

"No, you're right. I'd call Hayes."

She falls silent and remains that way until we're gathered in Larkin's kitchen, telling her about Burke.

"Duska's right. Stay with her. She has a phone, and she's close to town if you need to call the cops," Larkin advises. "Or you can stay here, as long as you don't mind an incredibly active and noisy little boy."

Jolene smiles, then shakes her head. "Thanks, but I'm staying at the cottage. Someone must have seen me in town with Duska and told Burke. You weren't with us, so he won't have any reason to come here. I've already put Duska in danger. I won't put you and Bash in danger too."

Right then, Bash comes into the kitchen.

Larkin steps over to Bash. "What are you doing up? Did we wake you?"

"Yes, I heard you guys talking." Bash rubs his tired brown eyes. "Sadie said I could come down. Just for a minute."

He stares at Jolene.

"Bash, this is my friend, Jolene."

Jolene smiles at him. "Hi Bash."

"Hi."

Larkin leans over and kisses the top of his head. "Go back to bed. It's late. I'll see you in the morning."

"Night, everyone." With that, he goes back up the stairway.

"Good night," we all say.

Moments later, we're getting ready to leave. But before we go, Sadie enters the kitchen with a worried look on her face. "Don't go out tonight, girls."

Suddenly we all see a bolt of lightning through the kitchen window, flashing in the sky to the south. The wind blowing in smells metallic. Rain's on the way.

Larkin lifts a brow. "Why, the weather? I checked it. It's going to get a bit stormy, but nothing we haven't experienced yet."

"No, not the weather," Sadie says.

"What then? You hear something about the Coast Guard or Mounties?" Larkin asks.

"No. I don't know what it is. Just a bad feeling, I guess."

"We'll be fine, Sadie," says Larkin. "Don't worry."

Sadie nods but looks unconvinced.

Once she's gone back upstairs, I look out into the darkness. Like Sadie, I feel the increasing cold and dread of night. Something feels heavy and ominous. I can't put my finger on what it is, but I too have misgivings about going out.

"Maybe you should stay home with Bash tonight," I tell Larkin.

"Sadie's always nervous when we go out, usually for no reason."

I nod but feel my chest clench a little.

Not Jolene, though. She claps her hands eagerly. "All right, girls, let's go have some fun." She says it as though we're off to Tahiti.

When we leave the house, feeling edgy, I keep an eye out for anyone lurking in the trees or a boat hiding out in the blackness of the ocean.

We jump on the boat and head out to the open sea, streaming against a sharp north wind. The barometer is plunging fast and the wind rises. Charcoal-grey clouds cross the sky. Behind them, moving fast, are inky black storm clouds. Within a half-hour, the temperature has crashed and sea spray is freezing on the deck and railings. The winds are gusting more than thirty miles an hour over the increasingly angry seas. The boat plunges into the trough and we see nothing but a wall of black water in front of us for a long time before being lifted up to the top of the wave again, only to repeat the stomach-churning cycle over and over.

Soon we're out at the rendezvous point, standing out on the freezing deck and keeping a watch all around. Our freezing hands grip the icy, metal railing.

The waves are choppy, full of foamy whitecaps that slam into us. Our breath whips away in the blasts of wind and my fingers are numb from gripping the side rail tight enough to keep me from losing my footing. My toes are numb too; I have to constantly stamp my feet to keep the blood flowing. I see Jolene doing the same.

She sees me looking at her and shakes her hands. "My hands are colder than my mother-in-law's smile!"

I laugh hard. It's the first good laugh I've had since Blade died. It's clear that despite Burke and the perils we face, Jolene still feels only exhilaration when we go out.

The seas turn even more ferocious, sending spray crashing over us and pooling around our feet. A howling gust of wind tears into us like a kick from a horse, throwing us violently to the deck. We all struggle to stand, grabbing the railing again to keep from being tossed overboard.

"This is dangerous, even with our life jackets," I yell at them over the wind. "If we fall overboard, we'll die of hypothermia. Let's go in the wheelhouse! They may not even be coming out in this."

Bent over, we start to make our way to the wheelhouse. Then, glancing back, I spot the silhouette of the sleek, narrow *Night Glider* moving toward us.

"Wait, they're here," I say.

We turn back around as the vessel slows and its captain manoeuvres it up close to our port side. Two men are standing at the starboard railing. One of them throws Jolene a line at the bow and she makes a grab for it, but the wind tears it away. He tries again, but the fury of the wind and sea is too great, and she misses once more. The man keeps reeling it in and tossing it; finally, on the fourth attempt, she catches it. Jolene lets out a "Whoop!" and then ties it around a metal clasp at the bow. Larkin does the same at the stern.

The crashing waves push the boats closer and the hulls bang into each other with loud thuds. Throughout the side window of the wheelhouse, I see the flare of a match being struck. The light of the flame illuminates the face of a heavyset man with a thick white beard and mutton chop whiskers. As the man lights his pipe, I notice his black pea coat and wool cap. The smell of tobacco carries out on the wind.

We all hang tightly on to the railings, our heads bowed to the turbulent wind. The sea bashes us continually, penetrating our clothes right through to our bones. I'm afraid we'll be exhausted and hypothermic before we even start working.

But finally, fifteen minutes later, the wind dies down and the seas settle enough that the men are able to start offloading.

Once finished, we watch the *Night Glider* slip away into the darkness just as I see lightning and hear thunder to the east. Another storm is moving in, and fast.

Larkin and Jolene start coiling the bow and stern lines and pulling up the anchor. I turn to go back into the wheelhouse when a movement in the distance to my left catches my eye. I stop and squint at the horizon.

And see the clear silhouette of a boat sailing by.

"Boat off the stern to the east! Looks like a Coast Guard cutter!" I shout to Jolene and Larkin, who are still pulling up the anchor. "Hurry, quick!"

They both nod and work faster.

I run into the wheelhouse and take my place behind the helm. Seconds later, Larkin and Jolene burst into the wheelhouse.

"They've turned and are steaming toward us!" Jolene says.

"Head for Skeleton Island," Larkins says, face frightened.

My heart in my throat, I ram the throttle forward and we roar away. My hands shake and I have to grip the steering wheel as tight as I can.

Suddenly, dark clouds scud across the sky. Within seconds, fat drops of rain dimple the ocean, pelting the windshield and deck.

Jolene cracks the door a few inches and looks out, battering us anew with rain and wind. "Hit the gas, Duska! They're gaining on us!"

"Keep watching and tell me if they get closer," I shout back.

"Don't let them! Go full throttle!" she yells. "Ow, the rain's tearing the flesh right off my face—"

"Never mind, come in."

She pulls her head back in and slams the door shut.

The clouds overhead open up even more and a deluge of rain hammers down on the roof. We race away in the heavy, pounding rain across the tempestuous sea. The boat rockets over the crests of wildly curling waves and then slams down into the inevitable trough, rattling our teeth.

When we reach the island, it looks like nothing but rock. No beach at all. I navigate around the rocky shore to the north side where I know overhanging branches hide a narrow gap that leads to a tiny cove. Rain continues to fall in great thundering sheets, stippling the surface of the sea. I manoeuvre the boat up close to the shore and back it in under a thick canopy of trees. I want to be able to take off if we need to and there's just enough room to slip the boat inside.

I shut off the engine and we drop anchor. We're hidden from sight, and mercifully protected from the chaotic seas. We stand without speaking, staring out the windshield, keeping our eyes out for the lights of the cutter.

After an hour, the wind drops but the heavy rain continues. Dark clouds conceal the moon like a bruise and ghostly fog rises from the water, hiding us even more effectively.

I let out my breath, not even aware that I've been holding it. "I think we lost them."

"Yes, but that was too close," Larkin says, and I hear a quaver in her voice.

"Close call, but what fun!" Jolene says.

Larkin and I share a smile.

Jolene sees us and laughs, seeming to thrive on the danger. "What?"

She reaches into the cupboard below the dashboard for my thermos, unscrews the tin top, and pours me a cup of hot coffee. She does the same for Larkin, and then lastly pours herself a cup from her own thermos.

"Thanks," Larkin and I both say.

"Cheers." Jolene holds out her cup, then taps mine and then Larkin's cups.

Larkin and I exchange another glance. Jolene is tougher than either of us really understood, and it's a good thing. It's rubbing off on us.

"We won't make it in time to meet up with Jean-Claude now," Larkins says. "We'll have to go straight to my place from here. Duska will drive you home tonight, Jolene. I'll get a message to Jean-Claude's nephew telling him what happened. We'll likely have to meet him at Schooner Cove tomorrow night to offload the liquor."

Jolene and I nod in agreement.

After two more hours, dawn breaks on the horizon. Rain continues to thud on the wheelhouse roof, flattening the island's trees and bushes and leaving big indentations when it hits the water. Nevertheless, the sky is growing lighter.

It's time to try to make it back unseen to Larkin's place.

An hour later, we make it and tie up at the dock. We hurry through the rain into the house, where we kick off our boots at the back door and shed our coats, hanging them on hooks on the wall. Larkin goes upstairs to get towels while Jolene and I sit at the kitchen table, drenched and shivering. The only sound is the plop of water dripping onto the floor from our clothing.

Larkin returns and we all start towelling off.

Hearing a scream from upstairs, we nearly jump out of our skins.

"Dad! Dad!"

Larkin leaps to her feet, tosses her towel on the table, and heads for the stairs. "That's Bash. He has recurring nightmares about the night our dad was killed. He wakes up shaking and wild-eyed. It's horrible."

"Oh, the poor little guy," I say.

Jolene looks at me, her expression sad.

Larkin goes upstairs taking them two at a time, and soon we hear her and Sadie's voices consoling Bash.

"We should go," Jolene says. "She'll probably want to stay up there with him until he falls asleep."

I nod, then stand and walk over to the stairway. "We're leaving, Larkin."

"Wait," she calls down. "Don't you want to finish drying off first? I can make some hot chocolate."

"No, we're fine," I say.

"All right. Be careful driving. And watch for the cops."

Jolene and I go outside, where curtains of rain are still falling. We race for the truck and leap into the cab.

I drive away, the wipers swishing back and forth. "I wonder if Larkin has nightmares too. She heard it all—the gunshots, the screams... and she saw her dad's body on the kitchen floor. She said it was the worst thing she's ever seen in her life."

The rain is picking up yet again, pummelling the dirt road and turning it to mud. I lean forward to see better as the rain slashes against the windshield,

"Yeah, I imagine she does. That's deep trauma, and she's so young. I've wondered how she copes with it."

I take my eyes off the road briefly to look at Jolene. "She has Sadie and us."

Jolene smiles. "We're there for each other. I mean, you lost Blade, too."

I nod, the image of Blade's shattered face filling my mind. I'm lost in my despairing thoughts, not paying attention, when I barrel around a turn onto the Oceanside Highway and see two RCMP cars parked side by side on the two-lane road just ahead.

"Roadblock!" Jolene screams.

I slam on the brakes and we fishtail a little. I peer out and see two Mounties standing in the space between the cars. Both are wearing yellow raincoats and hats and waving flashlights at us to drive toward them.

There's a thrumming in my brain. "I have to stop."

"You can't," Jolene says.

"Why not? We'll just say we're coming in from fishing like we planned."

"Can't. I've got the devil's rum in my bag."

"What!"

"When you and Larkin were walking back to the boat the other night, I bought some from Jean-Claude. It's damp in the cottage no matter how much wood I put in the stove. I like a hot toddy at night before bed. Warms me up."

"How many bottles do you have?"

"Six. I bought a burlock."

"Six!" I blurt, incredulous. "What are you, an alcoholic?"

She grins with shameless delight. "No, but I like a hot toddy when I have a cold… or the flu…"

"How often do you have a cold or flu that you need that many bottles?"

Her grin widens. "I'm stocking up in case prohibition lasts longer than we think."

"Jolene! You've put us in a bad spot."

"Just drive around them. There's enough room on the side of the car on the right."

The two officers' gesture with their flashlights. They're growing more adamant that I approach them.

"Are you crazy? They're standing right there. I could hit one of them."

"Nah, they'll move," Jolene scoffs. "It's either that or you need to make a U-turn and take off. But then we'll be heading back toward town. They'll radio ahead for another car to stop us. My cottage isn't far from here. We can make it there before they come after us."

My hands are slick on the steering wheel. My pulse is throbbing.

One of the cops starts walking quickly toward us.

"One's coming."

"Go!" Jolene yells.

Without another thought, I grind the gear into first, let out the clutch, and slam my foot on the gas. The truck takes off, the rear end sliding in a shower of pebbles and dirt.

My headlights illuminate the cop walking toward us. Thankfully, it's not Hayes. He stops and holds a hand up in front of the flashlight beam, motioning for us to halt. I veer around him but drive through a large puddle. Muddy water splashes up from my left-side tires, spraying into the air and cascading over his body and face.

"Woo-hoo!" Jolene bursts out laughing and slaps a hand on her thigh. "You got him good."

I punch the gas pedal almost to the floor and drive straight toward the second Mountie. Heart rocketing, I don't stop. At the last second, he leaps out of the way and disappears into the ditch.

Also not Hayes, I think in relief.

I keep my foot on the gas and race down the road, my knuckles white against the steering wheel. The whole time Jolene's killing herself laughing.

Minutes later, I turn into her lane and gun it for her cottage. I park off to the left side of the property, hidden beneath a canopy of trees. I shut off the engine, lay my head on the steering wheel, and rest my head on my arms. After a few minutes, my breathing slows, and my pulse calms.

I lift my head and look at Jolene. Tears of laughter stream down her cheeks. She's laughing so hard that she has the hiccups.

She reaches out and punches me on the arm. "Way to go! Boy, that was hilarious. I don't think I've laughed so hard in all my life. Did you see the cop's face when the water hit him?"

"No, I was too busy trying not to run him down."

"Too bad. It was so comical."

I look at her. She is incapable of fear.

Still grinning, she shakes her head in delight, relishing the memory. "Come on in. You should sleep here. The Mounties will be so furious, they'll be looking for your truck all night."

I reach with a shaky hand for the door handle, unnerved and exhausted by the whole episode. We might have gotten away, but both cops got a look at my truck. With the pouring rain, I don't think they saw our faces clearly, or saw my plates, but I can't be sure. I'm afraid it won't be too long before they show up at my house.

CHAPTER
TWENTY-FOUR

Two mornings later, at 11:00 a.m., wide shafts of warm sunlight fall across my face, waking me. I get up, though I'm yawning every two seconds and my brain feels like a bag of cotton wool.

As usual, I take my late breakfast of coffee and buckwheat pancakes with butter and maple syrup onto the back deck. Though my grief is unremitting, nearly unbearable, my appetite has been slowly returning. I sit on a wooden deck chair, setting my mug on the armrest and the plate on my lap.

It's Wednesday, the first of May, and the sky is a spectacular azure blue. The sun burns down, having chased away the fog hours ago. Birds sing gaily from the branches. The salty air is fragrant with the scent of the lilac bushes blooming beside the back porch of the house.

I fork up some pancake and chew slowly as I gaze out at the blue-green waves rushing onto the sandy beach. I feel uneasy. Every night, the sun sets a little later in the evening, forcing me to delay. In the evenings, before picking up Jolene, I restlessly pace the house until the sun finally drops into the ocean and darkness falls. Then, on the drive to Larkin's, Jolene and I continuously check the rearview mirror for any sign of Burke.

Then there was that close call with the roadblock. It's all so troubling, and that's on top of Hayes's obvious curiosity about us. Even worse is my growing attraction to Hayes himself, how often he's on my mind. That must stop.

After breakfast, I walk barefoot across the lawn and down the dirt path to the beach. I go up to the water's edge, where I sink my toes in the sand. A warm breeze whispers off the ocean, ruffling my housecoat. The foamy surf rolls up over my feet and then retreats again. It's cold but feels wonderful.

I take a deep breath and let the invigorating sea air fill my lungs. I run my tongue over my lips and taste brine.

After a few minutes of mulling things over, I decide that we really need to start fishing lobster to quell suspicion. I'm not sure who we can sell our catch to other than Jean-Claude, though. We could give some to Sadie and to families in town, the ones we know are struggling to put food on the table, and keep the rest for ourselves.

My mind calmer, I go inside and get dressed. I'll do the dishes and then some laundry, taking advantage of the warm weather and hanging it out on the line.

———— • ————

Later that day, the three of stand on the deck of the *Bad Reputations* at Larkin's dock. We're cutting up the mackerel we bought at Martin's Grocery, tossing the pieces into a bait barrel. Larkin and Jolene agreed to my plan, so tonight we're going to Blade's designated fishing area to set some lobster traps. No fisherman from town will be out there, and if the Mounties or Coasties see us we'll look legit. Then, in a few nights, we'll haul them back up.

"Larkin," Jolene says without looking up. "Duska and I were talking. Once prohibition's over, we were thinking we should start fishing. We'd be making an honest living, and we all love working at sea."

"I'd like that," Larkin says. "But who'd buy our catch?"

"Jean-Claude," she replies. "He'll be out of the rum-running business too, and he's a legitimate seafood distributor."

I really like them both, and we work together so well. Larkin, with her strong, steady manner, keeps me calm and steady, and Jolene, with her quick wit, can get a laugh out of me even in my deep grief. And I do struggle greatly with breaking the law and disobeying God. Most days, I can't look at myself in the mirror.

I give an enthusiastic nod. "I'm in."

Larkin smiles. "I'm in, too. It's dangerous work, but after this it won't faze us one bit."

We work in silence for the next half-hour, the only sound being the soft thud of the waves against the hull.

"Ahh!" Larkin cries out. "I cut my finger off."

I look over and see her holding her hand out in front of her. Blood is gushing from the open pinkie finger of her glove.

"Jolene, run in the house and grab a clean towel and some ice from the ice box!" I say. "You'll have to smash up a chunk from the fridge. Put the pieces in a bowl and bring everything to me."

Jolene leaps over the side onto the dock and races for the house.

Larkin slumps to the deck, resting her back against the wheelhouse wall. She holds her injured hand in the palm of her good one. Her right cheek is streaked with blood and her forehead glistens with perspiration.

"I'm going to be sick," she says.

I drop to my knees in front of her, remove my rubber gloves, and toss them on the ground. I pull a clean white handkerchief from the pocket of my overalls. "Let me see it. I'm going to gently pull off your glove."

She bites her bottom lip hard. "Go ahead."

I nod, carefully easing the glove off. Her pinkie finger's gone just above the knuckle.

Larkin can't seem to bring herself to look at it. "Is it bad?"

"No, not really. Just the tip's gone."

Her face turns a bloodless white. "Just the tip…"

"It's okay, Larkin," I say in my most comforting voice as I carefully wrap the handkerchief around her finger. "We'll take you to the hospital and get this fixed right up."

She gulps in a breath and gives me a brave nod.

A few minutes later, Jolene's back. She passes me a green towel and a ceramic bowl of broken ice chips. I take the towel, gesturing for her to put the bowl down on the deck.

"Hold the towel tightly around your finger, Larkin." I turn to Jolene. "Let's look for her fingertip. If we find it, we'll put it in the bowl of ice, and maybe they can reattach it."

Jolene looks mortified. "What?"

"Unbelievable." Larkin rolls her eyes. "Didn't you clobber your husband over the head with a pot? Finding a little chunk of my finger shouldn't bother you after that."

Jolene grins. "It wasn't a pot. It was a frying pan."

"Oh well then," Larkin says. "That's much better."

We all laugh, even though it's not that funny. It does lighten the grimness of the situation.

Jolene and I search the boat ramp for the fingertip. "It might still be in the glove, so look for a small piece of yellow rubber glove," I say. "We may have to get on our knees."

She drops down to her knees. "Right."

Only seconds later, Jolene shouts, "Found it!" She stands, triumphantly holding up a chunk of yellow rubber glove with a bloody fingertip visible at the lacerated end.

I pick up the bowl and move over to her. I stick my hand in the ice and make a hole in the centre. "Quick, put it in here."

"Take it out of the glove first?"

"No, just shove the whole thing in."

Jolene pushes it in and covers the hole over with the ice.

I pass her the bowl. "You hold this, and I'll help Larkin."

"I'm fine," Larkin says as she stands and walks between us to my truck. She turns her head and gives me a valiant smile.

I smile back, reminded once more that Larkin Wade, with her delicate features, may look frail and vulnerable, but she is one tough young woman.

CHAPTER
TWENTY-FIVE

We're in a cubicle in the emergency room of the town's hospital.

"We say we're fishing?" Jolene whispers.

I nod. "Yes, we stick with the plan."

We hear footsteps and the doctor pulls the curtain aside. "Hello, ladies, I'm Doctor Leduc."

"Hello," we three say in unison.

He turns to Larkin, a knot forming in his brow as he gently lifts her injured hand. "How did this happen?"

"I was cutting up mackerel for bait," she replies. "Knife slipped."

"Cutting up mackerel?" He flicks his eyes from Larkin to Jolene and then to me. Our faces are ruddy, our lips chapped. Our pants and shirts are splattered with fish blood and guts. We reek of it all. He smiles. "Helping your husbands out?"

Jolene scoffs. "We're cutting it up for our own use."

He cocks his head in disbelief. "You three ladies are fishing? On your own?"

"You're looking at Whaleback Cove's first ever fisherwomen," Jolene says proudly.

He looks surprised. "I thought that was taboo around here."

"It is," I say in a low voice. "We go out at night to avoid being seen."

"I'm impressed. You're brave young women. I'm glad to hear that's what you're doing, though," he adds. "An injured fisherman was in here yesterday talking about a rumour going around that some women from town are involved in rum-running."

It's like all the air is suddenly sucked out of the room. A tense disquiet surges in, silencing us.

"How interesting," Jolene says finally. "We wouldn't be cutting up bait mackerel if we were rum-running, would we?"

He watches us for another few seconds. "No, I guess not."

"Can you save her fingertip?" I ask, eager to change the subject.

He shakes his head. "I'm sorry, no, I can't. The fingertip shouldn't have been placed in the ice but set on top. The tissue is too damaged now."

"Oh shoot, my fault," I say. Jolene also winces in regret.

Larkin inhales a shaky breath. "It's just the tip anyway. No big deal."

The doctor lifts his brows. "I'll close the wound now then?"

"Yes, go ahead," Larkin says.

He peers out between the curtain opening and calls for a nurse. The nurse comes in and stands beside him. She takes in our bait-stained men's clothing and eyes us with distaste.

"All right. Please lie down now, Miss Wade," Dr. Leduc says.

Larkin goes stone-still on the bed, her face pale as sand as the nurse rolls a narrow table holding needles, thread, antiseptic, and bandages over to the bed. She drapes a white sheet over Larkin's abdomen and gently lays the injured hand on the sheet, covering it with a cloth except for the pinkie.

"Ready?" Dr. Leduc asks.

Larkin stares at the clock on the wall above his head. "Yes."

Twenty minutes later, the doctor stands back and helps her to sit up. "How are you feeling?"

"Fine," she says, though her voice is a bit shaky.

The nurse slips a sling over Larkin's shoulder. "Are you all right to walk, or would you like a wheelchair?"

"I can walk," Larkin replies, her bandaged hand resting in the sling.

I nod to the nurse. "We'll take care of her,"

"Yes, don't worry," Jolene chimes in. "We've got her."

The nurse leaves and Dr. Leduc writes out two prescriptions. He hands them to me before looking back at Larkin. "One is an antibiotic, the other is for the pain. Take one antibiotic daily and two painkillers every four hours. Try to eat something when you do take them. And keep your hand in the sling, and elevated."

Larkin nods. "I will."

He smiles at her. "Come back in two days for a cleaning and bandage change."

I walk up and stand on Larkin's right side while Jolene stands on her left. We help her off the bed and start out of the room.

"Goodbye, ladies. Be careful fishing." He says it with slight wonder.

"Do you think he really believed us?" I say once we're all settled in the cab of my truck.

"Hard to tell for sure," Larkin says. "If not, then too many people in town are getting suspicious. I'm starting to get worried."

"Me too," I say.

"Not me." Jolene wears a reckless grin. "Are we still going out to drop some traps tonight?"

I start the engine, put the truck in gear, and pull out of the parking lot. "No. Let's stay with Larkin. We'll make supper and watch Bash so she can rest."

"What? No, let's go fishing," Larkin shoots back. "Too many people are wondering what we're up to. I'm fine. I can wrap my hand in plastic to keep it dry."

Jolene and I both say no immediately.

"Come on," she protests. "I can do it."

"The doctor said to keep your hand elevated and in the sling," I say. "You can't work with one hand. And what if the seas are rough and you get thrown out of the boat? The plastic over your hand won't do any good then."

She laughs. "Saltwater is the best medicine for this."

We ignore that.

"Duska, Jolene, please? I want to go out."

Her pleas fall on deaf ears. We shake our heads.

Her face deflates. "Fine."

"It's just for a few days." I reach over and squeeze her arm. "After that, if Dr. Leduc okays it, you can come, but just to drive the boat."

She sighs and turns to look forlornly out the window to the harbour. "Agreed, but I'll only drive for a few nights. After that, I'm helping with the burlocks again. And I'll be fine alone with Bash tonight. It's just a fingertip. I don't need babysitters."

Jolene and I exchange looks again, then nod. "All right," we agree.

CHAPTER TWENTY-SIX

As darkness descends, I leave the house to pick up Jolene. I feel the dropping temperature and tension of this night's work.

A half-hour later, while an unhappy Larkin stays home with Bash, Jolene and I head out to sea. Ice fog covers everything, the sea and the boat. I can see my breath and the wind off the water slices through my coat and overalls, chilling me to the bone.

"It's freezing," Jolene says, her boots crunching on the icy deck boards.

"I know, weird weather. So up and down. There's nothing we can do about it but get this done as fast as we can," I tell her. "Keep your hat pulled down low over your ears, and wear your scarf over your mouth and nose when we're out on the deck."

"I'm fine." Jolene grins. "I don't care if it's minus-forty, I love doing this so much."

I notice how pale her face looks under the moonlight. While at Larkin's earlier, I'd noticed that her eyes were bloodshot. And she seems unusually weak and shaky. Through pole-thin, normally Jolene can carry crates of burlocks from the railing to the hold, and she can do it for hours, almost effortlessly. But when we were leaving the dock, I saw her sway a little and grab the rail. I didn't say anything because the boat had been rocking at the time. But now I wonder.

"You okay?" I ask.

"Yes. I'm a bit nauseous, but I'm fine."

"Are you sure? Your face is milk white."

"Positive. Just a stomach bug."

"All right then."

I start the engine and pull away from the dock. A blanket of fog has settled over the land and sea. When I look back over my shoulder, I can't see the boat ramp or the house, even though it was brightly lit when we left.

We motor out until we're close to the meeting site, at which point I ease off the throttle and idle. When we drop anchor, seagulls swarm the boat, drawn by the bait barrel.

We stand on the deck, scanning for the *Night Glider*. Clouds drift across the moon, obscuring the sea. We listen and watch carefully, for most rum-runners skim across the water without lights. We wouldn't them to ram into us.

But it's quiet and we're too early. We go back into the wheelhouse and grab our coffee thermoses. I pull out some sliced chicken sandwiches I brought along.

"I'm not real hungry, but they look good," Jolene says when I offer her one.

We leave the wheelhouse door open and keep our eyes on the water, watching for boats while we eat. Jolene does end up taking a sandwich and washes it down with coffee that's so strong that it must be as black as oil.

"Delicious," Jolene says. "Got another one?"

I offer an amused smile as she eats a second sandwich and three gingersnap cookies. "Not hungry, hey?"

Afterward we go back out on deck. Though we're anchored, the boat still pitches up and down in the troughs, lurching like a toy on the swells.

I look south where the *Night Glider* will be coming from. Using the binoculars, I scan the water until my arms ache. We're wrapped in impenetrable darkness and the waves are hammering against the hull. I pray they arrive soon because I want to get back to the safety of shore.

Jolene points to the south. I can't see anything.

"What is it?" I ask her, knowing that the mind can play tricks in conditions like these.

Suddenly, a dark shape becomes visible through the haze. A boat bursts into view as a spotlight mounted on the bow clicks on. The boat accelerates towards us.

"Inside, Jolene!" I scream, running into the wheelhouse. I fear it's too late.

I thrust the throttle forward and we take off so fast that the bow heaves up in the air. Jolene goes sprawling, but she scrambles to her feet and stands at the door, keeping it open a crack so she can watch the approaching vessel.

We roar away, and with each crest I feel my teeth slam together.

Suddenly, I hear something pinging off the railing. Then the portside wheelhouse window shatters. Gunshots!

"They're shooting at us. Get down, Jolene!"

She slams the door closed and ducks below the helm next to me.

Another shot hits the outer wall of the wheelhouse and terror rips through me. My heartbeat thundering in my ears, I grip the wheel and try to keep the boat on course.

"The Mounties or Coasties would warn us to stop before shooting," I shout over the howling wind coming through the broken window. "Has to be Frank, or pirates."

"Go! Go! They're almost on us!"

"It won't go any faster. Go down in the engine compartment and pour oil on the exhaust manifold."

She frowns, puzzled. "What?"

"The exhaust manifold's hot. If you pour oil on it, it'll create a smokescreen. There are cans of oil next to the engine. Dump it on quick!"

She opens the hatch to the engine area and jumps down inside.

I keep both hands on the wheel as I steer north toward Skeleton Island. I'm moving at full power, and the vibration of the boat's movements over the wheel is like a seismic shock that shudders right up my spine. It's all I can do to stay on my feet.

Soon a cloud of smoke billows out from the back of the boat.

"It's working," I shout. "Keep doing it."

There's no answer. Down in the engine hold, with the noise, I doubt she can hear me. But the smoke is growing thicker, so I know she's continuing the effort.

I can't see anything behind me now, and there aren't any more shots. I start to think we may escape this time.

Minutes later, Jolene comes up out of the engine compartment. "I used all the oil. Did it work?"

"I think so. Look out the door."

She opens the door and scans the sea. "I don't see anyone."

I let off the throttle a little, scared to keep pushing it at this speed.

When we reach Skelton Island, I back into our usual hiding spot and shut off the engine. We peer out the windshield. I'm so afraid that my pulse throbs in my temple; I press my fingertips against it to slow it down.

"All quiet," Jolene says, sounding as unfazed as ever.

"Go out on deck and listen in case they're sneaking up on us again."

She goes out while I keep my eyes on the water.

After a few minutes, she comes back inside. "Nothing. I think we got away."

I exhale a heavy breath. "Good thing this boat is so fast."

Jolene pumps her fist in triumph. "And great idea to pour oil on the manifold!"

"Not me. Larkin's advice."

"Do you have a shotgun or hunting rifle at home?"

"Blade has an old twenty-two he used to go rabbit-hunting with his brothers. Why?" Then it dawns on me. "Oh, no, no, Jolene. No guns on my boat."

"Why not? We could have been killed tonight. We need a gun to protect ourselves."

"No way."

She scowls. "You're being stupid."

I jerk my head to look at her. "I'm stupid?"

Jolene releases a pronounced sigh. "No, you're not stupid, but you're acting stupid."

"Nice," I say, steaming a little.

"What? What did I say? We need a gun. Bring the rifle next time."

I shake my head. Firmly.

"Think about it at least," she grumbles.

"The answer is no."

Jolene huffs to herself.

We wait an hour longer in silence, watching and listening. Then, because we won't be meeting up with Jean-Claude, we head to Larkin's.

In her kitchen, drinking mugs of hot cocoa, we tell Larkin the story.

"We have a shattered window and a bullet hole in the port side wall of the wheelhouse," I say. "A few bullets pinged off the stern railing but didn't damage anything. Mercifully, none hit the hull."

Larkin's mouth falls open. "No."

"I think Jolene and I narrowly escaped death tonight."

"Exactly," Jolene blurts. "Do you have a rifle here, Larkin? Duska doesn't agree, but I want to bring a gun on board."

Larkin's face goes as grey as stove ash. "No. My dad had a shotgun, but the cops took it. They still have it."

I stomp on Jolene's foot beneath the table and give her a look.

"Ouch," Jolene winces. "Sorry, Larkin, I wasn't thinking."

Larkin nods. "It's fine. I'll contact Jean-Claude and arrange another meetup."

We fall into a tense silence, all pondering the night's frightening events.

CHAPTER TWENTY-SEVEN

It's a splendid morning and I walk to town enjoying the bright sunshine. The warm air smells of the sweet scent of spruce and pine needles that litter the floor of the woods on both sides of the road.

I'm heading to the bank to make a boat payment and deposit a little into my savings account. But only a little. I don't want to arouse suspicion. I'll keep most of it in the metal lockbox in my closet. I know Larkin is doing the same, but Jolene, who doesn't trust banks, keeps all her money in the cottage.

"Didn't think clerking in a bookstore paid that well," says the teller, Vera Fremont, a tall woman with a long nose and skinny legs that reminds me of an egret.

She's nosy as heck, starving for gossip, and has always annoyed me. I smile sunnily at her. "Who knew?"

She pinches her lips together and doesn't say anything more.

As I'm leaving, the young teller at the end of the counter, Nelly Butler, catches my eye and waves me over.

"Hi, Duska. I'm so sorry about Blade. I wanted to attend his funeral, but they wouldn't let me have the time off."

I swallow hard. "I understand, Nelly."

She leans forward and whispers, "Listen, Vera's blabbing to every customer who comes in here how you and Larkin are able to keep making your mortgage payments and keep the boat."

I glance around the bank and see that everyone is eyeing me while pretending not to. "What she's saying?"

"That you two are lobster fishing."

I shrug, glad that it's all they're thinking. "I guess it's not a secret anymore."

"No, but still, you don't want all this attention. The RCMP members do their banking in here. She gossips to *everyone*." Nelly narrows her eyes. "And too many are remarking on how that's strange, with the lobster prices being so low."

I don't say anything but my pulse is rapid and loud in my ears.

"Vera and I both work ten to three, Monday to Friday," she says. "But Vera's lunch break is from eleven to twelve. Mine's from twelve to one. Why don't you come in when I'm here alone? I don't talk. I mind my own business."

My expression is wary. "Really?"

"Yes, you can trust me. We women need to support each other."

My eyes well up with gratitude. "Thank you, Nelly."

Her smile is kind. "My pleasure. I hope you girls make a million dollars."

I leave the bank and head home. If things keep going as well as they have, it's looking more and more likely that I'll pay off the boat loan and mortgage. Yet the pain of losing Blade never ebbs and I'm still stalked by an enormous cloud of shame. I miss my morning quiet time with my Lord. I miss His presence in my life. I've lost my way. Guilt gnaws at me, making me toss and turn at night. I wake each morning with fear and anxiety that isn't alleviated by my ability to pay my bills. But I remind myself that I have no other option, and it's only until the end of May.

CHAPTER
TWENTY-EIGHT

The next day, the three of us drive to town. A sudden spring storm just came through, like a door slamming in our faces, leaving the streets and sidewalks wet and bleak. The hushed grey rain clouds are slowly moving away.

After discussing my conversation with Nelly at the bank, we decide that too many people are talking about us. We really need to look like we're fishing. Today we're going to eat in Pruett's at the same time as some of the fishermen when they get back in town. We'll have a rough time of it, but we have no choice.

Also, since Burke is up and around now and looking for Jolene, she's decided to face him. Being with us in the busy diner is a good start.

We're all wearing knee-high rubber fishing boots, men's trousers, and long-sleeved flannel shirts under wool sweaters. No hats, a concession to the warmer weather.

Jolene stops in front of the diner and looks in through the big plate-glass window. "Looks like hell is empty and all the devils are here."

I look at her, surprised.

"What? I remember that line from reading Shakespeare in high school. It's always stuck with me."

Grinning, she opens the door with a flourish, stepping back to let me in first.

Larkin follows me inside and Jolene enters behind her. The diner is packed and noisy. The murmur of voices and clatter of silverware echoes around the room. It smells strongly of fried onions and hamburgers.

The only place left to sit is the last booth along the plate-glass window that looks out to the sidewalk and street.

The customers finally notice us and there's a collective gasp. The diner goes dead silent. Some of the customers stare at us with shocked expressions, while others make startled, amused mutters. A few with looks of revulsion. We're laughed at, reviled, loathed in many of their eyes.

I spot Constable Hayes sitting on a stool at the end of the counter and feel my heart somersault. He's in uniform. He swivels his stool sideways and eyes us. I avert my gaze and notice Blade's mom, Elsie, at a table in the centre of the room with another woman. Our eyes meet. She pinches her lips together and casts me a dark look. A moment later, she and the woman with her stand and switch chairs, so that Elsie has her back to me. Her cruelty feels like a punch.

Then, unsurprisingly, we are swiftly attacked.

"Men's clothing! And they're fishing. Scandalous!" Doreen Jolly says, loud enough for everyone in the diner to hear.

"Disgraceful," agrees Clementine Frost, who sits across from Doreen in the same booth.

At the next table, four men erupt into laughter at her comment.

"Satan has them firmly in his grip," hisses Clara Banks, a heavy, dour-faced woman with horse-like teeth.

Doreen nods and glares spitefully at Jolene. "There you are, Jolene Taylor! Your husband is looking for you."

Jolene snorts a short laugh.

"You laugh? You clearly don't understand your wifely duties," Doreen spits. "You need to go home and take care of him. Ephesians 5:22 says, 'Wives submit yourselves unto your own husbands, as unto the Lord.'"

"Is that right? Well, even the devil can cite scripture for his purpose, Doreen," Jolene says scornfully. "That's Shakespeare. You should try reading him."

Doreen slams her hand palm down on the tabletop. "The only book I read is the Bible!" she shrills.

Pastor Browne, the pastor of Jolene's church, sits facing us from a stool at the counter. "Mrs. Taylor, you need to learn from these other well-behaved women and be an obedient wife. Your place is at home making your husband happy, not running around town disobeying him."

"If I leave my husband, that's my business, not yours, Pastor, and certainly not anyone else's in this diner."

The room falls tense and silent.

Pastor Browne wipes his mouth with a napkin and tosses it onto his plate. "You and Burke are members of my flock, so it certainly is my business." He looks at her, concern on his face. "Divorce is a sin. There are no divorced women in Whaleback Cove. I don't want to see you be the first. Please, go home, Jolene." He turns his gaze from Jolene to Larkin and me. "Miss Wade, with your father gone, your young brother is your responsibility now. You are both mother and father to him. And you, Mrs. Doucette, need to conduct yourself as a respectable widow. You both need to do your duty and take care of your homes. No father, or…" He pauses. "…no husband."

Johnny, sitting at a table against the side wall seems to be enjoying all this. He adds, in a cutting voice, "Yeah, it's bad enough you killed your husband, you'd—"

"Johnny! I did not say that. That's uncalled for," Pastor Browne rebukes him.

Johnny ignores him. "Think you're smart, Joey? Mouthy thing, sassing the pastor like that. Embarrassing your husband in front of the whole town. And now you're fishing lobster? Who can blame Burke? If you were my wife, I'd give you a good slap myself, then drag you home and lock you in the house. Everyone in town knows if you were a better wife Burke wouldn't have to treat you like that, would he?"

"Johnny, that's enough!" Pastor Browne says.

Larkin looks angrily around the room. "Husbands or not, we have every right to fish, and we can't very well do that wearing dresses or skirts. And we're going to continue fishing whether any of you like it or not."

"Larkin, no." This, from Althea Driscoll, the town's biggest worrywart. "You're just a young girl. A good Christian. I don't think you understand that you've fallen in with some bad characters in these two."

Jolene grins at me, eyes twinkling. "Bad characters. Who, us?"

Althea wrings her hands when she speaks and looks perpetually fearful. "Don't carry on like this, Larkin. Think of your Christian testimony, your reputation. How will you ever marry? Who will ever have you?"

Jolene erupts into laughter. "Oh no, Althea," she says when she catches her breath. "What's that thing growing out of your left ear? Is that a tumour?"

Althea, who is also a hopeless hypochondriac, and with every little cough thinks she's dying, swiftly raises a hand to her ear. She gingerly feels around and stops on her ear. Her face goes white. She lurches out of her chair, hurries across the room, and flees the diner, one hand pressed against her ear.

"Off to the doctor, lickety-split," Jolene says.

"Jolene," I murmur.

"What?" Her shoulders shake with quiet laughter.

Pastor Browne shakes his head, then stands and walks to the cash register to pay for his meal. As he walks out, he stops by Jolene. "Jolene, please. Come and see me."

She stays silent and he leaves.

The pulse of hostility in the room is nearly unbearable. Surprisingly, though, I see compassion in a couple of the diners' faces.

Jolene taps on my arm. "Come on, girls." Coolly indifferent to their glares of contempt, she starts for the empty booth. A smile, then a full-on grin, crosses her face as she passes the diners, giving them all a wave.

With dignity, Larkin and I follow her across the room. I slide in opposite Jolene and Larkin slides in next to me. We pick up menus and study them, but warily. Will the owner, Leta Pruett, ask us to leave? If we refuse, will the men in here physically throw us out?

I don't look over at Hayes, but I can still feel him looking at me. It's entirely disconcerting and I keep my eyes glued to the menu.

I hear footsteps and then Leta is standing at the booth. We all look up.

"Are you going to tell us to leave?" Jolene asks.

Leta, a slender, energetic woman with shoulder-length silver hair, takes out a pad and pen from her apron pocket. "Not at all. I'm going to take your orders."

We smile with amazement.

Leta looks around the diner at the patrons and then brings her eyes back to us, shaking her head. "The foolishness in this town. Duska, Larkin, I'm sorry for your losses. Blade and Ethan were good men. I lost my Cleve when I was only thirty. It felt like my whole world flip-flopped. I was sure I'd lose the diner and my house. But I decided to run it myself. Since then, I've earned my own living. And no one bothered me one bit. It shouldn't make any difference if a woman runs a diner or fishes." She eyes Larkin's bandaged hand. "How'd that happen?"

"I was cutting up bait fish and the knife slipped."

Leta turns her soft hazel eyes on me. "Duska, your sweet Blade's death was an accident, nothing more."

I swallow past the sudden lump in my throat. "Thank you."

She leans in to whisper. "You might have a man, Jolene, but he's mean and nasty. I know he hits you. He's never fooled me. Rumour has it he, uh… fell and banged his thick skull so hard that he got a concussion. What a shame." She reaches out and squeezes Jolene's hand. "You stay gone from him."

Jolene sits speechless, Leta's kindness brings tears to her eyes.

"So what can I get you gals?"

"You might lose customers," Larkin cautions.

Leta grins. "Nah, I'm the only diner in town. I can't see any of this bunch going over to The Bluenose and paying an arm and a leg for the fish they just sold them."

We all chuckle.

"So, ladies, today's special is grilled haddock with mashed potatoes and carrots."

Jolene sets her menu down. "Sounds great. I'll have that and a coffee, please."

"I'll have the same, thanks," Larkin says.

"Me too." I set my menu down on top of Larkin's and Jolene's. "Only with fries instead of mashed."

"Coming right up," Leta says.

She walks behind the counter and passes our orders through the opening to the cook.

The diner goes as silent as a grave. Tension creeps back into the room.

"Leta, you'd better think good and hard about what you're doing," Dietrich Hann calls out to her from his stool at the counter.

Hayes, who's sitting two stools down from him, sets down his coffee mug with a bang. He gives Dietrich a hard look. "That's enough. These ladies have as much right to fish as any of you. They have as much right to eat in here as any of you. If you don't like it, feel free to leave. But no more of this meanness."

He looks sideways at me, his face tender.

After that, two patrons get up, leaving their uneaten meals on the tables. But the rest resume their conversations and eating. The diner grows loud with their voices and the clinking of silverware.

One young woman, Rhonda Nickel, catches my eye and smiles from the table across from our booth. I'm surprised but smile back.

When our food arrives, we hungrily dig in.

"I should have ordered the fries," Jolene says, eyeing my plate. "Those look good."

I nod. "Mmm, they're delicious."

She reaches across the table for a fry and I slap her hand away. We all laugh heartily, feeling cheered by Leta's understanding and encouragement.

I lift my plate and fork some fries on Jolene's plate. "Here."

"Thank you very much." Jolene grins and pops two into her mouth before I even have time to set my plate back down on the table in front of me.

Later, finished eating, we get up and walk by the customers. Some stare hard at their plates and don't look up. Others look away. But Doreen and her gang glare at us with pure hatred.

"Ignore them," I tell Larkin and Jolene, holding the door open for them. Larkin steps outside, but at the last moment Jolene stops and swings back around.

"Didn't I hear that your husband was institutionalized with a nervous breakdown last year, Doreen?" Jolene says, smiling sweetly. "No wonder. Poor man. Anyone living with you would end up in the bughouse."

Doreen puts a hand to her throat, her eyes bulging in disbelief.

"Jolene..." I say.

"What?"

"Stop it."

But I know it's pointless. There's no changing Jolene. She just laughs under her breath and follows me out the door.

——— • ———

That night, I stand at my bedroom window, ready for bed on this damp, chilly night. The sun sank into the sea hours ago and a canopy of low-lying fog hangs over it, clinging to the shoreline. The foghorn on the lighthouse at Big Harbour blasts its warning peal.

Still, I think of Nelly Butler, and then Leta and Rhonda, and feel a glimmer of hope at the realization that there actually are other women in this town who are on our side. And then, unbidden, my thoughts turn again to Constable Hayes and the tender smile he gave me in the diner.

CHAPTER TWENTY-NINE

The following night, I walk down to the beach and look out at the water. It's warmer than yesterday, and windless. The sea is like black satin, flat and glossy. But once again the air is thick and muggy with the promise of a coming thunderstorm.

I jump in the truck and head to Jolene's, turning the heater on every few minutes to clear the windshield, which keeps fogging up with humidity.

Later, on the drive to Larkin's, Jolene is unnaturally subdued. She had walked to the truck and climbed in with only a quiet hello. Normally she sprints, leaps inside, and wallops me on the arm.

"Everything all right?" I ask.

"Yup."

"Burke come around?"

"No, and he better not."

"His mom?"

"I'd choke her."

Only a mile further down the road, Jolene moans and leans over her knees.

"Jolene, what's wrong?"

"Nothing, I'm fine." She straightens up, but then just as quickly slumps back against the seat. "Wait, no. Pull over."

I pull over onto the shoulder of the road and put the truck in park. I turn on the dome light. "You're not fine."

She turns her head to me. Her face is a ghastly white. I've never seen anyone so pale.

"It's nothing," she says.

"Nothing? Jolene, you're sick."

"No, leave it. Boy, you're some cranky tonight."

I let out a breath. "I am not cranky, I'm concerned. You're the cranky one. But that's fine, because it's clear you're ill. I'm taking you back to the cottage."

"No, don't."

I start to say something, but she cuts me off.

"Give me a second, will you! I just need some air." She opens the door and climbs out, but as soon as she puts her feet on the ground, down she goes like a sack of potatoes.

I throw open my door and run around the front of the truck to her side. Jolene is lying on the ground, unconscious.

I shut the door, kneel, and lift her up, resting her back and head against my knees. "Jolene! Jolene!"

Her eyes flutter open, and she looks at me, her eyes glazed and faraway.

"Are you okay?"

Her face is drawn. She takes in a breath and then nods. "I just passed out. Help me sit up."

"Just passed out?" I repeat. "But why?"

"I didn't eat enough supper. I think my sugar's low, that's all."

I help her sit up and she leans back against the passenger door.

"Let's get you back in the truck," I say.

"No, the air feels good. Help me stand."

I help her to her feet. "This seems like more than just low blood sugar."

She shakes her head, dismissing my words. But she's avoiding my eyes.

"Jolene, you looked ill the other night, too. What's wrong?"

"Nothing!"

"Baloney. Tell me."

We stand facing each other on the shoulder of the two-lane.

"Only if you promise you won't stop me from rum-running."

"Now you're really scaring me. What is it?"

"I had rheumatic fever as a child. I recovered, but it damaged a valve in my heart. It doesn't open properly, so the blood flow is disrupted. I have a heart murmur, and my pulse sometimes is slightly irregular. Otherwise I've always been fit and healthy."

"But it's worsened?"

"Yes."

I wince. "How bad is it?"

She looks up at the moon, silvery white in the sky. "It started last month. I played sports in school and have always been active with no problems. Now… my heart pounds like a sledgehammer with less activity, and I get a bit light-headed. But this is the first time I've passed out."

"Less activity like loading and unloading heavy burlocks?"

She stares at the trees that line the side of the road. "No."

"Oh, I think so. Don't lie to me, Jolene."

She returns her gaze to me. "Maybe a little bit."

"Can't the doctors fix your valve with surgery?"

"Yes, but it'd have to be done in Halifax. Anyway, there's never been a need before. And it's not going to last much longer."

I tip my head. "I don't understand."

"There's something else."

"What?"

She turns her head away, and I stare at her until she looks back at me.

"Tell me, please," I press.

"Only if you promise that you won't tell Larkin."

"I won't keep anything from Larkin, and neither should you."

Jolene's huffs. "Fine. I'm pregnant."

My jaw goes slack and my eyes widen. "Ohhh."

"Yeah. That's what's going on. Pregnancy worsens this condition, but only in the first trimester."

I'm speechless for a moment. "How far along are you? Have you gone to the doctor?"

"Not yet, but I've just missed my third menstrual cycle, and I've always been regular. I have some morning sickness, too, although that's easing now."

"So you knew this when you came to me asking for a job rum-running."

"Suspected, but I wasn't sure. Not till I missed the third period. Sorry, but I couldn't tell you guys or you'd never have agreed."

"No, we wouldn't have. Does Burke know?"

"No. And he's not going to. Not if I can help it."

A sudden warm breeze rattles the trees, sending down a shower of pine needles on our heads. I raise a hand and remove my ball hat to shake the needles free.

"He's the baby's father, though," I remark.

"Too bad, so sad."

I'm speechless for a time. "Jolene, he has a right to know."

"No, he doesn't," she says in an irritated mutter.

"If he does find out, he'll be even more determined to find you and bring you back home."

"I know. That's why I have to keep rum-running and make as much money as I can. I can't go back to him, baby or not."

"Well, you're not going out with me tonight. You need to rest. I'll take you home now."

"No way. You can't go out alone. There's too much liquor for you to put in the hold yourself."

"I'll get one of the crew to come aboard and help."

She scowls. "I feel fine now. I can do it."

"No, you just passed out right in front of me."

"It was the first time, though, and I really didn't eat enough supper. It probably won't even happen again. It's supposed to end after three months. The symptoms *are* easing."

I consider it, and then nod. "All right, but only if you promise me that you'll let me know if you get dizzy, so we can stop. If you pass out on deck, you could pitch right over into the sea. You'd be gone before I could turn around in time to find you. You have a baby to think about now, not just yourself."

"I promise."

"We're running late. We'll tell Larkin later when we get back in."

We get back in the truck. I put the engine in gear and pull out onto the highway, all the while glancing at Jolene. She sits pale and subdued with her arm lying on the door and her cheek resting on her arm.

I drive through the dark streets to Larkin's, my mind churning with worry for Jolene and her baby.

Out at sea later, I scan with my binoculars for any sight of the *Night Glider*. I pray it'll arrive soon because I'm nervous for Jolene. I want to get this done fast.

"How're you feeling?" I shout.

Jolene shoots me a glare that would curl the deck's wooden planks. Her face, in the moonlight, is the colour of eggnog.

"Jolene?"

She ignores me and looks back out at the water.

"Jolene, are you dizzy?"

She whips her head around and stares at me with an expression like she might just throw me overboard. "Quit asking me how I am every ten seconds, will you? You're driving me mental."

I give up. When the *Night Glider* arrives, their deckhands seem unusually stern and alert. But we have an uneventful night.

At four-thirty, later than usual, I manoeuvre the boat alongside Larkin's dock. The first pink hint of dawn is showing in the eastern sky. Jolene made it through the night just fine, which is a huge relief.

I pull my gloves off and stuff them in my coat pocket. "Let's go in."

Jolene looks at the darkened windows of the house. "They're sleeping. I should have just gone up to the cottage after we met Jean-Claude. Would have been better than to wake Larkin up now."

I point at the kitchen window, where a light has just come on. "She's awake."

Jolene blows out a breath so hard her lips flutter. "Fine."

Larkin greets us at the back door, smiling. "Morning!"

"You're up early," I say.

"I kept thinking about you guys out there without me and couldn't sleep. How was it?"

"Went smoothly." I thumb behind me. "But Jolene has something to tell you."

"Oh, sounds serious. Let's be quiet, though. Bash is still sleeping. Coffee?"

"Yes, we're going to need it," I say as Jolene climbs up the steps and sails into the house.

After Jolene tells the whole story to Larkin, we sit silently at the kitchen table, drinking our coffees and staring out the window toward the sea.

Larkin pushes her chair back and stands. "I'm hungry. How about some toast? I have raspberry preserve jelly that's delicious."

"Sure," Jolene and I say simultaneously.

"I'll help you," I say, rising.

She waves a hand at me. She's no longer wearing a sling and can use that hand a little now. "No, sit down. You look tired."

I sit down and look out the window again. A rose and pearl-grey dawn is breaking over the sea. It's promising to be a lovely day.

Once the toast is ready, Larkin turns from the stove and sets a plate stacked high on the table. She goes to the fridge, takes out a dish of butter and a jar of raspberry jelly, and places them on the table. She passes us each a plate before setting one down at her place.

"Dig in." She sits down and starts to spread jam on her toast. "Will going through childbirth be dangerous for you?"

"Maybe a bit riskier," Jolene replies.

I feel my stomach drop. I'd been so focused on the dangers of her passing out while rum-running that I completely overlooked the dangers of delivering a baby.

Jolene sees my worried expression and her face tightens. "No, no, no! I know what you're both thinking. This shouldn't change anything."

"Yes, it should. And it does," Larkin says, but not unkindly.

I swallow some toast. "We're not just worried about you dying at sea. But what if we get caught, Jolene? We'll all go to prison. Do you want your baby born in jail?"

"Duska's right," Larkin says. "As soon as you deliver, they'd take the baby away. You'd never see her or him again."

Jolene opens her mouth and then closes it again. She stares through me.

"And another thing," I add in a gentler tone, for I can see how upset she is. "You shouldn't be alone in the cottage from now on. Move in with me."

Jolene cringes. "No way."

I'm insulted. "What's that look for?"

"Sorry. But we've talked about his before. I'd be a terrible roommate. I told you. I'm cranky and opinionated. I'll argue till the cows come home."

I snort. "Who told you that, Burke?"

"No, my mom," she says in all seriousness. "I drove her to despair. She said I was fifty percent angel and fifty percent demon."

We all laugh softly for a moment.

I shrug. "Well, so what? I'm a terrible introvert. I'd rather read a book than talk to anyone. And I'm anal about keeping my house clean."

She points a finger at me. "See, big problem right there. I'm a shameless slob."

"I guess we'll both have to make the best of it then."

Jolene gets up and paces around the room. "Okay, I'll agree to move in with you, but I'm not going to stop rum-running. I proved tonight that I can still do the work."

I look at Larkin and lift my brows. Jolene really is impossibly stubborn. Our words of caution are as futile as trying to bail out seawater from a sinking lifeboat with a teaspoon.

Larkin sighs. "The only way I'll agree to that is if you promise to tell us right away if you feel faint. And if your symptoms worsen, you promise you'll stop."

"Think of your baby, Jolene," I say.

She barks back, "I am."

"No, you're not. And it's selfish not to."

Chastened, a faint flush of red fills her cheeks and she falls silent.

Jolene huffs out a breath. "Fine, I agree. At least now you won't have to drive out to the cottage to pick me up anymore. I'll go home now, sleep, and then pack."

"And leave your whiskey at the cottage," I say. "You can't drink now, cold, flu, or otherwise."

"Are you serious?" she blurts.

"Entirely. And you should come to my place right away. We can go over to the cottage later to get your things."

"No, I'm going now. I've agreed to stay with you, but I'm asking for a last few hours alone. I'll pack when I wake up."

"All right," I say. "I'll pick you up around three, and you can eat supper at my place."

"Warning: I'm a fussy eater to boot."

"No surprise there."

"I'm going out tomorrow night, too," Larkin says adamantly. "I can drive the boat now."

"Fine," Jolene and I say together, too weary to argue with her.

CHAPTER THIRTY

At 3:00 p.m., I pull up in front of Jolene's cottage and go inside. She's in the kitchen. There's a suitcase and box of food on the floor.
"Ready?"
"Yup," she says with a glum tone.
"It won't be that bad."
"If you say so."

・

Once we're back at my place, Jolene puts her things away in the spare bedroom upstairs while I make us an early supper of baked chicken and mashed potatoes with green beans. It's a fine spring afternoon and my tulips and hyacinths have burst up from the ground.

I pick up the box of food Jolene's brought and carry it over to the counter. I open it, intending to put the food in the pantry when I spot a bottle of whiskey next to a can of beans.

Oh, that woman! I take it out of the box and dump it out into the sink, tossing the empty bottle into the garbage.

Minutes later, Jolene thumps noisily down to the kitchen carrying a basket of clothing. She sets it down on the floor, puts her hands on her hips, and looks around. "Boy, you weren't kidding. We could eat off the floor in here. Makes me nervous."

"Don't be. Supper's almost ready."

Truth be told, though I wouldn't have liked a roommate before, I now find living alone unbearable. Silent and empty, day and night, my footsteps echo sorrowfully off the walls of the unhappy house. The joy, the laughter, the life Blade and I shared in this house is gone. I'm glad for her company.

"It smells delicious," she says.

"No nausea?"

"None. And I'm so hungry right now, I think my stomach is eating my spine."

Jolene and her Nova Scotia sayings. I reach up into the cupboard for two plates, chuckling under my breath.

"I may be skinny, but I'm a good eater," she says. "More so now that I'm pregnant."

"I've noticed that. By the way, I found your whiskey."

Her eyes narrow. "Where is it?"

"Gone. I dumped it out in the sink."

Her mouth falls open. "No! Why? A little toddy won't hurt me."

"No, but it will harm your baby, Jolene. Did you bring anymore?"

"Anymore what?" she says sassily.

"Liquor. Is there any in your suitcase?"

"What are you, a cop now?"

"Jolene."

She casts me a dark look. "No."

"Good."

She goes to the back door and breathes in the warm breeze with its heady rose and lilac scent. "It's gorgeous here. You have your own private beach?"

"Yes. If you like, go have a look. There's a sandy path that leads right down to it."

"I'm just going to hang a few things on the line to air them out, if you don't mind. The cottage was damp and they smell musty."

"Not at all. Go ahead."

She picks up the basket and goes out onto the porch. I watch her through the kitchen window. She stands in the pleasant spring air for a moment, taking in my property. Then she steps down to the yard and over to the clothesline.

A few minutes later, I hear a man's voice, loud and angry.

I look out the window again, squinting into the late afternoon sun. Jolene is standing in the yard, her fiery red hair lifting in the sea breeze. Burke is standing in front of her.

"What do you think you're doing, Jolene?" he demands in a quiet voice laced with anger.

She's staring knives at him and doesn't reply.

I hurry outside and plant myself next to her. I also notice that he's no longer wearing the bandage. He's dressed in black pants and a red and white checkered short-sleeved shirt. His neck is thick and his arms muscular.

"What do you want?" I ask him.

His eyes are deep-set and inscrutable, like two grey stones. "I'm here to take my wife back."

Jolene gives a dry laugh. "I'm not going anywhere with you, Burke."

"Yes, you are, Jolene. You're my wife and you're coming with me now."

"No, I'm not. I want a divorce."

He stares at her as if at a stranger. "A divorce? Over my dead body."

"That'll work for me."

"You watch your mouth, Jolene," he chokes. It sounds like something's stuck in his throat.

"Leave my property," I tell him. "She's not going anywhere with you."

He flicks his eyes to me. A thick purple vein throbs in his forehead. "Mind your own business," he snarls.

"You're trespassing on my land, so this is my business. Go before I call the police."

Furious, he points a finger at me. "Stay out of this." He turns back to Jolene. "Get your things and come with me now, or I'll drag you over to the car myself."

"Don't you lay a hand on her," I warn.

"I told you. Stay out of this!"

I step between her and Burke. "Jolene, go inside, quick, and lock the door behind you."

"No, Jolene," he says.

She's already turned and run up the porch steps. He goes after her, but she's too fast. Within seconds, she's already inside.

I don't hear the door shut or the lock click, though. He stops and eyes the back door, as though having the same thought.

"Don't even think about it," I say. "If you don't leave now, I'll call the police."

"I'm not breaking any laws."

"Wrong. You're trespassing."

"You two think you're smart, don't you?" he sneers. "Well, you tell Jolene that she won't get away with this. She thinks she can bash me in the head and then leave me. Shame me in front of this whole town. She'll be sorry, believe me."

"Just go."

He glares at me for another few seconds, then mutters something under his breath and stomps around the side of the house. I follow him. He storms down the driveway to a red coupe. Clint is sitting behind the wheel as Burke gets in and slams the door.

Clint puts the car in reverse, backs up, then hits the gas and tears out to the lane, a dust plume rising in the air as they disappear from sight.

Jolene comes out the front door and hurries down the steps. She's holding a baseball bat in one hand.

"Good riddance," she says, but I can see that his appearance has unsettled her a little.

"Jolene, I don't think he's going to give up that easily. He'll be back. He might try to break in next time."

She shakes the bat in the air. "If he does, I'll be ready for him." She suddenly frowns. "He must have been watching your place. Probably saw me go inside with you carrying the suitcase."

"I think you're right."

We go back inside and stop in the kitchen.

"What about the baby?" I ask.

"What about it?"

"Are you going to tell him?"

"No."

"But he's the father. Bad husband or not, he should know."

"That's your opinion. I don't agree. It doesn't matter anyway. I'm giving it up."

I'm incredulous. "You're giving up your baby?"

"Yes. I've decided to give it up for adoption."

I hear my own breath go out of me. "Why?"

"Because I'm twenty years old and soon to be divorced. You know what this town is like. My child will be looked down on his or her whole life. And I believe a child needs both a mother and a father... a *good* father, not Burke. My baby will be much better off adopted by a good family."

I stare at her.

She looks both offended and confused. "Duska, are you mad at me?"

"Jolene, how..." I falter, take in a breath. "How can you give up your own baby?"

Her eyes cloud over with sadness. "It's not easy, but I've given it a lot of thought and it's the right decision."

I turn to the stove and turn down the damper. It's too hot in the room from cooking supper on the stove. "Burke's the father. He has a right to know. He doesn't even know it exists. You can't just give his baby up without his consent. That's not fair to him. And think, your baby will never know its own father or grandparents."

She scowls at me. "You want me to give my baby to a man who was filling up a bathtub so he could drown me? Or to the psycho parents who raised him? Are you crazy?"

I let out a dismal breath. I don't like either option, but I want Jolene to keep her child. I get two plates down from the cupboard and set them down hard on the counter.

"You're upset with me," Jolene says.

"I never said anything."

"You don't have to. You almost broke those plates."

I just shake my head.

She looks down at the floor, but then raises her head and flashes her eyes back to me. "I'm sorry that you're upset. But it's my baby, my life, and my decision."

"Jolene, you can keep your baby."

"No, I can't." She shakes her head in exasperation. "Why does this bother you so much?"

There's a pulsing tension in the kitchen. "Forget it."

"No, tell me. What is it?"

I'm quiet for a time before I say, with a broken voice, "Last summer, Blade and I found out we couldn't have children. I'm barren and the doctors said nothing can be done."

"Ohhh," she whispers, and then reaches out and softly squeezes my arm. "I'm so sorry, Duska. Truly I am. But I have to do what's best for my baby."

"Best for the baby," I echo, my voice hollow.

"Duska."

I see the hurt in her eyes, but I'm still fuming. I turn my back to her and begin pushing pots around on the stovetop furiously. I can't even think straight now.

"Duska, this isn't an easy decision for me," she says, reaching out to touch my arm again, but I pull away. "I've spent a lot of sleepless nights over this. It kills me, but it's for the best."

I can't hide my anger with her. I can't even look at her. I'll never understand her decision. I turn my head and stare out at the trees in the back yard, distraught for a reason I don't believe she truly understands.

"Duska?"

I hear Jolene's clothes flapping on the clothesline. I want to rip them all off and throw them into the sea. I feel tremendous resentment toward her.

I give a brisk shake of my head and don't reply. I make her a plate and set it on the kitchen table, but then take my own into my bedroom.

Jolene knocks on my door while I'm eating. "Duska, come out to the kitchen to eat so we can talk."

"No."

"Please, I have this thing about eating alone. I hate it."

"Cry me a river."

"Come on, Duska. It's not like you to be nasty."

"I'm not being nasty. I just don't want to see your stupid face right now."

There's a brief silence.

"Duska, I know you don't mean that," she says with unimaginable grace. "Please come out. I feel so uncomfortable. It's your house and I'm eating your food, in your kitchen, alone."

"I don't care. Go ahead, fill your boots."

"So now you're being nasty and sarcastic?"

"And another thing. Would you stop blowing your noise so loudly?"

"I don't blow my nose loudly," she says.

"Yes, you do. It blares through the house like a foghorn. And stop stomping around the house, too."

"What? I don't stomp around."

"You do. Up and down the stairs. It sounds like a bull moose is walking around in here."

It's quiet for a moment, but then she walks away and leaves me alone for the night.

———   •   ———

Since I'm up first the next morning, I creep from my bedroom down the stairs to the kitchen. I put coffee on the stove to brew, take cream out of the fridge, and set it on the table next to the sugar pot.

I'm at the stove stirring oatmeal when Jolene comes into the kitchen tying the belt on her housecoat. I have the back door open, the cool breeze carrying the sweet fragrance of lilac and rose into the house.

Jolene greets me with a cheery smile. "Good morning."

I stay silent.

She takes a mug from the cupboard, then over beside me at the stove and reaches for the coffee pot. "Mind if I help myself?"

"Probably best."

She looks at me and then lets her breath out.

"There's bread in the breadbox to make toast if you want. Jam and butter are in the fridge. Oatmeal's ready." I push the pot of oatmeal to the cold end of the stove.

"Thank you," she says, but I've already turned my back to her and am walking out of the kitchen carrying a bowl of oatmeal and a mug of coffee.

"You're not eating in your bedroom again?"

I go up the stairs without answering.

"Duska, please," she calls despairingly to my retreating back. "Let's talk."

"Bon appetit," I call down the stairs in a clipped tone.

"You know, I take back what I said about you being such a kind and gracious person," she grumbles. "You can be a spiteful thing, that's for sure."

I give a mean laugh, loud enough that she'll hear me, then go into my bedroom and bang the door shut.

All that day, whenever I'm in the kitchen or living room, Jolene comes in and lingers, hoping I'll soften and talk to her. But it doesn't happen.

We don't speak the next day either, and finally Jolene gives up. She slinks around the house like a shadow, tiptoeing through the rooms and hiding in the bathroom, running the water or flushing the toilet when she blows her nose.

On the second night, I break the silence. I have no choice; we have to go rum-running. I leave my bedroom and step into the living room, where I find Jolene standing at the window, staring out to the shadows in the front yard.

"I'm leaving for Larkin's at nine," I say. "Be ready."

"I am ready." Jolene closes the curtains and turns around. "Are you still angry?"

I'm about to say something unkind, but then see her sad face and hold my tongue. "No."

"You disapprove, though. I can see judgment in your eyes."

I tersely shake my head, offended by that. "Judgment? Jolene, you're giving your baby up."

"Yes, but don't you see that it's out of love for my baby that I'm doing this? It takes all the strength and courage I can muster to give my own baby away."

"Someday you're going to deeply regret it."

She stiffens. "How can I regret giving my baby a better life?"

"You don't know that. I think you'd be a wonderful mother."

"And you don't know that."

"I'm done talking about this. Drop it," I say with weariness in my voice. I'm too tired to argue anymore and we have a hard night's work ahead of us.

"Duska? I hate that you're upset with me," she implores.

I can see the pain in her eyes, and the horrible, desperate betrayal written across her face. I do regret my words, but I just stalk out of the house.

Before we reach Larkin's, Jolene tries one more time. "You haven't said two words to me since we left your place."

"So?"

"There's meanness in your silence, Duska."

I only shrug.

"Let's talk this over, or it's going to be a very uncomfortable night for us."

"Let's not."

Her voice now turns so frosty that it feels like an Arctic wind on my face. "I thought we were friends. I was wrong. No true friend would act like this."

Her words prick me with shame, but I hide it from her and stay silent.

Eyes distant, she turns her head and sullenly stares out through the windshield.

CHAPTER THIRTY-ONE

We're at the hospital waiting in an examination room for Dr. Leduc. Larkin's nervously swinging her legs off the side of the bed. Jolene sits in a chair and I'm standing next to her.

Jolene and I don't speak. In fact, we avoid looking at each other. But I'm not sure how much longer I can stay silent; Jolene's legs are drumming constantly against the tiled floor, and it's driving me mental. She's trying to act like her usual jovial self, but it's clear by the flare of indignation in her eyes that my words have bruised her.

Larkin has picked up on the tension between us and lifts her brows at me. I only shrug.

"Let's all try to get along, all right?" Larkin says to us. Though her tone is impartial, I feel chided.

We hear Dr. Leduc's voice approaching. A moment later, he parts the curtain and shuts it again behind him. "Hello, ladies."

"Hi," we all say in unison.

He turns to Larkin. "Let's have a look at your finger."

She grimaces but straightens her shoulders and holds out her hand. Thankfully, this time he doesn't bring up the rumours about women rum-runners and starts gently removing the bandages.

While he's working, I leave the room to go to the cafeteria to buy coffee.

"Where are you going?" Jolene says, following me out.

"I don't want company, thank you."

"There's that Mountie," Jolene says. "Hayes."

I follow her gaze and see Hayes coming out of a room on the right. He hasn't seen us yet, as he's stopped to write in a notepad. My breath catches.

"Let's go back," I say, but it's too late. He's looked up and seen us.

"Shoot," I murmur.

He looks at us with concern. "Hello, ladies. Everything okay?"

"Yes. Larkin had an accident cutting up bait last week," I explain, thinking it will bolster our story about fishing.

"Hope it wasn't anything too serious?"

"Sliced her finger off," Jolene blurts.

"No," he says.

I shoot Jolene a dirty look. "No, just the tip. It's not too serious."

"Glad to hear that."

I don't want him to leave just yet. "And you?"

"Car accident outside town. Minor injuries to one of the drivers."

He smiles and I feel a flare of happiness. What am I doing? It's mortifying. From the corner of my eye, I can see Jolene's head swivel from me to him and back to me. He closes the notebook and slides it into his jacket pocket alongside the pen.

I glare at Jolene, but it doesn't faze her. She laughs under her breath and I ignore it. She nudges me in the side with her elbow, grins, and tilts her head toward Hayes. I elbow her back. She doubles over, but I can see her body shaking with silent laughter. I want to strangle her.

Hayes notices and clears his throat. "I should get going. Give my best wishes to Miss Wade."

"We will," I say.

He walks away down the hallway, heading for the exit.

"What's going on between you two?" Jolene says when he's gone.

"What do you mean?"

"All those long lingering looks. He likes you."

"No, he doesn't. He just feels sorry for me. He helped me the day Blade died."

Jolene grins. "No, I saw you looking at him, too. You like him."

"I do not!"

"Me thinks thou protests too much."

"Wrong, Jolene, and cut it out."

I scowl as we walk back to Larkin's room. Unrepentant, she throws her head back and laughs and laughs.

"Jolene, stop. It's not funny. He's a cop. He's dangerous."

"Sorry, you're right," she says when her laughter subsides, but her grin never leaves her face.

After we drive away from the hospital, we head to Martin's and park out front against the curb. We all need groceries.

We're walking toward the door when we hear men's shouts coming from the wharf. We try to ignore the commotion, but it only grows louder.

"What's going on over there?" Jolene says, scanning the wharf.

Larkin shrugs. "Fishermen arguing. Nothing new."

Jolene crosses the street and steps into the alley between the post office and the library, where she can see the wharf clearly. She turns back to us, waving us over.

We join her and notice that three boats are moored in a line in their slips. The first one is Frank Defoe's boat, the *Augusta-Jayne*.

"What's going on?" I ask.

"It's the Defoes," Jolene whispers.

I look over and see Frank and Johnny on the stern of the *Augusta-Jayne*, facing each other, their arms up and fists clenched.

"Get away from me!" Johnny screams.

"Come on, let's go, ya big baby!" Frank shouts back, hunching his shoulders. He waves his fists and shuffles his feet in a boxing dance as he moves closer to his son.

"Get away from me, ya crazy old fool!" Johnny backpedals across the deck of the boat, then leaps over the side onto the wharf road.

Frank's face darkens. "What'd you call me? Come on, ya think you're a big enough man to fight me? Let's go!" He jumps onto the wharf road and goes after his son.

"Leave me alone!" Johnny yells, backing away.

"Where ya going? Be a man. Fight."

"No, cut it out, Dad!" Johnny cries, moving closer to the edge of the wharf.

Right then, Frank takes a swing at Johnny, and Johnny lurches back. His lower legs hit the low wooden wharf railing; arms windmilling desperately, he tumbles backwards over the side and into the harbour.

Frank bends over, slapping his thigh as he howls with laughter.

Johnny swims over to the wharf where there's a metal ladder. He climbs up slowly, his clothes dripping water. Frank runs over. When Johnny places his hands on the top rung, Frank stomps his booted foot down on his fingers.

"Owwww!" Johnny falls back into the cold, murky water. He swims back over and starts climbing again.

"Stay down there!" Frank yells.

Johnny moves down a few rungs, wraps his arms around the ladder, and shrieks up at his dad. "Let me up! I'm freezing."

Larkin shakes her head in wonder. "Do you believe this?"

"It's hilarious," Jolene whoops.

Billy Stoker runs down the wharf and looks over the side at Johnny holding onto the ladder. "Frank, let him up. He'll get hypothermia."

"Good," Frank growls. "Teach him not to mouth me back anymore."

Billy leans over the ladder and calls down. "Johnny, come up now."

Johnny climbs as Frank stands glaring down at him, but he doesn't try to stomp on his hands again. When Johnny reaches the top, Billy helps him climb over the last rung.

Johnny collapses and lies down on the road, breathing heavily and dripping seawater.

"You okay, Johnny?" Billy asks.

"No. I think he broke my fingers." Johnny holds his injured fingers in his good hand.

"He's fine," Frank snorts.

Johnny gets to his feet and glares at his dad. "You tried to kill me."

"Don't be so foolish," Frank says, looking around at the men on the wharf with a broad smile. "I was just teaching you a lesson."

"Wonderful parenting skills," Larkin says drily.

I nod. "Men like Frank love an audience, even if it means humiliating his own son in public."

Johnny looks embarrassed at the spectacle. He pretends not to see us or the group of four fishermen standing down on the wharf past Frank's boat, two with small grins and the other two laughing uncertainly; they're afraid of Frank.

He takes a step toward his dad but wobbles a little and has to stop.

"Look at him," Jolene laughs. "He doesn't know if he's coming or going."

"You... ma... ma..." Johnny stammers.

Jolene winces. "Ouch. That hurt my brain."

"What are you trying to say, ya big ba... ba... baby," Frank sneers. He turns and walks away, jumping onto his boat and vanishing into the wheelhouse.

Johnny starts to go after him but slips on the puddle of water under his feet and falls hard on the planks. He lies there, stunned, soaked, and wheezing.

Jolene dissolves into laughter and Larkin and I can't help joining in. When Johnny hears us, his face flames with humiliation.

He stands up and shakes his fist at us. "Shut up, you witches!"

"Oh boy, he's madder than a box of frogs," Jolene says.

That makes us howl even louder.

Suddenly I see Constable Hayes across the road leaning against his patrol car. The car is parked in front of a small, white-painted ice cream stand that's closed now for the season. He's smiling, which tells me he's been watching the whole time. .

Our eyes meet, and still smiling, he gives me a little wave.

"Did he just wave at you?" Jolene asks.

"No."

"Oh yes, he did. And he's smiling at you again."

I shake my head. "No, he's just enjoying this, too."

"I don't know," Larkin adds with a smile. "He does seem to like you."

"What are you talking about?" I try to deny it, but feel my cheeks feel scorched.

"Oh, ho–ho, look at you all red in the face!" Jolene laughs. "There's something there, isn't there?"

I want to choke her, but Larkin's standing between us and I'm afraid I'll bump her injured hand while trying to reach around to grab Jolene's throat.

"Jolene, stop it."

"Okay, sorry," Jolene says. But it's clear from her grin that she feels not an ounce of remorse.

She moves in between Larkin and me and takes my hand. "Don't be upset with me, Duska."

Jolene's such a funny and loving person that I find it impossible to stay angry with her. I also understand that my reaction to her decision to give up her baby comes from my own sorrow. She has the right to make her own decision, even if I don't agree with it.

"I'm sorry, Jolene." I squeeze her hand. "I'll respect and support your decision. I'll always be your friend."

Grinning, Jolene turns and pulls me into her, gives me a bone-crushing hug. "I knew you'd come around. You'd miss me too much."

I smile, conceding. "I would."

Later, we drive out of town, our groceries loaded in the bed of the truck. My emotions are chaotic. Larkin and Jolene are right. When I look into Hayes's eyes, something happens between us… some intense electric spark that pulls us toward each other. And though I try to hide it, I know that he feels it too. I find it confusing and upsetting. My Blade is barely dead a month, and I'm attracted to another man? My mind swims with sorrow and dismay.

CHAPTER THIRTY-TWO

I stand on the back porch with my coffee and stare out to sea. There's a veil of fog this morning that clings like gauze to the lawn, trees, and cedar shingles on the back of the house. Out in the bay, a foghorn peals its long, solemn warning. A sense of foreboding falls over me like a shroud.

When I go back inside, I hear Jolene move around upstairs. I push the dark thoughts from my mind and take out eggs from the fridge to start breakfast.

At two o'clock, we drive over to Larkin's. The sun is shining warmly now and the fog has vanished. It's a rare windless afternoon.

Larkin takes Bash into town for a doctor's appointment while Jolene and I stay behind to clean the boat and do some routine maintenance on the engine.

Jolene cleans inside the wheelhouse and I retrieve a jug of oil from the boatshed. I pop back out when I hear a vehicle turn into the drive. It's Jean-Claude's truck barrelling down the driveway. He brakes hard, kicking up a cloud of dust, and throws the door open.

"Duska!" he shouts, running over to me. "Where are da others?"

"Jolene's on the boat. Larkin took Bash to the doctor. What's wrong?"

"My boys..." He falters, swallows. "I can't find Louis and Andre nowhere. I checked dere cottage twice now, and dey not dere."

"They're probably just with friends and haven't had a chance to let you know yet."

"No. I asked all dere friends, and no one has seen dem since yesterday morning. Dey were supposed to meet me at my warehouse out at Cully Point at noon yesterday. We were going to take a load up to Amherst, but dey never showed."

I smile. "They're young guys. I'm sure they're just out running the roads."

"Non, dey good boys. Dey wouldn't do dat. Dey wouldn't worry me like dis."

"Maybe their car broke down somewhere out of town."

"Maybe," he says, but his tone is doubtful.

Jolene comes out of the wheelhouse and jumps onto the dock. She makes her way over. "What's going on?"

"Andre and Louis are missing," I tell her. "No one has seen them since yesterday."

Jean Claude's face twists with fear. "My boys… I have a bad feeling."

"Jean-Claude, they're not boys," Jolene says with a smile. "They're young men with a lot of money that's likely burning a hole in their pockets. I'm sure they're just out sowing wild oats. They're probably sleeping it off."

He goes silent, chewing his inner cheek while he stares out at the water.

I frown. "You seem awfully worried. What aren't you telling us?"

He exhales heavily. "I have a confess to make, me."

"What is it?"

"Last week, a customer told me dere was vinegar in the bottle of rum I sold him. He told me he heard from someone else in town that dey had vinegar in dere too. Someone replaced the rum with vinegar and then resold my rum."

"No!" Jolene says. "Who?"

Jean Claude shakes his head. "I don't know."

"And you never said anything to us about that?" I say.

"I didn't tink dey were telling the troot, me."

"But it's happened again?"

There's a ragged quality to his voice. "Yes, the last batch I delivered in Truro two days ago was all vinegar. And I checked the liquor in my warehouse. Dere's a lot missing."

Something topples down inside me. "No."

Jolene grimaces. "And you think it was your boys?"

He runs a hand across his mouth. "I don't know, me. I didn't tink dey would ever do dat, but who else? The only other peoples I've seen around my warehouse are teenager who drive down an old logging road and make party in the woods. Dey don't bodder me. Don't tink it was dem, no."

"Who else has access to the liquor in your warehouse?" I ask.

"Only me and the boys have keys."

"Any signs that someone else broke in? What about Frank and Johnny? Would they do something like this to you?"

"Doubt it. Frank works for a different mob, and he don't sell da booze." He swallows hard. "No one broke in. Locks good, no broken window. Has to be da boys."

We stand in stunned silence.

"Wait till I find dem! They'll wish Enzo found dem first."

Jolene chuckles at that, but I don't. The sun is hot on my face and I feel beads of sweat roll down my back.

"If dis gets back to Enzo, he'll have my boys and me killed. You girls too." His voice cracks.

I feel the blood in my veins turn to an icy slush. Enzo Marino runs the Boston-based mob Jean-Claude works for. His reputation as a violent mobster is well-known among rum-runners. Most mobsters kill their victims execution style, one or two shots to the back of the head, but not Enzo. We've heard stories about him having his victims, men and women, thrown in front of trains, or bound with chains and cement blocks and thrown alive into Boston Harbour.

Jean-Claude hauls in a breath. "I met Enzo last year when he come here to check on his operation. He has weird eyes, his pupils are too big, and he stare at you. But he don't blink, him. Give me da creeps."

"Why would your boys do this when they know it could get them and you killed?" Jolene asks in frustration.

Jean-Claude chews at a piece of jagged skin on his thumb, then spits it out on the ground. "I don't know, me. Dey know Enzo is dangerous. I can't believe dey did dis."

I feel the hair on my neck bristle. I've often heard the boys complain about how much Jean-Claude pays them. And last week, Andre bragged to Jolene that he just bought a brand new, fully loaded sports car from a dealership in Halifax.

A taut silence falls between us. The tide sloshes against the dock pylons and the boat's lines creak as it bobs on the water. A crow caws from the trees and I nearly jump out of my skin.

"Listen, you girls leave town till I find my boys. I need to find out how many bottles dey switch. I can give Enzo the money he's owed and get dis straightened out."

"Leave town for how long?" I ask.

"A week to be safe." He rubs the back of his neck nervously with one hand. "I'm going to check a few more places for my sons, and den I'll be at my warehouse. You girls come dere at four, and I'll give you enough cash so you can stay out of town."

"You don't need to do that, Jean-Claude," I say. "We have enough saved to do us until this blows over."

"I want to," he says.

Jolene frowns. "You really think Enzo will come for you over some vinegar in his bottles?"

He nods. "He know you work for me, so it's better for you girls to hide for now. Meet me at four o'clock. You know where my warehouse is?"

We shake our heads.

"It's eight miles outside of town, at the end of Seaforth Lane, out at Cully's Point. Oh, wait. My wife and daughters are at home. I don't have time. Would you go tell dem what's happening? Tell dem I said to go to my brother's place in Clare until I contact dem."

"Yes, of course," I say.

He reaches out and takes my wrist, squeezing it. "You girls go. Allez, cher! Allez!"

CHAPTER
THIRTY-THREE

We go up on the steps and I tap lightly on the door. There's no answer, so I knock a little harder.

Jean-Claude's daughter, who introduces herself as Manon, answers the door. She leads us down a narrow hall into the kitchen. On the walls I see wood-framed photos of Jean-Claude, his wife, sons and daughters, and grandchildren. Seven children and twelve grandchildren, I remember him telling me last week.

An older woman with short, curly salt-and-pepper hair sits at the kitchen table. Twin dark-haired and beautiful teenaged girls stand at the sink, one washing and the other drying the dishes.

"This is my mother, Berta, and my sisters, Claudette and Collette," Manon tells us. I make a note to remember that Collette has a blue apron on while Claudette's is yellow.

On the table in front of Berta sit two large mixing bowls. One holds wet ingredients, the other dry. To the side is a cake pan. She's holding a spoon and looks like she's about to combine the wet with the dry. The fire in the black enamel stove blazes, throwing out such heat that the room is too hot.

She pauses, spoon frozen in the air over the bowl. "What you mean, leave town?"

"Someone tampered with the mob's liquor," I explain. "He wants you to leave town until he can get this all straightened out."

"Are Louis and Andre with Jean-Claude?"

"No, uh... he can't find them," I say.

She stares at me in stunned shock. "Can't find dem?"

"Yes, no one has seen them since yesterday. Jean-Claude thinks they may have tampered with his liquor."

The spoon hits the table with a clatter. Her pale blue eyes, locked on mine, well up with tears. "No. Why he tink it was dem?"

Jolene replies. "The tampered liquor was in the warehouse. Only he and the boys have keys, and there's no signs of a break-in."

A sob catches in Manon's throat and she turns away from her job of stoking the fire in the stove. "Nooo…" She drops her head and stares emptily at the floor. "Those stupid boys."

"Where's Jean-Claude? Why didn't he come home to tell me dis?" Berta's chin is beginning to tremble.

"He's looking for the boys," I say.

Berta's hands fly to her face, covering her expression for a moment. Then she takes in a deep, tremulous breath. "The mobsters will come here?"

My breath feels ragged in my lungs. "Probably not, but Jean-Claude thinks it's better if you leave now."

"No," she moans. "Where are my boys?"

I pause and look away, but then turn back to her and speak in a gentle voice. "They're probably just with friends."

"Dey wouldn't worry me or dere father like this, no."

I glance at Jolene and we exchange silent looks of misery.

Berta sits immobilized, a look of raw terror on her face. "Maybe dis mobster did someting to dem."

"Jean-Claude doesn't think that," I tell her. "It's only been a few days. Once he finds the boys, he's going to contact the mobster and pay him for the tampered liquor."

Her terrified eyes remain locked on mine. Right then, I wish I was anywhere but here.

She turns her head to look out the window, but not before I see her face collapse with grief. She buries her face in her hands and weeps, her thick shoulders shaking.

Manon moves from the stove and stands by the side wall, looking out the window as though at some unseen terror.

After a moment, Mamon turns to us, her face aghast. "Not much scares my dad, but that mobster does. We've heard stories of what he does to people who steal from him."

Claudette cries out and it comes from deep in her throat. She lowers her head, too, and weeps. Collette quickly dries her hands on a towel and wraps an arm around her sister.

"They're just stories. They're not true," I say, though I fear it is true.

Claudette shakes her sister's arm free and runs out of the room. Her footsteps thump up the stairway to the second floor, and moments later a door slams shut. We can hear her muffled weeping from the kitchen.

Collette hurries out of the room and up the stairs after her.

Berta looks like her world has vanished out from under her. Devastated, her weeping grows louder and she squeezes her fists open and shut, open and shut.

"Oh, ma mere." Manon helps Berta to her feet, wrapping her arms around her shoulders. "Come on, we need to pack." Manon looks over at us. "Please, let yourselves out…"

With Berta clinging to her like a life vest, tears pouring down both their faces, Manon leads Berta out of the kitchen and down a narrow hallway to the back of the house.

Prickling heat rises to the back of my eyes, but I hold back my tears. Jolene also looks like she's trying not to cry. We shake our heads, then leave the house and climb into my truck in wretched silence.

CHAPTER
THIRTY-FOUR

We get back to Larkin's at the same time that she pulls into her driveway. Bash is in the front seat next to her.

Jolene and I jump out of my truck and run over to her car.

"Jean-Claude was just here," I blurt. "Something's happened."

"What is it?" She shuts the door and comes around the back of the car, carrying a small white paper bag with the drugstore's logo on it.

I tilt my head slightly at Bash. She leans down, kisses the top of his head, and hands him the bag. "Take this in the house for me. Help yourself to some milk and cookies."

Bash takes the bag and grins. "Okay!" he shouts, already racing for the house.

"Someone tampered with the bottles Jean-Claude sold to his customers, replacing the rum with vinegar. Now Andre and Louis are missing."

I hear the breath go out of Larkin. "Oh no. Was it them?"

"Most likely. There's no sign of a break-in, and only they and Jean-Claude have keys to the warehouse."

A flame of alarm blazes in Larkin's eyes. "Didn't Andre just buy a fancy new car?"

The wind has died away and the sun's rays are getting intense. My neck burns. "Yes, and they're always griping about how little they think Jean-Claude pays them."

"I don't know," Jolene says. "I still think it was Frank."

I see the fear in Larkin's eyes rise in waves. "Doesn't matter who did it. The mob will come after the Boudreaus."

Jolene scoffs. "I can't see the mob sending someone over five hundred miles, from Boston to Whaleback Cove, just because someone tampered with their liquor."

Larkin stares at her. "You forget who killed my dad?"

"No, but your dad worked for the New York mob, and he lost a ton of booze twice. That's different."

"I don't know," Larkin says, her voice tremulous.

"He wants us to meet him at the warehouse at four so he can pay what he owes us in full," I say. "Then we're to hide somewhere for a few days, maybe longer."

We stand in dazed silence for a moment.

Larkin speaks first. "I'll have to take Bash out of school. I'll tell them it's his asthma. Where do we go, though?"

"Halifax," Jolene suggests. "Let's stay in a fancy hotel."

"I'd rather stick closer," I say. "What about Coffin Island?"

Larkin shudders. "Wasn't that a cholera quarantine station in the late 1800s?"

Jolene grins. "Yup. Ships dropped off their sick passengers and crewmembers there. The island is just a big cemetery. I've heard the shoreline has eroded so much since then that you can see the ends of the coffins poking out of the banks. Some have even come completely free and floated away."

"Which makes it perfect. No one goes near the place," I say. "Blade and I went there once. The station's gone, but there's a small building set back deep in the woods. We found it almost by accident. It's rough, only one room, but it has a woodstove. We can bring blankets and quilts and sleep on the floor."

Jolene squints, pondering this. "But with the vehicles still here, and the boat gone, it'll be obvious how we left."

"Yes, but no one would ever consider that island," I say.

"True. Okay, it's creepy, but let's do it," Larkin agrees. "If Jean-Claude finds the boys and gets this straightened out, it could only be for a few days anyway."

Jolene nods. "What about food and water?"

"I have lots of canned meat, fruit, and veggies I can bring," I say. "There's a brook on the island with clear water. And there's lots of dead wood we can burn."

"I have plenty of preserves, too," adds Larkin. "I'll bring lanterns, flashlights, an axe, matches, pots, dishes… whatever else I can think of. I have enough of Bash's asthma medicine to last two weeks."

"What about your finger?" I ask. "You need the bandages changed."

"Dr. Leduc says it's healing great. I don't have to go back for a week. I'll bring bandages and antiseptic cream, and one of you can change it for me if it comes to that."

"Why don't we just agree to stay for a week to be safe?" I say. "At the end of a week, one of us can come back on the boat and dock at Larkin's, then slip a note to Jean-Claude's nephew and find out if it's safe for us to return."

Jolene and Larkin nod in agreement.

Birds sing from the trees overhead. The wind ruffles the leaves on the branches, carrying a salty, piny smell. Yet an ominous tension fills the air.

"Jolene and I will go meet with Jean-Claude," I say to Larkin. "You can start packing and putting your stuff on the boat."

She nods. "Good idea."

Jolene and I start for the truck while Larkin heads for the house. But before we can leave, we hear a car turning onto the lane.

"Great," Jolene sighs. "It's Sherlock Holmes."

I see an RCMP cruiser turn onto the property. Constable Hayes is behind the wheel. My heart pounds loud in my ears.

Larkin comes back to join us. "What does he want?"

"I don't know, but he's getting on my last nerve," Jolene grumbles.

Hayes pulls up next to my truck, steps out, and walks toward us. "Good afternoon, ladies."

"Good afternoon, Constable," Jolene says, as imperturbable as ever.

"Hi," I mumble.

And once again, to my utter mortification, our eyes meet and hold. I feel my pulse accelerate, then lower my eyes and focus on a patch of weed in front of my feet.

Jolene steps forward. "Actually, Constable, you came at a bad time. We were just leaving."

"Oh? May I ask where?"

"You may not," she snaps.

His warm eyes and soothing countenance can change, of course, and they do so now. His expression turns grave.

"We're just heading to town to run some errands," I explain, throwing a Jolene a warning glance.

"I see." His voice sounds cool. Has he picked up on my deceit?

I look up and meet his eyes, seeing there a mixture of emotions. Exasperation. Unhappiness. Concern. And then my throat catches and I feel that familiar jolt of connection. I feel like I've simultaneously betrayed Blade and disappointed Hayes. That spark feels inconceivable to me each time it comes. Why now, of all times?

He rubs his chin and draws a breath. "The talk in town is that two young men are missing. The rumour is that they and their father, Jean-Claude Boudreau, work for the mob selling illegal liquor."

A throb starts at the base of my neck. He knows. I feel a rush of sharp, clenching panic and want to jump in the truck and drive away. But I don't dare.

Jolene says, "And?"

"It's a treacherous business to be involved with the mob," he warns. "If the rumour's true, they'll be looking for the Boudreaus and anyone else involved. They're ruthless."

"Well, that has nothing to do with us," Jolene says with a dismissive snort.

There's a stiff silence. My pulse thrums in my ears.

Suddenly, two chipmunks on a tree branch behind us start a high-pitched trilling, shattering the quiet. Larkin and I jump a little; Hayes and Jolene do not.

He leans sideways and looks around back to the *Bad Reputations*, tied up at the dock. "Are you still selling your catch to Mr. Boudreau?"

"Yes, we are," I lie, managing to find my voice.

"I've learned that Jean-Claude is known to the police—for reasons other than selling seafood. Bootlegging and tax evasion being just two."

"Sounds like he has his hands in a lot of things," Jolene pipes up with such unforced boldness that it astounds me.

"I'm not sure you ladies fully appreciate the danger." His eyes seem troubled, his face achingly sad.

"The danger of fishing lobster?" Jolene says. "We know only too well."

"There's more. I've heard from a reliable source that a mob boss by the name of Enzo Marino is looking for the Boudreaus. He believes they replaced the liquor in his bottles with vinegar and then resold the stolen liquor at a higher price."

Larkin pretends to be absorbed in a lilac bush at the side of the property.

Hayes turns his gaze to me, and I look away, the tips of my ears blazing hot. "Do you ladies know anything about that?" His voice is still gentle, but persistent.

Jolene bristles. "Not much chance of that, since all we're doing is fishing lobster."

Once again, her fearlessness inspires me to be braver.

I wait for the throbbing of my heart to ease and then say, "Yes, we're just fishing. We don't know what anyone else is doing in town. And we don't care to know."

He examines my eyes more intently, and I'm sure he sees through me. There's something about the way he watches us, his alertness. We're not fooling him.

"Please listen to me," he insists, his gaze lingering on me. "Enzo Marino and his henchmen are stone-cold killers. They've committed heinous crimes. If you're involved in any way, I believe your lives are in peril."

"Enzo who?" Jolene says. "Never heard of him."

"Ladies, you can trust me. You don't have to be afraid."

Jolene huffs. "We're not afraid of you."

I feel a bead of cold sweat roll down between my shoulder blades, but I maintain my silence.

"I guess we're done then," he says in a subdued voice.

"Good," Jolene says cheerfully.

With a heavy sigh, Hayes turns and walks to his car. As he reaches for the door handle, he glances back over his shoulder. "Ladies, these are very bad men. Please be careful."

He drives away, with all our eyes glued to his receding car.

"He knows," I say.

"Yes," Larkin agrees. "And he's right about the mob. We need to get on the boat and get out of here. You girls go to the warehouse. I'm going to start packing."

CHAPTER
THIRTY-FIVE

Hayes leaves the Wade home and heads back to town. There, he parks in Pruett's lot and shuts the engine off, his mouth set in a thin line. He sits for a moment looking out through the windshield to the harbour, all the while drumming his fingers hard on the steering wheel.

Duska looked me right in the eyes and lied, he thinks. *She's a liar and a criminal, and I'm a cop! Yet I still can't get her out of my head.*

He stares out to the water, his mind reeling, feeling more than ever that he has to stop this absurdity. Those women's lives are in grave danger. Even if the mob doesn't come to town, he knows with certainty that one day soon Duska is going to be arrested, either by him or another officer.

I can't stop wanting to help her, though...

How far would he go? His feelings are complicated. He keeps thinking of how scared she looked. Scared yet striking. His heart liquifies every time he sees her. He wants so much to protect her, to hold her.

Has love unexpectedly found him? Would he do anything illegal for her, anything to put his career in jeopardy?

He sits there, conflicted, grappling with his decision, knowing that the outcome for Duska and her friends won't be good, no matter what he decides. The realization that he would even consider helping them is appalling.

Feeling his throat tighten, he rolls down the window and takes in a deep breath of fresh sea air. After a minute, he sits up straighter and runs a hand hard over his face.

No, he could never do anything illegal.

I'll do my job, he thinks. *I'll follow the women until I catch them in the act… and then I'll arrest them. They'll go to jail, but they'll be safer there than out on the streets with the mob after them.*

It's not an easy decision. But it's the right choice for any police officer and Christian with any integrity.

The image of him arresting Larkin, of her walking into prison, makes something collapse inside him.

CHAPTER THIRTY-SIX

I back the truck out of Larkin's driveway, race down Schooner Lane, then pull out onto the highway and cover the eight miles to Cully Point as fast as I can, turning off the highway onto Seaforth Lane. The road is long, narrow, and rutted, twisting and turning for a half-mile before it reaches its dead-end. Jean-Claude's warehouse sits off to the left, surrounded by thick woods on all sides. It's a large, grey-shingled structure with a big overhead door over which the sign reads "Boudreau & Sons Seafood." Jean-Claude's five-ton truck is parked in front of the overhead door.

It's quiet around the warehouse, which makes me nervous. I park around the side of the building where we'll be out of sight if anyone drives into the lot.

We climb out and walk to the big door. Just as we near it, we hear a car turn off the highway onto Seaforth.

"Car," I say, stopping so fast that Jolene bumps into me. We run back around the side of the building, hearing the sound of rocks flinging up from the car's back tires and pinging against the bumper.

The car brakes, coming to a sliding stop in front of the warehouse.

"Bonjour," Jean-Claude calls out, but there's a tremble in his voice.

A spark of fear passes between us. I motion to Jolene, letting her know that I'm going to creep up to the corner and peer around the corner of the building. Terror turns the blood in my veins to ice as I see two men dressed in dark suits pointing revolvers at Jean-Claude.

Jean-Claude walks toward them with his hands held out, pleading. "Non, non, wait…"

Jolene slips up behind me. "Who is it?"

"Mobsters, I think," I whisper. "This is bad."

We hear Jean-Claude cry out: "Where's my boys?"

"They're fine," the shorter of the two mobster replies. "We'll go meet up with them when we're done here."

"Have you hurt dem? Listen, my boys didn't do what you're tinking."

"Let's talk about it in your office, Jean-Claude," the other man grunts. "You got a safe in there? Boss wants his money back."

Jean-Claude backpedals away from them.

"Don't give us no trouble," the man says.

The men grab Jean-Claude by the arms. They lead him over to the door, their guns pointed at his head. One man opens the door and then they drag Jean-Claude into the warehouse as he kicks his legs and tries to wrench his arms free from their grip. The door bangs shut hard behind them.

I moan inwardly, sick with fear. "They took him inside. They want money from a safe in his office."

"And then they'll kill him," Jolene says grimly.

We listen in the still air but hear only the buzz of insects and the rustle of the leaves on the trees.

"We have to help him," I decide.

"How? They have guns."

"We can throw rocks against the building. Maybe that will scare them enough that they'll take off and leave Jean-Claude inside."

And that's when the office door bursts open. Jolene jumps and I drop to my knees. The two men drag Jean-Claude back out, his hands bound now, his nose bloody. The taller man is holding a white cotton bag, probably stuffed with cash.

The taller man opens the back door of the car and pushes Jean-Claude inside before getting in beside him. The shorter man gets behind the wheel. Then the engine starts and the car rumbles back the way it came down the dirt road.

"Let's follow them," says Jolene. "Maybe we can help somehow."

"My truck will never catch them."

Her face falls. "Poor Jean-Claude."

"It sounds like they're taking Jean-Claude to the boys, meaning they're alive. Maybe they won't kill them now that they have the money. Maybe they'll just talk to them, or at worst beat them up."

"You're probably right."

Although we don't say anything further, I know that neither one of us truly believes that.

"I think we need to stick to the plan," Jolene says. "We go to your place, get our stuff, and then meet up with Larkin on the boat. Coffin Island is the safest place for us right now."

"No, we have to help the Boudreaus. Let's call Constable Hayes and tell him what's happened. Jean-Claude must have a telephone in his office. We can use that."

"We can't. We don't have a second to spare. What if those mobsters torture Jean-Claude and his sons? Those young boys will give them our names."

"There's no way I can just jump on the boat and leave. I'll call Hayes and disguise my voice."

"All right. But I'll make the call. My voice is deeper. I'll sound more like a man."

Before we can move, we once again hear a car turn off the highway onto Seaforth. It's accelerating fast.

A rush of adrenaline goes through me. "Someone's coming! In the truck, quick!"

I take off running, with Jolene right behind me. I jump in behind the wheel just as Jolene vaults into the passenger side.

My chest heaving, I slam the truck into first gear, let out the clutch, and hit the gas. The rear end fishtails and then grips.

"It sounds like the mobsters' car," Jolene says, looking out the back window. "Why're they coming back?"

"I don't know, but there's only one road in and out. We have to hide."

Jolene looks around. "Where?"

Suddenly, I remember the old logging road in the woods, the one Jean-Claude told us about, where teenagers go to party. I drive behind the warehouse and notice a narrow gap in the trees. This must be the road. I pray that it goes deep into the forest.

I floor it, shoving the gear into second, and then quickly into third. The tires shudder over the rough road, whipping up dirt that pings against the undercarriage.

My eyes locked on the narrow track, I grip the wheel so hard that my knuckles turn white. The trees shoot past in a dark blur. We hit the bumps hard enough to lift us right up out of our seats; our heads nearly hit the roof of the cab.

Jolene looks out the back window. "Faster. If they heard, they'll be coming after us."

I press the gas pedal even harder, my bones shuddering as we hurtle over potholes.

We come to a fork in the road and I only hesitate for a second before turning right onto another even narrower lane. We bump so violently over ruts and dips that we feel every jolt in our backsides.

The track becomes narrower and rougher and the truck lurches from side to side. The trees are thick, their limbs stretching out like ghoulish arms, raking the hood and windshield. I slow down, look right, and spot a narrow break in the trees. It's so narrow that it's almost invisible. If I hadn't glanced that way right at the exact second, I'd have missed it.

I brake.

Jolene raps on my arm. "Why are you stopping? Keep going!"

I point to the right. "There's a small gap there. I think we can hide in it."

She looks out through the passenger side window and studies the slim opening. It goes into the brush for about ten yards before vanishing abruptly.

"You'll never get the truck in there." Jolene shakes her head. "It's not wide or deep enough. We'll stick out too far."

"What if the road we're on now dead-ends? I can't turn around. They'll be right behind us and we'll be trapped." I say, making my decision. "I'll back in until we can't be seen. If not, at least we'll be facing the right way to smash them if we have to."

I drive ahead a few feet, shove the gear in reverse, and back into the bush. When the truck hits the tall grass, I give it more gas. The tires spin on the thick pine needles but then gain purchase. I wince at the sound of the brush and trees scraping the sides of the truck.

The back bumper eventually gets hung up on branches and I can't go any farther. I quickly put it in park and shut off the engine. Towering pine and fir trees grow all around us. Their canopy blocks out most of the light, leaving us in darkness. We're hidden good, but the front of the truck is chrome and I'm afraid it might glitter if the car's headlights shine on it.

"Let's cover up the front of the truck with branches, quick," I say, throwing open the door and leaping out.

We break off old branches and pick up any deadfall lying on the forest floor, then drape them over the front and hood, even the cab roof. Once finished, we get back in the truck, our breathing ragged, and peer out through the gap we left in front of the windshield.

"I don't know," Jolene says. "I don't feel like we're backed in deep enough."

"Probably just teenagers anyway," I say, but inwardly I'm sick with fear. I roll my window down in order to hear the car coming.

The croaking of frogs and ticking of the cooling engine fills the quiet air. The breeze is thick with the scent of rich soil and pine needles. A chipmunk leaps from a low branch onto the hood, startling us. We jump slightly.

"Go away, stupid chipmunk," Jolene grumbles.

It scurries over the side of the hood and down to the ground.

Then we hear a vehicle rattling as it bounces over potholes in the road. I hear the whine of its gears as the driver shifts down.

"They're coming…"

Within a few seconds, the vehicle rumbles closer. Its transmission grinds and its undercarriage creaks. Numbness slides through me as I watch it slowly pass.

"It's them," I whisper.

"Where's Jean-Claude?" Jolene says in a low voice. "He's not in the backseat."

"Probably lying on the seat, or the floorboards."

"He must have told them about us meeting him at the warehouse. Why else would they come back?"

"I guess with a gun pointed at your head, you'll talk."

But the car continues up the lane. We sit, terrified and drenched in sweat, waiting for them to return.

Minutes later, we hear the car labour back toward us in low gear. It passes in reverse, not having had enough space to turn around, pitching from side to side as its tires sink in and out of the ruts. The passenger's window is down and we hear one of the men swear loudly when a big pine bough scrapes the side of the car from the front fender all the way to the back.

Jolene laughs. "Goodbye, fancy paint job."

Its brake lights flash and it stops right in front of the gap to our hideout. We fall silent. It sits there, its engine idling.

The passenger side door clicks open and my heart throbs wildly.

They've spotted us, I think, ready to turn the engine on. But then the passenger leans out of the door and studies the damage. "Branches are scratching the paint right off the car. Let's go. They're gone."

He pulls his head back in and slams the door. The brake lights go out and the car begins moving again. We watch until the sound of its engine fades before releasing our long-held breath.

Jolene looks at me. "Now what?"

"We wait to make sure they're gone. Not too long, though. We have to get help for Jean-Claude and warn Larkin. She's alone with Bash. There's no time to go to my place and grab our stuff. We go to straight to Larkin's, call Hayes, get on the boat, and leave—fast."

"You still want to call Hayes?"

"Yes."

She nods in agreement.

We sit, ears pealed, eyes fixed on the road, our faces slick with sweat. We wait fifteen minutes, all we dare. It's almost five o'clock now and dusk is falling.

I start the engine, shift into first, and nose the truck out onto the dirt track. About halfway down the lane, a deer jumps out of the trees and darts across the road only inches in front of the truck's bumper. I slam on the brakes and just miss hitting it.

"Whoa!"

"Lucky deer," Jolene says.

I take my foot off the brake and press down the gas, slower now. We emerge at the warehouse and don't see anyone else around. I drive past the structure, down the long lane, and out to the main road. As we head toward town, my eyes flick to the rearview mirror every few seconds.

CHAPTER
THIRTY-SEVEN

Larkin's face twists with fear. "Oh no, poor Jean-Claude and the boys. We can't just leave now."

"Jolene's going to call Constable Hayes," I tell her.

Jolene goes into the living room, where the phone sits on a side table. Meanwhile, Larkin looks at me with a strange, vacant expression, as if she doesn't know where she is or who she's looking at. A tremor goes through her and her knees start to buckle.

I point to a kitchen chair. "Sit down, Larkin."

She nods and starts toward it, her steps clumsy. Then she lurches and I reach out fast to steady her. I lead her to a chair and she collapses down on it. Her entire body trembles and her feet thump softly on the floor. She sees me looking at them and pulls her legs up on the chair, wrapping her arms around her calves to stop it.

"What have I done," she says. "They'll kill the Boudreaus, and then come after us. They'll kill Bash."

"Where is he?"

"Upstairs. He's finishing packing."

"Is everything else on the boat?"

"Yes.... Uh, I don't know. I can't think straight."

Jolene comes back into the room. "Hayes is on patrol, but the dispatcher said he'd radio him. He asked, 'What is your name, sir?' So disguising my low voice actually worked. There's nothing else we can do for Jean-Claude. We need to leave now."

Though she sounds calm, I can see her pulse throbbing in her temples.

"Bash, bring your suitcase and come down, please," Larkin calls out, standing and feeling stronger now.

We hear footsteps and the thump of a suitcase hitting the steps. Bash steps into the kitchen and promptly bursts into tears.

Larkin hurries over and takes the suitcase from him. "What's wrong?"

"I heard you saying someone is going to kill me," he sobs.

She leads him over to a chair, sits down, and pulls him up onto her lap. "No, Bash, no."

But he's distraught and his sobs grow louder, echoing around the kitchen.

Larkin rocks him in her arms. "No, no, nothing's going to happen to you."

He cries harder and then starts coughing and wheezing. An asthma attack.

Larkin points to a white paper bag on the counter by the sink. "Can you pass me an inhaler from the bag?"

Once I get it, she places it between Bash's lips, her hands shaking.

"Draw in a breath now, Bash," she says as she squeezes the end of the inhaler. After another dose, Bash's coughing and wheezing stops. He's breathing much better. "You're safe, Bash. In fact, we're all going on the boat now. We're going camping."

He looks up at her. "Camping?"

"Yes, it'll be so much fun, you'll see." Larkin kisses him on top of his head. "All right, little guy."

He gulps in a tremulous breath but gives her a smile.

Bash consoled, we walk out of the kitchen and outside to the back porch. We go down the steps, pass through the lawn, and make our way quickly to the dock. It's early evening and growing darker by the minute.

Larkin stops and I almost bump into her. She turns around, wincing. "Shoot! I forgot Bash's medicine. The inhaler's on the table and there's more in the white bag on the counter."

"I'll get it. You guys keep going."

Suddenly, we hear the sound of a vehicle roaring down the highway. It slows and turns off the highway onto Larkin's lane.

My heart thrashes in my chest. "On the boat, quick!"

Jolene leaps over the rail onto the deck and then helps Bash over. And finally, Larkin.

I run back to the house and up the steps to the porch. I stop and listen. It's silent. Feeling like it's now or never, I go through the open door into the kitchen. It's dark inside, but I don't dare turn on the light. I run to the table, grab the inhaler, then cross the room and get the white bag. I stuff it into my coat pocket and start for the door.

I hear a click as someone turns on the kitchen light, which illuminates the men's faces. The air leaves my lungs and my throat closes. I feel a gust of heat on my face, like the winds of hell.

One man stands in the doorway by the light switch. He's wearing a black suit with a dark overcoat and black hat. He has a narrow, badly pockmarked face. One eye is milky blue, the other brown. His mismatched eyes are devoid of human emotion.

The other man, older, is dressed the same, other than that his suit is dark brown. He's standing next to the kitchen table and pointing a gun at me. He's heavyset yet has a strangely skinny neck. His amber eyes are as shiny as glass.

I recognize them. They're the same mobsters who took Jean-Claude away.

Night fog slides in through the open back door. I turn to run, but the older man darts around the table and stands in front of the door, blocking me. I hear a humming sound in my ears, like a swarm of wasps is encircling my head. My knees go weak and the room sways under my feet. I lean back and grab the edge of the counter to brace my legs and keep from collapsing.

"Hello, darling," the older one says, his voice low and menacing. "Where are your friends?"

"They left town," I want to say, but my breath catches at the back of my throat. No words come out. Just a grunt.

"Answer me, darling."

I look away. I have no saliva. My throat is so dry, I can't speak. There's a fleck of spittle at the corner of his mouth.

He emits an odd musky odour like cucumbers, the same odour that comes off a copperhead snake. He steps over, stands right in my face, and speaks quietly, his voice so whispery silent that a tremor goes through me: "Where are they?"

"Gone." It's all I can manage. Just normal breathing is a struggle.

He eyes me with a cold gaze. The younger one watches me but makes no sound. Both men's hearts are black with evil. I want to scream from terror.

The older man sees my fear and smiles cruelly. "See, there's no malice intended here. I just do my job. You tell me where your friends are and I'll put a bullet in the back of your head. You won't feel it, you'll be dead before you hit the ground. You're going to die tonight, that's a given. Enzo wants to make an example of you all. Nothing you can do to stop that. But it can be slow and painful, or quick and easy. It's up to you."

The older one speaks with a disturbing calm; the younger one never speaks. They're a hideous, terrifying pair and I have to turn my head to the window to keep some composure. The sky is clear tonight and filled with stars... a beautiful evening, which seems so unfair.

Oh, Lord, help me.

The older one steps closer and a puff of his fusty cucumber odour hits me. Nausea surges in my throat. I keep my face turned to the window, trying to not gag on the stench. Still, I can feel his eyes burning into me.

"Where are your friends?" he says in that tranquil voice.

A chunk of wood shifts inside the stove, hissing and snapping, the fiery glow reflecting on the walls. It's like flames of Hades, and Satan, that ancient serpent, lurks in the shadows, watching his two minions carry out his work.

Terror incapacitates me and I can only emit a strangled groan.

"What's that, darling?"

My back is coated with cold sweat. I'm taking shallow, raspy breaths. I know, with a deep, heart-wrenching sadness, that I'm going to die.

But I can save my friends. Tears start behind my eyes, but I hold them back. I can't lose courage. I'll die before I tell them. I console myself with the fact that dying won't be so bad, for it means I'll be with my Blade again.

The older man sighs. "All right then. We'll do this outside. Don't want your friends coming back here and finding you first." I feel a stab of hot pain as he clamps his hands around my neck. "It's a shame it's come to this, darling. The grown men we've dealt didn't have an ounce of your courage. They cried like toddlers, begging us to spare their lives while on their knees, grabbing our ankles while they tried to bribe us with the money they stole from Enzo. But you've done none of that." He smiles in admiration. "You'd make a perfect mobster's wife."

I shudder at that. "Never."

He smirks, still gripping my neck with one hand, and pulls me through the door into the damp, dark night. My knees weak, I walk, unsteady on my feet. We go down the steps and across the yard, moving toward a dense wall of trees at the side of the property. I can see the *Bad Reputations* tied up at the dock from the corner of my eye but don't look over. The men aren't interested in it right now and I don't want to do anything that might change that. I pray that Larkin and Jolene are watching the men lead me into the woods and will unmoor the boat and let it slip away until it's safe for them to start the engine.

The air is sharp with the tang of brine. The tide's coming in and the waves rush over the pebbles on the beach. I believe that I'll never smell or hear the roar of the sea again. I inhale deeply and take one last quick glance at the water.

"There's a spade leaning against the shed," the older man tells the other. "Get it."

They're going to dig a grave in the woods and bury me. Blood surges to my head, filling my ears with a noise like a howling wind.

"Where?" the younger one says.

The older man's grip loosens slightly as he turns his head to look back, jutting his chin to the side of the property. "Over there."

I seize my only chance while he's distracted and tear out of his grasp and run toward the dense woods. I lift my legs high and sprint for my life, the men's shouts echoing behind me. Branches scrape at my face and ferns and undergrowth grab at my feet, nearly tripping me. But I keep going.

After five minutes, I stop behind a wide oak tree. I lean over to breathe, gulping for air, my lungs afire.

The air smells of decaying fir and pine needles and rich soil. The moon is out now, but the branches overhead block its light. I look back, but it's almost pitch black in the woods. Pockets of long shadows fall everywhere. The men could be right behind me and I wouldn't know.

My heart hammers. My breathing is ragged. I clamp my lips together, hold my breath, and listen. I hear the wind in the trees—

And then, over that, the snap of a twig on the forest floor. New terror fuels me on as I take off, running for all I'm worth.

I smack face first right into a huge spiderweb strung between two trees. I swipe at it, but it's stuck to my face and tangled in my hair.

Behind me, I hear the men's footsteps closing in. Icy panic drives me on again and I break into a run, branches slapping and slashing my face. I hardly feel it. It's hard to run and breathe at the same time. My calf and thigh muscles ache and blood runs down my face.

I run until my lungs are bursting and I can go no further. I hide behind a stand of spruce trees, catching my breath and rubbing my cramping thighs. There's a soft flapping of wings as a nightbird takes flight from a tree overhead, and then it's quiet again. I stand dead still and hold my breath.

A crack breaks the still of the night like a rifle blast. They're coming.

A moment later, I hear footsteps approaching. They're perilously close! Terror clutches my heart. I want to bolt, but there's no time; they'll see me.

Desperate, I look around and behind me, then spot a fallen jack pine. Its trunk is rotten and it's split in the middle. Brush and ferns grow on three sides of it, hiding the log from the direction the men are coming from. I slip over to the fallen tree and crawl into the hole where its roots once sunk deep into the earth.

I scoop up some decayed leaves and throw them over my body. Then I lay on my back, arms at my sides, staring up through the soaring trees to the starless sky. Clouds have crossed in front of the moon and I doubt they can see me.

The hollow stinks of mould, rot, and death. My pulse booms in my ear, drowning out all other sounds. I hold my breath to try to slow my heartbeat and block out the stench.

The crunch of dry pine needles grows louder as the men draw near. Beads of sweat roll down my forehead, stinging my eyes. I lift my head an inch and peer to my left. Right then, the moon appears from behind the clouds and white light spills through the treetops, revealing the dark silhouettes of the men approaching. One of them is holding a gun.

They stop, standing silent in the shadows of the trees, listening for me. The urge to get up and flee is overpowering. It takes everything in me to stay put. I don't move. I barely breathe.

Suddenly, I hear a rustling of dry leaves underneath me and feel something writhing up from the depths. Then something cold glides up onto my left thigh. I lift my head slightly and look down into the eyes of a fat black snake slithering over my legs.

A shock of horror goes through me. I drop my head back down and bite my bottom lip to stop a scream of horror. I'm biting down so hard that I taste blood.

I feel more movement, this time on my right leg. Something is sliding up my side and across my belly. Another snake, longer.

My legs shake, violently. Tears fill my eyes. I've disturbed a den of snakes. Tangled together and agitated, they're twisting in a frenzy to get free.

A third black snake pokes his head up and stares at me. It slithers over my chest toward my face, then stops and lifts his head. Its tongue darts in and out, eyes locked on me. I let out a low moaning wail unlike any sound I've ever made before. My whole body trembles, as if I've fallen through thin ice into freezing water.

I have an unspeakable fear of snakes. Panic explodes in my chest. I have to get out of here! I'm about to rise when I hear the crunch of footsteps, followed by the men's low voices only a few feet from my hiding spot. I freeze.

I lay there in muted horror, able to feel my heartbeat through my jacket as a snake glides across my cheek. I feel a prickling behind my eyes and have to bite my bottom lip to keep from weeping.

The snake slides off my face, and from the corner of my eye I see it slip over the side of the log. I hear it plop down on the ground, then the rustle of leaves as it slithers away. Two other snakes are now moving over my legs.

My ears are humming. I'm sweating wildly. I will myself to calm down. They're harmless. They're more afraid of me than I am of them.

I close my eyes and hold my breath.

Another snake glides over the edge of the log and falls to the ground. Seconds later, the last snake does the same.

I open my eyes but still hold my breath, listening. The men's voices are soft over the crackle of their retreating footsteps on the forest floor. Soon the sound of their passage is gone.

Still, I force myself to wait another five minutes.

I lift my head a little. It's too dark to see more than a few feet through the trees, but the way seems clear. I strain to hear the men, but there's only the whisper of wind and the low chirr of insects. But I don't want to move too quickly in case they're hiding in the shadows.

Copying the snakes, I slip over the trunk and drop to the ground on the other side. I lay still there for a moment but hear nothing. Then I crawl over to an oak tree and hide behind it, my blood drumming in my ears.

My back is damp even though the air is cool, but I stay there until I'm breathing more calmly.

At last I wipe at my bleeding face with a handful of leaves. I decide to go back and see if the *Bad Reputations* is still at the dock. If so, I may still be able to board in time for Larkin, Jolene, and I to make our escape.

I get to my feet and take off at a brisk walk. The ground is covered with a quilt of fallen fir and pine needles, but on top of that lies dead branches and leaves. I'm fearful of snapping any twigs and hold my hand out in front of me to protect my face, creeping as lightly as I can, though it's impossible to move soundlessly. Ahead stretches more trees, more silence, more shadows...

And then hear a crack. Someone stepping on a dead branch.

I crouch behind two birch trees, heart thrashing.

From the darkness, I hear Jolene's voice call out in desperation. "Duska!"

Uncontainable relief washes over me. "Here, I'm here..."

"Where?"

I step out of my hiding place. "Over here."

Jolene bursts out of the trees and we rush into each other's arms.

"Oh, Duska, we thought they killed you," she sobs, hugging me so tightly that I'm afraid my ribs are going to break. She releases me, smiling ecstatically as tears trail down her cheeks. "How did you evade them?"

"I hid in the cavity of a fallen tree." I swallow hard. "There was a snake den in it. It was horrible."

"Horrible?" she frowns. "What, are you afraid of snakes?"

I pause for a second. "Petrified. Where's Larkin and Bash?"

"Back on the boat. We saw the mobsters walking you into the woods, so we got off and hid in the forest on the other side of the property. We saw them come out, then search the boat and the sheds. Then they left in their car and I came looking for you. But we have to go now. They'll be back."

We run for a time, until we emerge from the trees onto the yard. The kitchen light is still on in the house and the boat is at the dock, engine running. We race across to the dock, sprinting faster than we've ever done in our lives.

CHAPTER THIRTY-EIGHT

At 7:00 p.m., Hayes is parked off the highway just a little down the road from Whitecap Lane, where the Wade home sits. A thin veil of fog rolls in from the sea, slithering through the trees.

He hears the roar of an engine and sees a dark sedan hurtle onto the highway and speed toward town. His stomach lurches when he sees its Massachusetts licence plate. Flicking on his siren and emergency lights, he gives chase. At first he's sure the car is going to try to escape, but finally it slows and pulls over onto the shoulder. He eases behind it and studies the car. Two men sit inside.

Hayes bows his head and prays silently for protection before climbing out and walking up to the driver's side door. He shines his flashlight first on the driver, and then on the passenger.

"Good evening, officer," the driver says.

"Going a little fast, weren't you?" Hayes says, noticing that the men's faces are sweaty. It's a humid night, but not enough to warrant that kind of sweat.

"Was I?"

Hayes sweeps the backseat with the beam of his light and then brings it back to the driver. "May I see your licence and registration please?"

The driver doesn't move. He locks his eyes on Hayes, who notices that the man's eyes shine reptilian yellow in the light. Hayes moves the beam once again to the passenger. There's a deadness in both men's eyes that makes the hair on his neck stand up.

He steps back and moves to the rear passenger door, shining his light on the seat and floor. He's looking for guns, but also giving himself time to regain his composure. He's never had to use his revolver, but he might have to today.

He unsnaps his holster, draws a breath, and moves back to the driver. "You're a long way from home."

"Yes."

The wind rises up and moans through the trees, carrying a strange sulphurous odour.

Hayes eyes both men. His nerves are on edge. His senses heightened. An icy sensation creeps into his stomach

"Where are you gentlemen headed?"

"What's it to you?" the passenger blurts, leaning forward to look past the driver. He smiles, cruel and predatory.

"We're headed to a cottage we've rented on the coast," the driver says, casting the passenger a quick warning look.

Hayes doesn't dare take his eyes off them. They're clearly mobsters. His right hand hovers over his holster.

"Licence and registration please, sir," he orders.

The driver takes his time pulling his wallet out of his overcoat pocket and removing the licence. He finally hands it and the registration to Hayes, who shines the flashlight on the documents while keeping one eye on the men.

"Where on the coast is this cottage, Mr. Deluca?" he asks.

Deluca pauses. "Uh… Shelburne."

"You're headed the wrong way then."

"Oops."

Then Hayes's car radio crackles and he hears the dispatcher's voice calling him.

"Excuse me, gentlemen." He walks back to his car but keeps his body turned sideways to prevent showing them his back.

Suddenly he hears a noise, a soft thump coming from the trunk of the men's car, followed by a low, muffled cry.

Hayes reaches for his sidearm and whips around. He steps up to the driver's side door and points the revolver. "Mr. Deluca, please step out of your vehicle and bring your keys." Hayes shines the light on the passenger and aims his revolver at him. "You! Place your hands up on the dashboard. Do it now!"

The passenger does so but takes his time, staring at him with the half-smile of a sociopath.

"Don't you move," Hayes says. "Not one inch."

After a pause of a few seconds, the door clicks open and Deluca steps out.

"Walk slowly around to the back of the car."

The man obeys, and they both stop there. Hayes keeps the revolver levelled at Deluca.

"Open the trunk."

Deluca shakes his head. "Don't do this," he whispers.

"Open it, now!"

Deluca shrugs, then slides the key in and the trunk pops open.

With his gun trained on Deluca, Hayes leans over slightly and peers into the trunk. Three men—faces bloodied, mouths covered with cloths, hands and feet bound, eyes wide with terror—stare up at him.

The passenger door swings open and a gunshot shatters the quiet night. Hayes feels a sting, like the slice of a razor as a bullet grazes his earlobe. He hits the ground and rolls over, dropping the flashlight but hanging on to his revolver.

He leaps to his feet and sees Deluca jump into the driver's side, the passenger leaping in on the other. Hayes reaches into the trunk and manages to yank one of the men out. The man falls hard to the ground as the front doors slam shut and the engine starts up. Hayes reaches in for the other two captives, grabbing their bound arms and hauling them up and over the side of the trunk as the car starts to drive away. The men tumble to the ground and Hayes falls over on top of them.

The constable rolls forward, then kneels, aims, and fires a shot over the car's roof. He fires again, but the car speeds away, kicking up a thick cloud of dust and pebbles in its wake. It hurtles around a curve in the road before its red taillights vanish from sight.

Hayes grabs his flashlight and then runs to his patrol car. He leans in and radios the dispatcher for help. Too late, the dispatcher gives him the message about the mobsters having kidnapped the Boudreaus.

Leaving them bound, Hayes puts the Boudreaus in the backseat of his car. He then jumps in behind the wheel and races down the lane to the Wade home.

He brakes hard in the driveway, then climbs out in the muggy nighttime air. Heat lightning flickers to the east as he faces the house, silent and dark as granite. His heart pumps with fear.

Am I too late? he wonders. *Have the mobsters killed Duska and the others?*

He climbs the porch steps, revolver pointed straight ahead, and steps through the open front door into the foyer.

"Mrs. Doucette! Miss Wade! This is Constable Hayes. Come out now. The men are gone. You're safe."

He moves to the kitchen next, where the light is on and the back door open. Over the sound of the surf, he hears the low roar of a diesel engine in the distance. He runs outside just in time to see the *Bad Reputations* racing away over the water.

Duska's face fills his mind. They're fleeing!

He doesn't want to report them, but there might be other mobsters in town, or on boats out at sea, hunting for them.

With his blood pounding in his ears, Hayes sprints back to his patrol car. He radios the detachment and tells the dispatcher to alert the RCMP patrol boats and the Coast Guard.

He starts the engine, stomps on the gas, and speeds toward the town wharf where the RCMP patrol boat is docked. Blood rolls down from his wounded earlobe, pooling on the collar of his uniform jacket. He takes each turn on nearly two wheels. The trees whiz by in a flash of deep green. In the back, the men bounce into each other, groaning in pain.

CHAPTER THIRTY-NINE

I'm at the helm, my heart thundering, as we set a course for Coffin Island. The boat idles as low as possible and glides across the moonlit water. Jolene is at the port side, Larkin at the aft, searching the water with binoculars.

"Duska!" Larkin shouts. "Boat to the north, about five hundred yards!"

I see the lights of a boat in the distance, just sitting on the water. I veer to the south when she adds, "There's two boats!"

We're running without lights, so I ease off the throttle. We're far enough away that they haven't spotted us.

"Kill the engine," Jolene says through the open wheelhouse door. "I hear yelling."

I shut off the engine and turn to Bash. "Stay in here and stay down low."

He nods and sits on the floor.

I join Larkin at the aft side and listen for the men's shouts. Then there's a blood-curdling scream that carries over the water.

"Something terrible is going on over there," Larkin says in a tense whisper.

Jolene, carrying binoculars, comes over to us with a frown. "It's Burke and Clint on the *Bianca Lynn*, and a rum-running boat called *Swift Seize*. It looks like the rum-runners have boarded Clint's boat. Why would they do that?"

Larkin sweeps the boat with her binoculars. The wheelhouse and deck lights are on. "There's burlocks on the deck," she reports. "The same ones we transport for Jean-Claude. That's Jean-Claude's liquor!"

The three of us exchange shocked looks.

"So Burke and Clint are the ones who tampered with Jean-Claude's bottles," Jolene says, nodding slowly. "Burke knows how to jimmy a lock. That's how they got into the warehouse. I wonder if this was Burke's idea of revenge. Maybe he hoped the mobsters would blame us and then kill us. He'd be rid of me then."

"No, Jolene," I say.

"Wonder how they got caught," Larkin muses.

"Oh, they're both as dumb as a box of rocks," Jolene says. "They could never plan and carry out something like that."

Looking through my binoculars, I see Burke and Clint kneeling on the deck while three men stand in front of them. Two are dressed like deckhands, but the other wears a black suit and overcoat, and a fedora; he's holding a gun.

A mobster.

One of the deckhands shouts at Clint while hitting him on the head with an oar. Blood pours in jagged lines down his face. Burke's face is also bloody.

As I watch, the two deckhands lean over and pick Clint up by the legs and arms and carry him over to the railing.

Slowly, horrifyingly, we start to understand what's about to happen.

"No, don't!" Clint screams.

Without a word, they swing him back once and throw him over the side.

Clint hits the water hard and vanishes. A moment later, his head pops up, but it's barely above the surface. His clothing is weighing him down. He's struggling to stay afloat, his arms flailing in desperation. He swims toward the stern of the *Bianca Lynne*, reaches it, and lunges up out of the water, grabbing for the edge.

A deckhand walks over. "Drown, you thief!" He lifts the oar over his head and brings it down on Clint's fingers.

Clint shrieks and falls back into the sea, sinking below the surface. When he surfaces again, he opens his mouth to scream, but water gushes in. He makes a gurgling sound in his throat.

The two deckhands move toward Burke, who staggers backwards, tripping over a coil of rope on the deck. He falls on his back, thrashing wildly, eyes bulging with terror.

"No, don't," he pleads.

One man grabs him by the shoulders and the other takes his legs. They lift him up and carry him over to the side.

"No! No!" It's a cry of raw rage and fear.

"Steal from Enzo?" The mobster laughs. "Now you're fish food."

The deckhands swing Burke back and forth twice, then heave him over the side. He crashes into the cold, dark sea and is gone.

All the air rushes out of my lungs at the terrible scene unfolding before me.

Seconds later, Burke surfaces, arms thrashing, mouth open in terror. He, too, reaches up for the side of the boat, but the same oar comes down on his head. There's a lull in the wind for a few seconds and the sickening thud carries to our ears.

Dazed, Burke falls into the water and slips under. He's submerged for a few seconds before bobbing back up, gasping and choking.

"Even if he manages to stay above water, he'll die of hypothermia," Jolene says with despair.

I'm surprised by her show of feeling. But then, she loved him once.

Burke raises an arm in a last feeble plea, but the deckhand only laughs and pushes his head under the water with the oar. Burke's arm falls, making a tiny splash as it hits the water, and then his head slips beneath the sea.

The water turns calm again and there's a horrible silence in the air. Burke is gone.

The two boats, tied together, drift closer toward us. I squint. Is that Clint rising on the crest of a wave? He's still crying feebly for help, swallowing seawater, coughing and retching while being dragged away.

"Let's throw some life rings in the water," I say.

Suddenly, a squall rises up from the water and hits us from the south. The waves begin to church in the violent winds. I look back to find Clint again, but his head is small above the water. The deadly sea has him in its grasp.

Each time the throttling waves smash into him, he slips further into the water. Then I realize that he's being swept toward us! Jolene throws a life ring over the railing, but he misses it. I reach down with a gaffer to try to snag him, but to my horror he careens by me too fast. Our eyes meet for a second and I see the hopeless, terror-stricken look on his face. I watch helplessly as he's carried away and swallowed by the sea. The shock of it turns my body into a sheet of ice. I can't get air into my lungs again.

"Hey!"

The waves have carried the two boats closer, and the mobster has seen us. But before they can react, we hear the loud roar of two approaching boats. The *Bianca Lynne* and *Swift Seize* are quickly illuminated by two bright spotlights.

"This is the RCMP!" a man's voice orders over a loudspeaker. "Prepare to be boarded."

One of the patrol boats pulls up next to the port side of the *Swift Seize*. Mounties are out on the deck, ready to board. The other patrol boat is about two hundred yards behind and moving toward the starboard side of the *Bianca Lynn*.

They haven't seen us yet.

I turn to Larkin and Jolene. "Let's lower the lifeboat on the port side. You two take Bash and row back to Larkin's place."

"We can't do that," Larkin says.

"You must. Jolene has her baby to think of, and you have Bash. You can't go to jail. They haven't seen us yet. Go, please."

Jolene frowns. "What? No! Start the engine! Let's get out of here!"

I shake my head. "I can't do this anymore, Jolene. I don't want to do this anymore. I'm finished breaking the law. I'll face the consequences, but you have to go now, for your baby. You too, Larkin. For Bash."

"She's right, Jolene," Larkin says, but with sorrow.

I pull the bag from my coat pocket and hand it to her. "Bash's medicine."

Larkin nods, takes the bag, and runs into the wheelhouse while Jolene and I hurry around to the port side. Using the ropes, we carefully lower the lifeboat into the sea. It's sheltered from the swells and wind and sits rocking on the water.

Jolene scrambles down the ropes and sits on the middle bench, keeping it even steadier.

Larkin and Bash appear with their suitcases and I drop them down to Jolene, who stows them in the bow. Then, with Bash clinging to her back, Larkin inches down the rope. Jolene helps them get settled on the stern bench.

Jolene picks up the oars and slides them in the locks. As she starts rowing away, she looks up and smiles sadly. Larkin and Bash give me mournful waves.

I say a silent desperate prayer for them, for they have a formidable row ahead of them. It's twenty miles back to shore in that little wooden dinghy.

Returning to the wheelhouse, I try to keep the boat sideways to shield them from the sight of the patrol boats. Moments later, a spotlight hits the boat.

"Halt, *Bad Reputations!*" a voice commands as the patrol boat proceeds toward me.

I feel a rush of bittersweet relief that this is all finally over. I walk out to the deck, wincing against the bright light, and wait, resigned to my fate.

Strangely, as fast as it hit, the storm is gone, leaving behind a windless humid night.

CHAPTER FORTY

On the town's wharf three hours later, I stand handcuffed and broken. I watch as two Mounties lead the captain, crew, and the mobster from the *Swift Seize* down the wharf toward a patrol car. I glance over at the *Bad Reputations*, tied up at the dock. The Mounties tore it apart looking for liquor and found nothing. But they did find the hidden compartments and charged me with rum-running.

Doesn't matter. I'm glad it's over.

The sun is rising in the east. Bands of tangerine orange, soft lilac, and magenta streak across the sky. It's a spectacular sunrise and I watch it while drawing in a deep breath of the briny air, knowing that I won't experience this again for many years.

The RCMP sergeant stands in front of me. "Who else was with you?" he growls.

"No one. I was alone."

His face is heated. "I don't believe you."

Constable Hayes comes up beside me and drapes a blanket gently around my shoulders. "Sergeant, she's telling the truth. I saw the boat leaving the Wades' dock. There was only Mrs. Doucette aboard."

The sergeant eyes him with a weighty stare. A mixture of disapproval, irritation, and disappointment.

Finally, he gives a little grunt. "Think about this. You could destroy your career."

"She was alone," Hayes repeats.

"There's no place in the RCMP for a sentimentalist, Hayes."

Hayes nods. "I understand."

The sergeant scowls. "Fine. It's your life."

Once the sergeant leaves, I look at Hayes. The depth of his kindness stuns me and we hold gazes for a moment.

"Thank you," I say.

"For what?" His voice is quiet and sad, and also slightly hoarse.

A shadow crosses his eyes and something catches in my throat. I understand that we aren't to talk about this ever again. I see how painful this is for him, how much this decision is costing him as a police officer and a Christian.

He slowly turns his eyes away from me. His face distant and cool, he takes me by the arm and walks me over to his patrol car.

My heart is shattered with remorse. Whatever I thought was happening between us is forever gone. I've destroyed that, too. I've hurt him badly, and my grief is just as powerful and heart-wrenching as it was on the day I lost Blade. I hate myself.

We walk past the crowd of townspeople collected at the side of the wharf entrance. I hear murmurs and laughter, see condemnation and recrimination in some of their eyes. I feel assaulted by it but walk with as much grace and dignity as I can muster.

As I pass Sophie, my friend and former boss, she releases a cry of such despair that it reverberates out over the harbour. The sound pains me more than the glares of the townspeople. I feel the depth of her sorrow in my heart.

———   •   ———

Later that day, I sit in a small, windowless interrogation room in the town's RCMP detachment. The commander looms across the wooden table. He came into the room a moment ago but hasn't said a word. He's just glaring at me while tapping his fingers on the tabletop.

I remain silent, waiting for him to speak.

"Who else was with you?" His voice booms off the walls of the bare room. "The rumours are that three women worked for Jean-Claude."

"Lobster fishing, yes. But rum-running, no. I worked alone."

His eyes flare. "If I find out you're lying, I'll make sure the judge tacks on a few more years."

"Your men searched the boat. There was no one else."

"Fine, if that's the way you want it. We don't have women's cells, so you'll be lodged in the men's along with the others arrested today. We'll put you in the last cell and hang some blankets for privacy. In the morning, you'll be transferred to the Halifax jail to await your trial and sentencing," he explains, his eyes stony and uncaring.

"Have you found the Boudreaus?" I ask.

"Yes, they're in our cells right now. The two mobsters who kidnapped them were going to kill them. Luckily for them, Hayes stopped it, though the henchmen did escape. The mobster we arrested along with the captain and crew of the *Swift Seize* will be charged with murder in the deaths of Burke and Clint Taylor." He pushes his chair back, then stands and eyes me with disgust. "When are you people going to learn that working for the mob only leads to prison or death?"

He walks out of the room to end the conversation, his footsteps echoing like gunshots in the hallway outside.

My body turns leaden. I'm glad he's gone. I sag back against the chair, relieved that the Boudreaus are alive but still worried sick about Larkin, Bash, and Jolene. Were they able to make it back to Larkin's place? What if the dinghy flipped or was carried out to sea?

I'm in a very dark place. I've reached the lowest point in my life and I have no one to blame but myself. Larkin, Bash, and Jolene could be dead. I've destroyed my relationship with my Lord and Saviour, as well as my testimony as a Christian. I've hurt Hayes and may have ruined his career.

I'm going to prison. I've ruined my life. Humiliation, guilt, and sorrow engulfs me like a tidal wave. I bury my face in my hands and weep in the stark chill of the room.

CHAPTER FORTY-ONE

At 6:00 p.m. that same night, Asher Hayes, his heart crushed, drives his patrol car through the streets of Whaleback Cove. The town is buzzing with the news of the arrest of the captain and crew of the *Swift Seize*, the mobster, the Boudreaus, and Duska Doucette.

A search is also underway for Burke and Clint's bodies. The news of their deaths has shocked the entire community. After tampering with the mob's liquor, and then reselling it for a higher price, they stupidly bragged about it to their friends. And of course it didn't take long for the news to reach Enzo Marino.

Though the Boudreaus weren't directly responsible, they nearly paid the terrible price. They'll be transferred to Halifax in the morning where they'll face charges for bootlegging and tax evasion.

Duska's arrest is more personally devastating. Though she has no prior criminal history, and no contraband liquor was found on her boat, she admitted to rum-running. He feels hollow at the thought of her sitting in jail, waiting to be transferred to Halifax. That charming yet solemn smile, that wounded heart, will only get more battered by a lengthy prison sentence.

It wasn't meant to be, he tells himself. What did he think would happen between them? A cop and a criminal? A grief-stricken widow? He had foreseen this, hadn't he? It wasn't a surprise. *Forget her now, once and for all.*

Letting out a heavy sigh, he starts the car and drives out to Whitecap Lane. Once there, he drives slowly past the Wade home. The lights are on and Larkin's car is parked alongside Duska's pickup in the driveway.

He drives past the house, and parks under the darkness of the canopy of overhanging branches. He gets out and makes his way down the edge of the property to the dock. There, tied up and bobbing on the water, is a lifeboat with the name *Bad Reputations* painted on its bow.

Hayes walks back up to his car, starts it, and drives down the lane. He brakes in front of the house.

The living room curtains are open, and he waits and watches. Soon he sees Larkin and Bash walk past the window. Seconds later, Jolene enters, cups her hands around her face, and presses her forehead against the glass. She sees his car but just stands there watching him.

Ignoring the whispers of his already battered conscience, Hayes takes his foot off the brake and presses the gas. As he drives past, Jolene gives him a cheery wave and then closes the curtains.

He pulls out of the lane onto the main road and heads back to town. Though he knows he shouldn't do it, he's going to stop in at the jail and secretly let Duska know that her friends made it home safe. She has enough to worry about without adding that. One last thing he can do for her before erasing her from his mind forever.

CHAPTER FORTY-TWO

June 7, 1930

I get off the bus on Waterfront Street and survey the downtown. It's quiet, the fishermen have gone hours ago, and few people are out on the sidewalks. I turn and start walking out in the direction of Rowboat Lane.

Once home, I stop in my driveway and take in my house and the ocean behind it. I close my eyes and stand for a moment with the warm sun kissing my face. I draw in a deep breath of the fresh salty air.

Inside, I open the windows to air out the rooms. The place is spotless, thanks to Jolene and Larkin, who, using the spare key I kept under a rock by the front step, have been coming over to take care of the place.

In the kitchen, I find milk, cheese, butter, and a cooked chicken in the fridge. Larkin and Jolene brought it over yesterday. They also stocked the cupboards with bread, coffee, tea, and canned goods, and the root cellar with potatoes, carrots, peas, and squash from their own gardens' fall harvest. They wanted to meet me in town when I got off the bus, but I told them that I wanted my first day home alone.

I make a chicken sandwich for lunch and eat it while standing at the kitchen sink, looking out the open window at the ocean. The sunlight glitters like gold on the water. The breeze carries the intoxicating scents of salt, lilac, and rose, such a wonderful change from the musty prison air that smelled like damp towels left in a hamper too long.

For the first time in just over a year, I feel the tension drain from my body and my nerves relax. I missed my home, the ocean, almost as much as I miss my Blade. It's so good to be back. I now understand fully what Blade meant when he said that man schemes and God smiles. I've learned a hard lesson about obeying and trusting God.

Later, I go out to the garden, which needs a lot of work. I grab a spade from the shed and start turning the ground over pulling weeds. It's back-breaking work and my face is slick with sweat.

I hear a car pull up in my drive, but I just keep working. I don't want to talk to anyone.

"Good afternoon, Mrs. Doucette," says Constable Hayes.

I turn around and it's like an electrical jolt goes through my body. It settles into a warm vibration. He's not in uniform. He's wearing a blue cotton shirt, tan pants, and a dark brown jacket.

"Good afternoon, Constable," I say, disconcerted. *Why is he here?*

"I'm off-duty. Call me Asher."

"And you can me Duska."

"Duska," he says, so softly that I feel a warm tug in my heart. He smiles, then shades his eyes with a hand and gazes out at the water. "You have a beautiful piece of property. The view is breathtaking."

"Yes, it is."

He drops his hand and turns his eyes to me. "I hope you don't mind me dropping over unannounced. I saw you get off the bus. Wanted to say hi."

I wipe the sweat from my brow with my fingertips. "Yes, I was released early for good behaviour. Although I'm sure the large groups of women who travelled to Halifax and marched on the Legislature for my release are the biggest reason."

"I read that in the newspaper. Good for them." He draws in a soft breath. "I wanted to visit you in prison, but I was worried about word getting back to the detachment commander. He'd get more suspicious and it might have been bad for you."

My heart wobbles in my chest. He wanted to visit me? I'm speechless.

There is a long silence.

"Getting your garden ready, I see," he says.

"Yes." I stick my spade in the dirt and put my foot on top to drive it in.

"Looks like you could use a hand. That's a big patch to turn over."

I look up, startled. "Are you offering?"

"I am."

"Then yes, I could. There's another spade in the shed." I surprise myself. I really didn't want any company, but I can't deny that I'm glad he's here.

He walks over to the shed and comes back with the spade. He removes his jacket and hangs it over the wooden railing on the step.

We work in silence, the sunshine hot on our backs, the light wind off the water rustling the branches.

Once it's done, he turns to me. "That looks like it. I guess I should get going."

I smile. "Thanks so much for your help."

He smiles back. "You're welcome. Ah, Duska, I was wondering if I may call on you some time."

Stunned, I look at him, unblinking.

"Or not," he says.

"It's just… I mean, you're a cop. And I'm a convicted felon."

He nods, staring out to the water. "Have you decided to go straight?"

I'm about to answer when I see that he's grinning.

"Ha-ha," I say.

He chuckles.

"But yes, my short-lived life of crime is over."

"So may I call on you?" he asks again.

A rush of happiness bursts in my chest. "Yes, I'd like that."

His eyes are tender. "Good, I'm glad. Bye for now then."

I watch him walk away, and then blurt out, "Wait, uh… Asher. You must be hungry after all that work. Would you like a cup of coffee and a piece of pie?"

He turns around. "I'd love some, thanks."

"Larkin brought over a freshly baked blueberry pie. I can't eat it all myself."

He grins. "Ha! Pie is my downfall. I'll put a good dent in it."

We sit on the back porch, bathed in the warm breeze and bright sunshine. Birdsong fills the air as we eat pie and drink coffee, our conversation easy and relaxed.

"I'm off on Sunday," he says. "I'm going to attend morning services at the Lutheran church. Would you like to come? If it helps, Jolene attends now with Larkin."

"I heard that. Yes, I would. I attended services in prison on Sundays, after praying and asking God's forgiveness. The first night there, I was laying on my bed, scared and broken, when I turned to my Bible. I opened it to Jeremiah 29:11: 'For I know the thoughts that I think toward you… thoughts of peace, and not of evil, to give you an expected end.' That hit me like a sledgehammer. After Blade died, I thought my life was over. I let hopelessness overwhelm me. I made bad decisions because I didn't trust God to take care of me. It was a horrible feeling, being away from God. I never want to let that happen again."

When he speaks, his voice is achingly gentle. "Sometimes when we fail, and we all do, Duska, it's hard to remember that God is in control."

I nod.

"There's a potluck lunch downstairs after services," he adds. "Why don't we stay for it?"

I lift my brows. "Are you sure? People will talk."

"Let them. Pick you up at ten-thirty?"

"Yes, and I'll bring a casserole."

We fall into a comfortable silence, looking out at the glistening water as the sun dips in the west and soft lilac and flaming crimson streaks fill the sky. After a moment, he reaches over and gently takes my hand in his. I let him, giving his hand a soft squeeze.

EPILOGUE

November 24, 1930

The dawn sky is clear and the air cool and fresh. I inhale deeply, then exhale, watching my white breath spiral out in front of me. My steps are light as I leave the house and climb into my truck. I drive to town and turn onto the wharf road.

Larkin is already parked there. Sadie, Bash, and Jolene stand next to Larkin's car. Jolene holds her baby girl, Matilda Rose, in her arms.

I get out and join them.

"Goodbye, sweet Mattie," Jolene says, kissing her before handing her to Sadie. "Take good care of her for me."

"I will." Sadie smiles and pulls the baby into her chest. The little one is bundled in blankets. "We'll have a fun day, won't we, Mattie?"

I smile, recalling the letter Larkin sent me in prison, the one explaining that Jolene had given birth to Matilda Rose and had decided to keep her. Apparently Jolene's face had glowed with love as she held her.

A month later, Jolene sent me a photograph of her sitting at a table holding Mattie in her arms. Jolene lovingly gazed at her baby girl while tears of joy spilled down her cheeks.

Larkin gives Bash a hug. "Have a good day and help Sadie with Mattie after school."

"I will," Bash says. His voice, because of a new medicine, doesn't sound raspy.

Voices and laughter rise into the air and the smell of coffee wafts over. Tables are set up along the shore facing the wharf. They're piled high with plates of sandwiches, donuts, coffee, and tea. It's dumping day, the first day of lobster fishing season, and most of the townspeople are gathered at Pruett's, and along the shore, to cheer the fishermen off.

Leta, carrying a tray of sandwiches out of the diner, is walking to one of the tables when she spots us. "Morning, ladies! Help yourself to the food and drinks. Take some on your boat for later."

Nelly Butler, Rhonda Nickel, and a few other women stand at the table. Smiling, they also wave and shout, "Good luck, ladies!"

Doreen Jolly and her sour-faced crew stand nearby. Although they don't shout insults, they glare at us. We don't care. They are a very small, miserable looking group.

I watch as an RCMP cruiser comes down Waterfront Street. It stops along the curb and Asher climbs out. A sudden uncontainable swell of happiness rises in my chest.

He threads his way through the crowd toward us. "Good morning, ladies."

"Morning, Constable!" Jolene hoots out, way too exuberantly.

"Jolene…" I say.

She grins. "What?"

Asher smiles at me, and he and I move away a few feet. It's gone quiet on the wharf and the sidewalks. Everyone is watching.

He leans ahead and kisses me softly on the lips. "Be safe out there, Duska."

Then he turns and walks back to his car, the townspeople all staring. Some look shocked, their mouths hanging open. But most just smile and nod as he passes.

Before getting in his patrol car, he looks over his shoulder to give me one last tender smile.

I join Jolene and Larkin again.

Larkin squeezes my arm. "I'm so happy for you, Duska. He's a wonderful, kind man."

"He is, but we're just friends for now. I need to take it slow."

Jolene's eyes are way too bright. She grins and nudges me with an elbow. "With that kiss? Sure you are! Ha! *And* what fun to date a Mountie, with the handcuffs and all. Certainly adds some excitement to things, doesn't it?"

"My word, Jolene!" Larkin says. "What are we going to do with you?"

She throws her head back and laughs, as incorrigible as ever. "Not a thing. Let's go."

We start walking down the wharf to our boat, our shoulders straight, our chins held high. We reach the boat, painted nectarine orange and white, and stop to relish this moment, our first day of lobster fishing together. The deck is filled with traps and there's a barrel on either side of the wheelhouse door; one holds bait, the other seawater for our catch. We've already decided that after lobster season ends in May, we'll start fishing herring and mackerel in June.

While I was in prison, Bill Tucker, who it turned out was sympathetic to our plight and believed women had as much right to fish as men, sold Larkin and Jolene this boat for almost nothing and promised to buy their catch. Larkin and Jolene made repairs and renamed it the *Nauti-Girls*, Jolene's idea. Larkin wanted to name it *Redeemed*, but she gave in after Jolene's unrelenting pestering.

They fished mackerel and herring, and then lobster, though still at night, and from Larkin's dock. Until I joined them in June, they'd also made my mortgage payments. But today is the first day we're going to fish in the daytime and leave from the wharf with the men.

Callum and his two deckhands walk past us, heading to his boat.

"Good luck, ladies," Callum says over his shoulder with such kindness that the three of us all exchange incredulous looks.

"Good luck, men," Jolene says. "If any of you run into trouble, the *Nauti-Girls* will be there to help."

They halt and face us. It's a creed that all fishermen bound by their comradeship live by. If someone is in trouble, their fellow fishers come to their aid. But will they want us rescuing them? Will they come to our aid if need be?

Callum smiles. "Appreciate that. And the same goes for you ladies."

The other two fishermen nod and smile, then continue down the wharf.

On shore, some men are even waving and shouting "Good luck, ladies!" Two little blond girls jump up and down while screaming and waving excitedly. We wave back and that just makes them scream even louder.

Jolene winces. "Whoa, those little girls are louder than a couple of howler monkeys."

Laughing at that, we leap aboard. I go into the wheelhouse while Jolene and Larkin unmoor us. I'm eager but nervous, for dumping day is the most dangerous day of lobster fishing. Each boat's deck is stacked with traps, and it's easy for the load to shift and the boat to capsize. The seas are mild, but still, I'll take it slow and careful.

When Larkin and Jolene come inside, we hold hands tightly, bow our heads, and pray for God to protect us and the other fishermen. When done, we all hug, sharing indefatigable spirits, our hearts thrilled with excitement for our new and bright futures.

I step up to the helm and start the engine. "Ready?"

"Yes," Larkin says, her face glowing.

Jolene grins and gives a fist pump. "Yes! Hit the gas! Let's go!"

The sun is rising on the horizon and is a fiery red glow onto the sea. I ease the boat away from the dock, point the nose toward the open water, and set a course out of the harbour. Ahead of us, I see a long line of fishing boats steering toward the grounds. The people of Whaleback Cove want nothing more to do with rum-running. Prohibition is over. Lobster prices are up again.

Callum's boat is the last in line. I push the throttle forward and follow him, looking ahead to where the sea and rising sun meet. My joy is complete.